MASTERPLAY

WILLIAM F. WU

POPULAR LIBRARY

An Imprint of Warner Books, Inc.

A Warner Communications Company

POPULAR LIBRARY EDITION

Portions of this novel were originally published in slightly different form as "On the Shadow of a Phosphor Sheen," *Isaac Asimov's Science Fiction Magazine*, July 1979; and in the anthology series *There Will Be War*, edited by Jerry Pournelle, as follows: "Interim Justice," Vol. IV, "MasterPlay," Vol. V, "HeartPlay," Vol. VI, "Frozen Justice," Vol. VII, and "Final Justice," Vol. VIII.

Cover illustration by Jim Warren

Popular Library books are published by
Warner Books, Inc.
666 Fifth Avenue
New York, N.Y. 10103

A Warner Communications Company

Printed in the United States of America

First Printing: August, 1987

10 9 8 7 6 5 4 3 2 1

THE LAW OF THE GAME

▼ ▼ ▼

Ken Li, Master Gamer, had fought a record tournament, defeating one hundred ninety-nine opponents to earn the right to become a resident Master at the Headquarters of the Gaming Masters' Guild. From chariot combats to the Wars of the Roses and beyond, Li had played his way to victory on a multitude of computer-generated, holographic battlefields. Now, as one of the top masters in the nation, Li along with his fellow Gamers would refight historical battles to determine the outcome of lawsuits which otherwise might remain bogged down in the overburdened courts for years to come.

But what Ken could not foresee was that the Guild Act—recently passed to enable the courts to order trial by gaming whether both plaintiff and defendant agreed to it or not—would soon place him in a situation that would force him to choose between his own future career and the life of his closest friend…

▼

MASTERPLAY

This novel is dedicated to:
Henry Robertson

ACKNOWLEDGMENTS

Thanks are due to many people who helped during the writing of *MasterPlay.* Among them are:

Brian Thomsen, Jerry Pournelle, John F. Carr, and George H. Scithers for their aid in editing and suggestions.

Diana Gallagher Wu for companionship, suggestions, and encouragement.

Rob Chilson, Michael D. Toman, and Ted Reynolds for observations, encouragement, and friendship going back a long way.

My parents, Dr. William Q. Wu and Cecile F. Wu, for their support over the years.

CHAPTER One

Ken Li leaned toward the window of the luxurious shuttlecopter and squinted into the bright sunlight. Below him, the World Headquarters of the Gaming Masters' Guild was growing larger, no longer a dot lost in the sprawling city, but now resembling an architectural model like those displayed in hopital lobbies. He continued to watch as the shuttlecopter descended toward the rooftop heliport so he could enjoy his excitement and anticipation to the fullest.

This was it. At age twenty-nine, after years of first apprenticeship and then later gaming in the master class, he had finally made his way to the center of his profession. A rare opening had occurred here at WHQ and two hundred *master gamers* had competed for it in a tournament stretching across fifteen months.

Ken Li was the only survivor.

When the shuttlecopter had landed gently, Ken stood up in the aisle and looked down at himself. He had dressed carefully for this occasion, in a loose white dress shirt of some silky synthetic, worn open at the collar, and a hand-tailored, solid turquoise sport jacket with silver buttons. Dark blue dress slacks and white loafers completed the picture—an extreme one—which made him smile with self-conscious irony as he smoothed the sides of his jacket. He knew the message conveyed by his appearance: that he was professional, successful, vain, and a bit eccentric.

Well, he reflected, that message was fairly honest. With a big grin for the wide-eyed, pretty, red-haired flight attendant who opened the door, he picked up his empty briefcase, slung the strap of his black shoulder bag over his shoulder, and moved out to descend the steps.

With an unerring but amused sense of drama, Ken strode regally down the metal steps with his back erect, looking out across the paved rooftop with apparently casual interest. The wind from the propeller overhead blew his hair forward. Two men stood at the bottom of the steps, awaiting the flight's only passenger.

As Ken neared the bottom, he looked directly at his hosts for the first time. He recognized one as Kirk Emerald, Director of the Guild's Executive Committee and one of the founders of the Guild. Ken was pleasantly shocked and then humbled. He hadn't expected *him*.

"Master Li." Emerald, a tall, slender man with a full head of white hair tossed in the shuttlecopter's stiff breeze, extended his hand. "I'm Kirk Emerald. Welcome to World Headquarters."

"Thank you. I'm glad to be here." Ken shook hands, smiling up at the man who towered over him.

"This is Lou Crandall." Emerald gestured to the man beside him.

"Oh, of course. Pleased to meet you." Surprised again, Ken shook hands with the heavyset man in his forties.

"Ken, I'm glad to meet you, too. After all the corresponding we've done, it's about time. I'm honored to be your new contractor."

Ken wasn't fooled. Crandall was one of the top contractors in the business, and he could do more for Ken than Ken could do for him. "*I'm* honored to sign with you. Thanks for meeting me. I really appreciate it." He included Emerald in his eye contact. "Thanks very much."

Lou took a cigar wrapped in cellophane out of his inside jacket pocket and started tearing at the wrapper with his teeth. "That's the great part of having this heliport on the roof, Ken. You don't have to go very far to meet people." He laughed good-naturedly.

Kirk Emerald clapped Ken on the shoulder as they turned and started to walk. "No need to be formal anymore. You're one of us now."

So Ken Li came to World Headquarters.

Ken was introduced at the Guild Hall reception desk, an impressive black marble structure in the main lobby. After that his hosts said farewell, and a reception clerk escorted him up to the suite of rooms that the Guild was providing for free, temporarily. Most of his belongings were somewhere on the way from Ann Arbor, Michigan, in a van. Now he simply set down his briefcase, his shoulder bag of books and cameras, and one suitcase of clothes.

The suite was large, spacious, and airy. One wall of the sunken living room was a huge window looking out over the city. The furnishings were contemporary modular rectangles of pastel orange, yellow, and blue. The video screen on one wall could be keyed for any of the games being played in the Guild Hall, provided public access had been granted. In addition, old tapes could be called up from the Guild Hall Library. The bedroom contained a broad, firm bed and an entire wall of entertainment consoles for video, film, radio, or audio pastimes. The kitchen was fully equipped with electronic appliances, and the refrigerator, bar and pantry were fully stocked, not only with staples but also with champagne, black caviar, dim sum, and sushi.

Ken explored with a mixture of amazement and giddiness. He laughed aloud at the large sunken tub and shag carpeting in the bathroom and then, shaking his head at the wonder he felt, he washed up and changed into a clean, light blue shirt. He checked his watch, composed himself with a deep breath, and went out to see the Guild Hall. His giddiness would remain in the suite, as it would not befit a master gamer of the World Headquarters.

Later, just before five-thirty P.M., Ken wandered casually

down a wide, carpeted hallway to the Summer Palace banquet room where the reception in his honor was to take place. It was decorated in the style of the opulent Summer Palace in Beijing. Ken smiled to himself, amused that they had chosen this banquet hall, out of many, to honor him. Quite a crowd was already visible in the room, through the open doorway, where shelves of ancient Chinese antiques and art lined the walls under glass.

"Well, well." He spoke aloud to himself, grinning. Then he stuck his hands into his pockets and walked up to the short line at the door. As he waited, he gradually became aware that everyone inside the banquet room, and everyone ahead of him in line, was wearing a long red ribbon. When his turn came, he inclined his head toward the people filing into the room. "Where, uh, do I get a red ribbon?"

A young, slender man in a black dinner jacket looked up at him. He wore a green ribbon reading HOSPITALITY on his lapel. "You should have received it over a week ago, sir. That is, you did preregister, didn't you? We don't have registration here at the door."

"Well, I was told to be here at five-thirty." Ken smiled amiably, not wanting to cause the young man any trouble and rather enjoying the irony that he might be kept out of his own reception. "I'm Ken Li and—"

"*Oh*! Master Li?" The young man's eyes grew wide, and his face suddenly started turning pink. "Uh—well . . . just a moment, Master." He stuck his head inside the door of the banquet room and shouted in a hoarse stage whisper. "Donna! I need help!"

Ken glanced behind him and smiled awkwardly. The line was still forming, and the young man's discomfiture embarrassed him. When he turned to face forward, the young fellow had been joined by a stunningly pretty woman, also wearing the green hospitality ribbon.

"Can I help you? I'm Donna Wong." She smiled and held out her hand.

"Glad to meet you. I'm Ken Li." He shook her hand, which was small and warm and gripped his firmly.

Donna was about five feet four, with high, even cheekbones and a square jaw. Her lips were full and her nose was straight and a little wide. Wavy, shoulder-length black hair framed her face as her eyes met his. She had a strong Cantonese look, he thought.

"*Oh*—Master Li. I'm sorry if there was a mix-up. Um—we were expecting you to come down with Lou Crandall." She waited for a response, watching his face with an open, pleasant smile.

"Ah—that's my fault. I forgot all about it. He did tell me he'd swing up to my room to get me. I was exploring the Guild Hall and just came over here when it was time."

Donna nodded without taking her eyes off his face. "I see. Well, Lou has your ribbon." Her smile remained as she gazed at him.

Ken realized, suddenly, that even though she seemed impressed with his looks—or his status, more likely—and even though she was not going to embarrass him outright, she also had no intention of letting him in just because he claimed to be the guest of honor. He laughed lightly and reached for his wallet. "May I show you some identification?"

"I—wait. There's Lou now." Donna looked past him and waved.

"Ken!" Lou called out as he came striding down past the rest of the line. "Hi. Came down early, eh?"

"I'm sorry, Lou. I forgot you were coming up to my room . . . and it's a little eerie up there alone, if you ask me."

"No harm done. Here, pin this on." Lou handed him the red ribbon. "Okay, hon?"

"You know my name, Lou," Donna said firmly.

"Aw, yeah, all right. Sorry." Lou gripped Ken's shoulder. "C'mon, let's go in."

"Okay." Ken grinned at Donna, gave a little shrug, and followed the contractor.

The room was already crowded. Lou worked his bulk slowly along the wall toward the bar, and Ken took advantage of the trail he blazed. The big contractor looked back over his shoulder and waved him forward.

"C'mon, Master Li! Don't be shy. What do you drink, anyhow?"

"White wine." Ken laughed at Lou's gruff and friendly manner. His personality would be an asset for their working together.

"White wine it is. Yeah, here you are." Lou handed him a cold glass. "Well, you'll get a formal introduction to the crowd later. In the meantime, here's a toast."

"Oh?" Ken grinned and raised his glass.

"Here's to the new arrangement that brought you here—to the Guild Act. May we all prosper." Lou clinked glasses with Ken and took a healthy swallow.

"Ah, yes. Here's to it." Ken sipped the sweet white wine modestly. More than a few gaming careers had been poisoned by alcohol, and he had long ago determined to remember that. Lowering his glass, he turned to survey the crowd. He was certain that he had heard of many of the *master gamers* present, but he didn't know any of them by sight any more than Donna Wong had known him.

Richard Ross was looking at him.

Deep in the crowd, the tall, lanky man with reddish-blond hair stood with long, lean arms folded across his chest, a glass of beer clutched in one hand at an awkward angle. He was watching Ken with a self-conscious smile. As soon as their eyes met, Ken began weaving his way through the crowd toward him, and he started toward Ken.

"See you later," Lou said quietly, behind Ken. "He gives me the creeps."

Ken, jostled by someone in the press of people, still managed to reach out and shake hands with Richard.

"Welcome to World Headquarters," Richard said with that familiar, strange tone of his that seemed to hint at sarcasm.

"Thanks. I'm glad to be here. Back in the old hometown again."

Richard waved his glass of beer slightly in his other hand. "Let's see . . . we haven't seen each other since I was visiting the Detroit Guild Hall a couple of years ago. You've uh, been moving up in the world."

Ken shrugged, uncomfortable with an apparent compliment from his old friend. "I have to say, this Guild Hall makes the others look like outhouses."

Richard laughed shortly. "Yeah. Trouble is, everyone here knows it." He tilted his had back for a sizable swallow of beer. "You realize, of course, that you've got it made now, just by being a *master gamer* slotted in this Guild. You can do anything here but fail."

"Well, I guess that's true. It's true in any Guild Hall, though." Ken shrugged again.

"Not like it is here." Richard sneered and waved his glass around at the crowd. "Our esteemed colleagues have the souls of circling buzzards. I've been here, what, over eleven years, and I've never been rated lower than six in the entire world. They know it, too—and every one of them would like my slot near the top."

"Or at the top, frequently." Ken grinned.

Richard laughed genuinely, then. "Yeah, sometimes." He frowned again. "Just keep in mind—no one here even discusses failure. Success is expected, and to hear people talk, that's all that happens here. We all know better, but that doesn't matter. Every master here just says . . . it's a *good* life." He laughed and shook his head. "I guess you'll have to be here awhile to feel it, but it'll come."

Ken nodded, watching his childhood friend take another long draft of his beer. Richard had been a young phenom when he had attained master status at age nineteen. He had always been extremely competitive, with his anxiety and insecurity about winning always near the surface. Yet his knowledge of military history and tactics was unmatched by any other master, past or present.

On the other hand, Ken was not exactly in the habit of discussing failure—or even considering it—himself.

"Ironically," said Richard, "I won't be under the gun quite as much anymore. Now it's your turn."

"What? How so? If anything, people have been falling all over themselves to welcome me."

Richard laughed with a sarcastic twist to his smile. "Oh, yeah. They'll always be like that on the surface. Do you realize why you're here—in depth, I mean?"

Ken was in no mood to guess. "Suppose you tell me."

"All right." Richard shrugged. "Before the Guild Act was passed, we had a fairly stable number of games contracted. One slob gets mad at some other jerk; their lawyers can't work it out, and so they mutually hire masters to play for their dispute. The old trial by combat, right? You with me so far?"

"I don't need lectures. What's the point?"

"Now, under the old rules, we were only contracted by mutually agreeable private parties—the government had nothing to do with it. With the Guild Act passed, the very same slob can now sue the very same jerk for a game, and under certain provisions a judge may grant it whether or not the defendant agrees to trial by combat."

"You haven't told me one single item yet that's new to me. Every master who reads the trades knows all this."

Richard eyed him tightly. "And you still don't get it? What it means to you?"

"The Guild expects more games to be contracted than ever before and has opened new slots in Guild Halls all over the country. I got the one here. That's all."

Richard laughed derisively. "Not hardly. You are the new gunslinger in town. Every master here will be gunning for you. And the members of the public who hate us for the Guild Act will center on you as the most visible representative of the new order."

Ken looked down at his glass pensively. "Hmm. I hadn't thought of that. I remember reading that some people are against the Guild Act. I don't see why, really. Nobody likes being sued. Why should getting sued for a game be any worse than getting sued for anything else?"

Richard waved his free hand in dismissal and finished his beer with the other. "You got me. I don't care, anyway.

Plenty of people love watching our games and betting on them and making us celebrities. That's good enough for me." He fixed his gaze on Ken's eyes. "Maybe I should demonstrate my point myself. You up for a practice game?"

That was a gunfighter's gaze, Ken thought, staring back up at his friend. "Sure. Name the time and place."

"Tomorrow morning. I'll reserve the room. Meet me at the registration desk at ten o'clock."

"Done."

They continued to stare at each other until Ken returned to his glass. "I still think you're being too hard on the other masters. I was friends with lots of my colleagues back in Michigan."

"That was Michigan. You notice how no one has approached you while we've been talking? Every one of them knows who you are. I mean, you do rather stand out in this crowd."

Ken grinned. "I just thought they were avoiding *you*."

Richard laughed, and his pale face flushed slightly. "Could be, at that." He raised his empty glass. "I'm going for a refill. Want one?"

"No, thanks. Think I'll mingle."

Richard vanished into the crowd, and Ken turned to look around. The crush of well-dressed men and women were talking in the normal fashion for any cocktail party, but he could see people occasionally glancing at him as they spoke. That made sense; the reception was in his honor, after all.

Donna Wong, in a striking dress of lavender lace, was circulating, talking to people briefly and then, with a quick smile, moving on. Ken hesitated, then began working his way toward her. He intended to make running into her look like an accident, but when she saw him, she changed direction to meet him.

Ken stopped where he was, smiling at her, and watched. Her dress was long, made of lace over satin with white trim. She seemed to be of a medium build, but the cut of her dress really disguised her below the neck. Meanwhile, he noticed with amusement, she was looking him over too—this outfit he had so carefully selected to make the impression he wanted.

Judging from the look on her face, it had worked just fine.

"Master Li. Can I get you another?" Donna gestured to take his glass with a big smile.

"Oh—no, thanks. This is fine."

"You haven't turned red." She put her upper teeth on her lower lip in a teasing expression.

"It hasn't been long enough yet; that's all." Ken laughed. "And call me Ken, will you?"

"Sure."

Ken kept on smiling at her, feeling a bit awkward. Her eyes were so plainly enjoying looking at him that he wasn't sure how to act. He was tempted to gaze at her with equal enthusiasm, but then, nobody would be talking.

Just before the pause became a burden, he nodded toward her green ribbon. "Are you catering? Or are you associated with the Guild?"

"I'm an apprentice gamer." Her tone was proud. "I came to it later than most, but I'm perking right along."

"Really? I . . . thought you were just an attendant or something. How far along are you?"

"I've already applied for a qualifying game. Right now, all the masters here are so backlogged that none of them are playing qualifiers. I'll get it eventually, though. In the meantime, I'm practicing a lot and passing the time with projects like this."

"That sounds like a good program." Ken suddenly realized that he could offer to play against her in a game that would test her ability to become a master, since he was unbooked. He immediately dismissed the idea, since he wanted to get to know her better. Becoming her opponent would only be an obstacle.

"Now." Donna took his arm. "I'd like to escort you up to the front where Master Emerald is getting ready to introduce you to the assembled multitude. You don't have to do much. Just smile and wave at the right time, and it'll all be over."

"Yes, Lou explained it to me this afternoon." Ken responded to the pressure of her on his arm and started moving toward the front of the room. "Well, even if I'm in a room full of future opponents and competitors, at least I feel like it's a family. You know what I mean? The Guild is like home."

Donna looked up at him, and her face was close to his. Her full lips were pursed in a tight smile. "Well, Ken . . . Master Li. Perhaps you should know that some of us are very much against the Guild Act that brought you here."

Ken blinked in surprise. "Even gamers are against it?"

She nodded. "Not very many—in fact, here in town, I may be the only one."

"But . . . you're really against it? Seriously?"

"Definitely."

"I don't understand how anyone—"

"Shh." She laughed and put a finger to her lips. "Master Emerald is about to start. We'll talk some other time."

Ken smiled self-consciously as she stopped at the side of the dais, still holding his arm. He took her advice when the time came; Kirk Emerald called his name in clear, dignified tones and extended his arm toward Ken. Ken stepped up onto the dais, waved with a quick smile, and hopped down next to Donna again to the welcoming applause.

The introduction broke the reserve of the other guests. When Kirk Emerald had finished his announcements and returned the gathering to its party atmosphere, Ken found himself surrounded by bright smiles and extended hands on all sides. He was disappointed to see Donna back away and leave him to his new colleagues, but he was glad that his status as an outsider had ended. Whatever happened to him next in this crowd would happen to one of their own.

CHAPTER Two

Early the next morning, freshly showered and breakfasted, Ken hurried down a silent, carpeted, dimly lit corridor after Richard, whose steady, long-legged stride set a brisk pace. They passed long rows of heavy closed doors and kept turning corners set at irregular angles. Ken could see brass nameplates on each door, shining slightly in the weak overhead light. Finally, after Ken had completely lost his way, Richard stopped to open one of the doors with a key.

Without speaking, Richard snapped on the room light and walked inside. He had worked himself into a fierce, competitive mood for their practice game, Ken realized, and would not be sociable again until after they had finished. Ken waited for Richard to choose one side of the big room, then took the other for himself.

The practice room was a large rectangle, just a bit bigger than the ten-meter-square playing field outlined in black on the floor. The playing field itself was a plain white synthetic substance that took holograms particularly well; Ken could never remember what they called the stuff, nor did he really care. Outside the square, the room was luxuriously carpeted and furnished with a multiple beverage dispenser and private rest room.

Ken sat down in the padded chair centered along one side

of the playing field. It had a console that allowed him to adjust the softness or firmness of the seat, back, and arms, and to shift all their angles to the minutest degree. Ken liked a hard seat and back, the back straight up behind him. Years ago, in high school, his Latin teacher—a silver-haired woman who had corrected students' mistakes without the need to consult her text—had decreed that no one could "cerebrate" if he was comfortable. As near as Ken's own cerebrum could tell, she had been right.

Across the field from Ken, Richard was adjusting his own seat. Above the center of the field, Ken could see the opening in the ceiling that housed the projectors. He reached down to his left and brought up the keyboard on a swiveling steel arm. It held twelve horizontal rows of keys, twelve keys to a row, plus larger buttons and dials running vertically down each side. Across the top, a small video screen completed the board.

Across the way, Richard glanced up at him with an intense scowl. Trying not to laugh nervously—he was too knotted up inside to be truly amused—Ken waved a hand. Richard hit a button, and the game opened.

The field was suddenly lit up from above with three-dimensional miniatures. A city from ancient times sat on the coast of a large sea or ocean; the surrounding region held two sizable armies, still some distance from each other. The terrain was generally flat, and rolling slightly, covered by the green of plowed fields and patches of forest separated by open country.

Since this was a practice game, both gamers had sixty seconds before the game would come alive in a computerized simulation of tactical warfare. Ken read on his video screen: "Tunis. 255 B.C. Carthage. Xanthippes." Officers' names, Victory Conditions, and odds for the battle followed. That was all the system would tell him.

Ken was taking the place of the Spartan mercenary, Xanthippes, who had come to Carthage and taken command of the Carthaginian army. As *master gamers*, both Ken and Richard were expected to know all the details of the battle, including the personalities of individual officers who were on record historically and the abilities and cultural tendencies of the troops. These were all programmed into the game.

Tunis, Ken thought. His heart was pounding. This battle had been fought in the Punic Wars, well before the time of Hannibal. Xanthippes had defeated a Roman army led by its Consul Atilius Regulus, whose decisions would now be made by Richard.

Ken flexed his fingers nervously. He, as Xanthippes, had units representing four thousand cavalry, twelve thousand foot soldiers, and one hundred elephants. The battlefield would be on level ground. He sat quivering with intensity, not certain that he could defeat Richard even now, but anxious to play him close, at the very least. As the seconds passed, he could feel his confidence ebb, to be replaced by an old, familiar feeling of intimidation.

The game activated.

Ken's Carthaginian Army was on the near side of the field, represented by tiny figures. They were too small to discern clearly with the naked eye as individuals, but they functioned most of the time in military units that were fairly easy to identify.

Ken picked up the metal sensory band from its hook on the arm of the chair. He fitted it around his head, turning it so that the transparent eyepieces and small audio speakers were properly placed. The sensory band was controlled by the keyboard; unless he activated it, he would see and hear normally.

The Carthaginian armies were usually comprised of foreign mercenaries led by Carthaginian officers. Ken remembered that his army was an exception. The Romans had landed outside Carthage, isolating the city from its recruiting field and part of its food supply. So two thirds of Ken's army were Carthaginian citizens with training but limited experience, led this time by a mercenary.

Ken began tapping the keys to arrange his units. On the far side of the field, Richard was setting up his Roman legionnaries. He had a slight numerical advantage, with fifteen thousand infantry and five thousand horses. However, the Carthaginian cavalry had possessed more fighting quality, and the figures had greater combat power to reflect this.

Since Carthage had won the real battle, Ken did not tamper with the Spartan's plan. Like Xanthippes, he put his elephants in the front line as shock troops, followed by his infantry, with his cavalry on the wings. It was a fairly standard arrangement: the elephants, charging across the level plain, should trample the front lines of legionnaries and throw the rest into confusion, to be finished off by the Carthaginian infantry. The mobility of the cavalry would prevent any flanking movement by the more numerous Romans. Richard's numerical superiority could be nullified by the elephants.

Ken activated his sensory band and moved into the battle scene as Xanthippes. The great gray elephants lumbered forward, raising their trunks and trumpeting. He could choose between an on-scene viewpoint, from the spot where his game persona was at any given time, or he could use the larger perspective of the gaming seat, with a near total loss of detail.

Ken hesitated, then pulled out of the sensory band again. It was most useful at crisis points and had little to offer when the large pattern of the battle was still developing. He happened to enjoy it a great deal, but that was a matter of pleasure, not business.

Behind the elephants, the lines of infantry began to move forward. Both wings of cavalry fanned out slightly to prepare for action. Ken would meet any flanking motion by the Roman cavalry with his own, but he doubted Richard would try it. The two sides were too closely matched for such a move to work on level ground.

The Romans marched forward. Even with his naked eye Ken could see the red hairline that was the great red plumes of dyed horsehairs worn by the Roman legionnaries. The formation looked a little odd to him, but on close examination he found the different units to be in conventional order.

He selected the combination of keys he wanted and directed his elephants, through the tiny figure of Xanthippes on the field, to charge.

The front line of Carthaginians began to move out ahead of the others. The Roman infantry halted its forward progress. Ken held his breath, watching.

The gray line of Carthaginian elephants advanced up the field, meshed with the lines of Roman infantry, and continued to charge forward, between the files of legionnaries. Ken's stomach tightened. The elephants, now rampaging out of the control of their drivers, were stampeding harmlessly through gaps in the formation. The Romans closed files behind them and resumed marching.

Ken swallowed. The Roman formation had looked odd because Richard had spread the files apart while keeping the positions of his troops otherwise conventional. Ken remembered that the Romans had used this technique on later historical occasions, such as Zama, but not at Tunis. Since the only historical limitation on this formation had been the vision and decision to use it, the computer allowed it as an option. Richard, of course, knew better than anyone when to use such variations.

The two front lines of infantry clashed, and Ken concentrated on the screen and his keyboard. The computer considered morale factors, and the Romans gained an advantage from surviving the elephant charge intact, while the Carthaginians lost morale for the same reason. Ken's infantry held but did not move forward. The wings of cavalry met on each side and spread out farther as they fought for position against each other.

Ken hit the keyboard as quickly as he dared, holding back a little speed for fear of making a mistake. His confidence had been rattled. He watched his front line carefully. Through Xanthippes he encouraged the mercenaries to hold their ground. The Carthaginian left, in particular, was hard-pressed by the Romans. Ken's right was advancing slightly, but he was not sure what to do next. In the real battle, the Carthaginian elephants had thrown the Roman right into chaos and the Carthaginian infantry had crushed them. Here the balance was still undetermined.

On the wings, the Carthaginian cavalry was commanded by two separate officers programmed by the computer. As Xanthippes, Ken could issue them new orders, but if he did not, those officers and their men would perform as they had historically. Ken's cavalry, with a fighting superiority that more than offset their fewer numbers, threatened to drive their Roman counterparts from the field. He figured he should not interfere.

All at once, then, he realized that the Romans were trying to disengage themselves. It was a complicated maneuver; if the Romans retreated too quickly, their formation would break and become a rout. In these circumstances, with the Carthaginians still strong and aggressive, that was nearly inevitable. Richard, however, was pulling his legionnaries back in good order, despite the pressure from Ken's lines. The Carthaginians began to advance faster, destroying their retreating enemy at a faster rate than before. Still, the Roman infantry, anticipating help, maintained their fighting order. The game computer allowed this because of the renowned discipline of the Roman legions and Richard's delicate handling, Ken surmised, of the necessary orders.

Both wings of Roman cavalry, fleeing the Carthaginians, fought their way between the two bodies of infantry and slowed the Carthaginian advance. The retreat of the Roman infantry gave their cavalry room to maneuver. Then, as the Carthaginian cavalry closed on the Roman cavalry from each side, the mounted Romans fought a holding action to allow their infantry time to escape.

Ken ground his teeth as he punched the keyboard. He was seriously damaging the Roman cavalry, but his own infantry could no longer close with the retreating legions. Ken hated losing, and his stomach felt cold as he watched the Roman infantry pull away.

It was a risky and costly maneuver on Richard's part, and not one he was likely to try in a real game. He had tried it to find out if he could sacrifice his cavalry to save his infantry.

In a way, he was just playing around—experimenting. Ken realized that the insult to him was unintentional, but he was still disturbed by the fact that Richard could succeed even though he had not taken Ken very seriously.

Resigned, Ken halted the advance of his units. His refusal to pursue the fleeing Romans activated an assessment by the computer. After a wait of thirty seconds, during which the two gamers could resume new maneuvers, the field froze. The game results appeared on the video screen above Ken's board.

Ken read them with disgust for himself.

"Victory conditions: None.

"Tactical position: Stalemate, advantage Carthage.

"Strategic position: Stalemate, advantage Rome."

The list went on, giving statistics and elapsed time, but Ken ignored the rest. He was angry with himself and embarrassed.

Richard punched a button and erased the game, leaving only the blank playing field again. He visibly relaxed and lounged back in his chair. Then he remembered his sensory band and leaned forward a moment to pull it off. "You lost," he called out, grinning. His bushy blond hair was sweaty. "Welcome to World Headquarters."

Ken swung his own keyboard out of the way and took off his sensory band. "Stalemate, actually." He adjusted his seat to recline and fell against the backrest, aware that he was hot and soaked in sweat.

"Technically true." Richard turned to one side and hung a long leg over the arm of the chair. "Actually, though, the strategic position favors Rome. Atilius Regulus still has enough of an army to keep Carthage isolated, and the Romans can get new horses from the surrounding country. Carthage is still threatened and would have to fight again under these circumstances. If the Romans wait for the return of their reinforcements in the spring, Carthage could be finished."

Ken shrugged and shook his head in concession. At this point, he just wanted to forget it.

Suddenly Richard jumped up. "Never mind! I'm celebrating. Let's run down to the Club for brunch, on me. Champagne time."

"Okay." Ken slid out of the chair. He understood that Richard had been unable to make friendly conversation before the game, when he had been in a competitive frenzy. "What's the celebration about? Not beating me, surely."

Richard laughed. "Are you kidding? Let's get settled downstairs, and I'll tell you all about it."

Again, Ken followed him through the labyrinth of Guild hallways. They had been deliberately constructed this way to increase the privacy of gamers who often did not wish their colleagues to know when they were practicing or with whom. No formal rules governed such information, but a tradition of discretion in the Guild had a rigidity bordering on that of law.

The Guild Club was a formal dining room and lounge on one of the lower floors. It offered linen and sterling silver for the settings, a staff in black tie and tails, crystal goblets, and fresh flowers clustered around scented candles. Heavy curtains adorned the walls; they proved to be, Ken found, copies of famous medieval European tapestries. Money was not exchanged on the premises; only masters who gamed out of this Guild Hall could eat or host meals here, and the staff was expected to know them by sight and to accept their signatures without further verification.

When they had ordered an elaborate brunch, Richard flipped out his napkin and set it in his lap. "Gene called me early this morning—uh, that's Gene Graham, my contractor. He's wangled an offer for me to play in the very first game contracted under the provisions of the Guild Act. Hey, I'm going right back to the top."

Ken was impressed, though a pang of envy hit him, no doubt strengthened by his disappointment over the morning's practice game. "Really? That *is* grounds for celebration. Let's see—you're rated number two right now?"

"Yep—what's his name, DuVeau, is number one at the

moment. They tried to get him first, of course, but apparently he's booked four or five months ahead."

"I don't know much about him, but he must be good." Ken watched as the immaculately dressed waiter wheeled up an ice cart with the neck of a bottle of champagne jutting out at a jaunty angle.

Richard frowned and shook his head. "I was in the top ten long before he was, and I'll be here long after. Matter of fact, he's older than we are."

"Think he's a flash in the pan?"

"Ha! Flush is more like it."

Richard nodded his approval of the champagne, and they both watched as the cork was popped and the bottle poured. When the waiter had retired, Ken lifted his glass. "Congratulations. Here's to Victory Conditions."

Richard clinked glasses with him. "Ah, yes—here's to Victory Conditions. Thank you."

Brunch arrived promptly, and Richard devoted his attention to it with a nervous, energetic earnestness that Ken remembered well. As they ate in silence, he began wondering if the pressure to succeed had gradually created an obsession with winning in his old friend. It was not easy to tell, because Richard had always been ferociously competitive, and he may have simply thrived here in a naturally conducive environment.

Another thought occurred to Ken about their practice game. "That maneuver you were trying with me earlier. Are you, uh, working on a masterplay?"

Richard looked up in surprise, hesitated, and then grinned self-consciously. He reddened as he finished a mouthful of food. "No, not exactly. To be honest, it's hard to plan a masterplay. If people could figure them out in practice games, at their leisure, they'd do it all the time."

"And then they wouldn't be masterplays." Ken nodded. "You have what, three of them?"

"Four."

"Two more than anyone else. That's a major contribution

to the field." Ken was not being generous; this was the plain truth.

"Actually masterplays will become a problem if they're ever common. Think of it—a masterplay is a maneuver that always works in the game it's developed for. So—"

"Given that the opportunity develops. It may not—"

"Yeah, yeah, of course," Richard snapped. "But, like I was saying, *if* the situation for a masterplay develops in a game, and the maneuver is already in our professional repertoire, then the game is essentially over. We'll have standard solutions for every game, and I guess they'd have to be reprogrammed or something."

Right now, though, there aren't very many masterplays in the books, are there?"

Richard grinned again and shook his head. "Well, no. It's a long way off." He returned to his plate.

A masterplay, thought Ken. It was a special mark of prestige, a pure artistic accomplishment that went beyond winning games and charging fees and drawing clients and crowds. A master with a mediocre career would always be known for creating a masterplay; a master with an otherwise stellar career might never feel completely fulfilled without one. Richard's place in Guild history was already assured. Only the extent of his prestige had yet to be established.

Their childhood sometimes seemed to be in the distant past and sometimes seemed very recent. They were *master gamers* now, accomplished performers with a greater knowledge of their field than most military historians. Great civil decisions rode on their tides, and now, with the Guild Act passed, even greater decisions would follow. They were too young to remember the entry of games into private disputes. The game sets had only had a few battles to choose from back then, though all had been classics. The technology was primitive.

And Ken and Richard initially were two introverted, socially backward kids in an upstairs bedroom, setting up toy plastic knights. A carefully tumbled landscape of books, boxes, and blankets on the floor formed rugged peaks, treacherous valleys, and unscalable castle walls. Set aside, stacks of various histories provided countless scenarios and suggestions for their vivid visions.

"Okay," Richard announced from his own side of the floor. He had his back to Ken and was maneuvering nine thirteenth-century men in armor down the cascading folds of a blue blanket. "Mace-face is leading his puny band down into the valley now, sneaking up on the camp down there." Carefully he lifted a large armored individual with an upraised mace and knocked over a sentry with it.

"The Norman cavalry is having trouble," said Ken from his side of the room. He wheeled about seven toy knights, actually from the Wars of the Roses, and sent them into retreat. They didn't resemble Norman cavalry at all, but they did have horses and lances. "The Saxon shield-wall has held and reforms while the Normans regroup for another attack." He knew that Richard was listening with only the barest of attention, just as he was, but that didn't matter. This way, they could enact whatever battles and time periods and strategies they wanted. This included manipulating defeats into victories and deciding on their own who would live or die. Both of them always won, and the victories were always shared.

Richard sat back suddenly and considered. "All of these kinds of people were descended from Roman tradition—mixed up with the Franks and other barbarians, of course. I wonder what would have happened if some descendants of Carthage had lasted into medieval times."

"Yeah," Ken said without interest. He was trying to form a new shield-wall on the fold of a bedspread with nine Saxons and two temporarily converted Vikings, who looked similar enough, but they all kept falling down.

"No good, I guess," Richard continued. "Even if Carthage had survived the Romans, the Vandals went through later, anyway. So did the Arabs, too, in the 700s." His voice grew pedantic. "Tarik invaded Europe in the year 711—the easiest date to remember in all history."

"Hm." Ken tried to fix the name in his memory, to go with the date, but he didn't know how to spell it. He had never been as good with dates as Richard, but he had a better grasp of concurrent events and their interrelation. Then Richard gave him an opening.

"I guess those Carthagians were doomed from the start," he said, and turned back to his half-completed battle.

"Carthaginians," Ken corrected him.

Richard clenched his jaw and took on a firm look. "The city is Carthage—so, Carthagians, stupid. It's the easiest way to change it."

"I *read* 'Carthaginians' someplace," Ken said haughtily.

"I presume," Richard said with equal loftiness, "that's C-a-r-t-h-a-g-i-n-i-a-n."

"Yep," Ken said, thinking that Richard must be the only ten-year-old he had ever known who said *presume* out loud in sentences.

They looked at each other, and the undercurrent of childhood rivalry rose up in a mutual giggling ferocity that set them leaping at each other. Growling and yelling and laughing, they grappled and rolled in a narrow space of the floor that was still clear. Both were slender and limber, making them quick at close quarters. Richard had the reach, being considerably taller—and he looked thinner on account of it—but Ken was more aggressive. As they rapidly approached their usual stalemate, someone's foot flicked into a battlefield and knocked over a few miniature stalwarts. Instantly, they both froze.

"Whose was it?" Richard panted, holding an awkward pose.

"Yours, I think." They untangled themselves gingerly and returned with extreme care to their battles. Fallen fighters were resurrected, to be killed according to plan instead of by accident. Although their backs were turned to each other, they repaired the damage with a shared reverence, and in silence.

* * *

Ken smiled wistfully at the memory. They had both acquired a certain polish over the years, yet the raw material underneath seemed unchanged. All they had ever done was study and play wargames. Gaming in the master class was a way of life for Ken, yet, compared to Richard, he almost seemed like a dilettante.

CHAPTER Three

Later that evening, Donna drew her feet up onto the couch and wrapped the hem of her long flannel nightgown over them. "Really, Sharon, it just sort of happened. I mean, *I* don't believe in love at first sight. I really don't." She laughed and wrinkled her nose playfully. "Except now." She knew she'd get a rise out of her friend with that.

Sharon Wills rolled her eyes and put her fists on her hips in an exaggerated gesture. She was sitting on the floor by the coffee table, and her broad-shouldered, angular frame threw an intimidating shadow across Donna's bright, colorful painting of Fa Mulan on the far wall. "It's not that I'm not interested, but you asked me to run you through this exercise. Mooning about a total stranger won't help you get master status." Sharon laughed, then, and sighed. "All right. I'll put water on. Do you still have some of that—what do you call it? The expensive imported tea from high altitudes?"

"Monkey-picked tea. Sure." Donna slid her feet into her embroidered red silk slippers. "Just remember *why* it's so expensive—just think of all the poor monkeys that pitched over the edge of cliffs trying to reach those hard-to-get tea bushes. You can use up a lot of monkeys that way."

Sharon laughed and stood up, smoothing her rust-colored turtleneck down over the waistband of her jeans. "That's terrible. But, uh—speaking of 'hard to get' . . . you know what I mean?"

Donna followed the taller woman into the kitchen. "Yeah, I suppose. I just don't want to play any games. I used to do that with men, and it ruined everything. Always. I'd rather be honest."

"I'm not arguing with that." Sharon raised her voice as she ran water into a white, flexible container over the sink. "You could find a middle ground, though, couldn't you?" She opened the transparent door of the flasher and set the two-liter container of water inside. Then she stepped back and winced as she pushed a button. The flasher lit up, buzzed, and went off.

"What are you afraid of?" Donna asked. "I've seen you do that before. It's all sealed and insulated and everything." She opened the door and took out the boiling water.

Sharon took the lid off Donna's elaborate blue and white Ming-style teapot and sprinkled leaves inside. "You trust those damn contraptions too much. They told you it was sealed, but for all we know, it's flashing us at the same time it's flashing the water."

Donna picked up two cups and started back to the living room. "Maybe you don't trust enough. I trust my instincts about Ken, too." She hesitated, debating whether to say her next thought. It was nothing new to Sharon, anyway. "I'm not exactly without experience, you know." She smiled tightly.

"I know. That's what I'm worried about." Sharon knelt and began to pour.

Stung, Donna said nothing.

"You like it weak, right? I'll let mine steep longer."

"Yes, thank you. Um—okay, I'm going to start the exercise. Illegitimate foreign duke, by right of conquest."

Sharon consulted her sheet of paper. "Right. Second son, by designated inheritance."

Donna leaned forward from the couch to accept her cup of tea. "Younger brother."

"Nephew."

"Cousin once removed, plus war and signed agreement."

"Son." Sharon sighed. "All right, wait a minute. I give. Somehow your love life does seem a little more pressing than the right by which medieval rulers of England took the throne. You still want to tell me about him?"

"Sure!" Donna spoke earnestly. "Sharon, I'm really not the way I used to be anymore. I'm not. I have a lot more self-confidence and direction and everything. Really, Sharon. I'm not looking to be used again. It's been a long time since I was into the really self-destructive phase of my life."

Sharon sipped her tea and then gazed into it thoughtfully. "All right, I'm sorry. But I'm still worried about you. The way you talk, you sound so vulnerable. You're just so . . . gushy over this guy. I haven't seen you like this in a long time." She looked up, softening her words with a smile. "You aren't going to revert on me, are you?"

"No." Donna shook her head. "I won't revert. I know who I am now. I'm Donna Wong and I'm an apprentice gamer and I'm going to be a master. That's a far cry from the confused mess I used to be. And I came out of it the hard way, too, all by myself. I won't revert."

"I'm glad to hear you say so. But, uh, what about him? Didn't you say he was this new guy the Guild brought into town after some big elimination tournament?"

Donna nodded enthusiastically. "He impresses the hell out of me. He's the last survivor out of two hundred masters from around the world. But you know—I didn't realize who he was when I first came out and saw him. That's when it really happened—the moment I laid eyes on him. It really did."

"Maybe I have him confused with someone else, but . . . isn't he the one who represents everything you're against?"

"Well . . ." Donna wrinkled her nose again, this time uncomfortably. "He's the one you mean. That's true. It's just that, well, political opinions can change. I'll just have to change his mind." She looked up apologetically and laughed. "That's all. I'll just have to change his mind."

Sharon gave her a reluctant grin. "I don't know about you, sometimes. You're incurable, I guess."

"Yeah. I'm also determined."

Ken tossed the morning paper down on the couch next to him and looked around the Guild Hall lobby. The city was full of comfortable, affordable places to live—but none were available anywhere near the Guild Hall. The Guild Hall wouldn't be the only location in his life, he knew, but until he made more friends in town and learned his way around again, his career was about all he had. Finding a place to live nearby was only sensible.

The problem was, he couldn't find one. Well, the Guild would continue to put him up without charge for at least a month, and probably longer if he convinced them that he was seriously looking. In the meantime, his suite upstairs was opulent, even decadent, but also empty and boring.

So was his morning, for that matter.

People had been bustling through the lobby ever since he had settled there, after having breakfast served to him in his sunken bathtub up in the suite. That idea, too, had been overrated, but he had wanted to try it upon learning that the Guild Club offered room service. He had been reading the paper here in the lobby ever since.

People were still weaving briskly around the black marble pillars and tall potted plants placed throughout the lobby. Most of them stopped at the reception desk before hurrying on. The gold carpet was deep and new; Ken reflected that a lot more foot traffic would have to pass through before it became worn. He suspected, however, that it was replaced regularly, long before any wear became obvious.

"Ken? You busy?" A woman spoke near his ear, from behind him.

Deeply grateful for someone to talk to, Ken turned and found Donna Wong coming around the end of the couch.

"Well, hello!" He started gathering the newspaper to move it out of the way. "No, I'm not busy. Would you like to sit down?"

"Are you sure? I don't want to take up your time." Donna sat down gracefully, though, and crossed her legs.

Ken laughed. "I wish someone would. It's been a dull day so far; I can tell you that."

"Really? You mean, you've moved into a new place and everything already? And now you don't have anything to do."

"No, no. I'm looking for a spot near the Guild Hall, and the decent places around here are all taken. So right now, I don't have much looking to do." Again, Ken became aware that she was gazing at him with a smile that seemed unrelated to anything either of them was saying.

"Yes, I'm afraid the area is saturated with gamers. I live just a few blocks from here myself. It's a nice area." She nodded sympathetically.

"It's funny. Right now, I have the most outrageously fancy suite I've ever seen. The trouble is, it's too much. It doesn't seem like a place to live. It looks more like a set for a movie."

"Have you been meeting people and all? Getting acquainted?"

"No, not at all." He laughed. "Lou introduced me to a few people at the reception after my formal introduction to the crowd, but that's about all."

"Are you shy?"

Surprised, Ken laughed lightly again. "No, I wouldn't say so. On the other hand, I haven't been collaring people in the lobby just to say hello, either."

"Oh, that's not what I meant." She flashed a bright, pretty smile of amusement. "But everyone knows who you are. I'm sure it would be easy if you got started."

"Maybe later in the day. This morning, everyone coming through here has been pretty preoccupied." Ken shifted on the couch to face her. "Can I ask you something? You said at the reception that you came to gaming late. How did you get involved in gaming?"

"Speaking of the reception, I meant to say good night to

you when the party was breaking up. I got caught up on hospitality duties, though."

"That's okay. Uh—"

"Oh, sorry. Yes, I . . . well, it sounds like such a cliché. But I had never watched a game until I was twenty-three. A friend took me to be a spectator at a game played over some kind of huge corporate merger or something. Anyway, it was the Battle of Zama. I was fascinated."

"Really? That's all it took?"

"The very next day, I started calling around to find out what becoming a gamer would involve." She spoke proudly.

"I've never known anyone who actually became a master from that kind of start. It's a cliché for spectators to identify with gamers, and to dream about gaming, but hardly any of them ever make that decision in adulthood. Those of us who make it usually start as kids."

"I'm the exception, then. I've almost reached master status, but I have a long way to go before I reach your level."

"You wouldn't say that if you'd seen me yesterday," Ken said, laughing.

"Oh, I doubt that. What happened? Nothing serious, I hope."

"Richard Ross and I played. He beat me badly, as usual."

"As usual? You just beat out two hundred other masters for this position. I know you're good. So does everyone else in the Guild."

"Correction—I beat one hundred and ninety-nine other masters. I was the two hundredth."

"Touché." Donna closed her eyes with a smile and shook her head tightly. "Of course."

"Actually, Richard and I are old childhood friends. He's always beaten me, as a matter of fact. That's why he made it into the Guild Hall at World Headquarters long before I did."

Donna watched him, still smiling, without saying anything.

"Uh . . . as a matter of fact, I thought about asking him to put me up until I find a place, but I decided it would be a mistake. He's too intense." Ken forced a laugh. "I'll have to suffer here, in lonesome luxury."

"You can stay with me."

"What?" Ken wasn't sure he had heard her right.

Donna smiled warmly. "No obligations, no strings attached. I have a nice two-bedroom condo. You'd have to sleep on the couch in the living room, though. The second bedroom is full of junk."

"Uh . . ." Ken smiled and sort of shrugged.

"To tell the truth, I wouldn't mind a little company for a change. It would break the routine."

"Well . . ." Ken still didn't know what to say.

"You don't have to decide now. And if you don't want to, that's fine. It's just a suggestion. Oh, and remember, you'll still have the suite here to fall back on. So think about it. I'm not going to pressure you."

"Okay. Sure." Ken finally gathered his wits. "I do appreciate the offer."

"I think I've taken enough of your time. As a matter of fact, one of the reception clerks has been trying to get your attention for the last couple of seconds. I suppose you ought to see what he wants." Donna uncrossed her legs and rose.

Ken looked back over his shoulder and saw a clerk waving the earpiece to a videphone. "Oh—uh, yeah. I've got a call. Okay, thanks for the, um, offer. Would—would you like to have dinner with me tonight?"

"I would, but I have a girlfriend coming over. She's helping me keep my history fresh. Maybe another time?"

"Sure. Gotta go. Bye!" Ken gave her a big smile and hurried toward the reception desk. He could feel her gaze following him as he crossed the lobby. When he took the earpiece from the clerk, he made a point of not turning around. He didn't want to see her quit watching and walk away.

"Hello?" Ken shifted the small videphone screen toward him and saw Lou's broad, smiling face. He had a freshly lit, oversized cigar between his teeth.

"Ken, I got a hot one for ya." Lou was obviously excited. "You sittin' down?"

"I don't have anything to sit on, except the floor." Ken laughed. "What is it, Lou?"

"All right, bucko. You're the celebrity hotshot they brought into town on account of the Guild Act, right?"

Ken shook his head, but he managed to keep smiling. He didn't know Lou well enough yet to hurry him along. "I guess so. If you say so."

"So, it's only right that you play in the very first game contracted under the new act, isn't it?" Lou laughed gleefully. "I got you the offer, bucko. Great, huh?"

"Yeah." A flood of mixed emotions came over Ken. "Uh—wow. You got me a contract already?" He was fumbling for words.

"Not *a* contract; *this* contract. You, uh . . . you do understand what I'm talking about, don't you? You don't seem too excited."

"No! I am. I understand. Really, Lou. Yeah, of course I want to do it." Ken tried to sound enthusiastic, but he could feel his confidence ebbing. Yet, only yesterday he had gotten off the shuttlecopter, ready to take on the entire Guild.

"That's better. Tell you what. Swing by my office any time today and we'll go over details. The sooner the better, though. Okay?"

"I'll be up soon. Right away. Bye." Ken handed the headset back to the clerk and sighed, watching the small screen go blank. This was what he had played for, fought for, and worked for. He was in World Headquarters, playing the most important game the Guild had offered in many years. Even now, he knew that he probably could defeat almost any master.

The problem was that he would be playing Richard.

CHAPTER Four

Ken left his meeting with Lou in a flurry of excitement and apprehension. He stopped in his suite just long enough to change out of his formal clothes into a one-piece white shimmersuit, though he kept it switched off for the time being. Moments later he strode out of the Guild Hall, anxious to get away for a while.

He walked fast for the nearest Overhead stop, burning up nervous energy in the warm spring sunlight. When he saw the four linked monorail cars swooping around a curve, he broke into a run and just made it. The river bottom was only two stops away.

Being a *master gamer* was a high-pressure occupation for everyone, but Ken had adapted to that fact. He converted worry into motivation and found that the edge of panic in a game could give him an added drive. Fear of failure could be useful, and that was now the source of his energy.

Yet even Ken Li needed a break.

He stepped into a car that was almost empty. The smooth acceleration dropped him into a cushioned seat, and he squinted out across the city as the Overhead glided north. The track wove a path through downtown, skirting a grand old Art Deco skyscraper and then curving around the shining, clustered towers of the Board of Trade. He leaned close to the window to see forward to the river bottom.

This section of the city was in transition. New bars and restaurants intruded on a broken-down riverfront and crowded against older dives frequented by local residents. Ken had visited here occasionally in previous years.

The Overhead took a precipitous plunge down the slope of a bluff overlooking the water and came to a sudden, but gently calculated, stop. Ken stepped out on a platform high above the river, a secure position even in floods that would wash away the entire neighborhood below. The train slid away across the river, and he trotted quickly down the stairs with the brisk, down-current breeze whipping lightly at his hair and sleeves.

Before stepping off the platform into the throng on the sidewalk, he paused to switch on his shimmersuit. It lit up in concentric, rainbow-colored circles of varying sizes that shifted, flowed, and jumped in response to his pulse. The flash drew attention away from his face, aiding anonymity when he was in a mood to want it.

Ken swung into the crowd and moved along, finding that most of the people right here by the Overhead stop were professionals like himself, dressed for leisure. It was a safe midday crowd, but one where he might run into other masters. He walked quickly past the row of glittery new establishments, enjoying the view of the river and its banks below him on his right.

A large construction site marked an unofficial barrier. He had to slow down in the bottleneck of pedestrians on the makeshift boardwalk, trying to edge around the filthy plastic supports of scaffolding without smearing his suit. The street here was being chewed to rubble by some giant mechanical bulldog driven by a tanned and tattooed young man. It was a prelude to converting the street into a wide pedestrian boulevard. One block later, the neighborhood was unchanged.

The crowd was gone. Instead, sullen knots of ragged people stared at him from a long line of large old crumbling houses. The windows were papered over or boarded up. The yards, long untended, sported a healthy young growth of weeds and clumps of grass, flourishing in the late spring sunshine.

Right on the corner, a rambling old tavern presented a new facade of royal blue brick. It was an older establishment that hoped to attract enough of the new business to survive. He had seen it on a previous trip. A new sign hung on the front, bearing barely legible, pseudo-medieval script with the name QUAY HALL.

Ken stepped inside and found himself in near darkness. The place was crowded, though, and the dull roar of conversation and laughter filled the room. Then, as his eyes adjusted from the sunlight, he realized that heads were turning toward him, one after another, and staring.

His shimmersuit was still on, blinking and glowing in the dark, speeding up as his pulse raced with embarrassment. He turned it off with a self-conscious grin and eased into the crowd. People made way for him and returned to their conversations.

The bar stools were full, so he had to flag down the bartender over several heads. She was a blonde in her late thirties, a little heavy, who wore a name tag that read MARCIE.

Instead of speaking, she raised her eyebrows at him.

"A Kirin," he called.

She nodded and moved away into the shadows and colored shafts of light behind the bar.

The decor was a cheap attempt at medieval European atmosphere. Wooden shields lined the walls with simple heraldry rendered in inexpensive paint. Behind the bar, mirrors were separated by rough wooden shelves that held little statuettes of knights and ladies.

Ken grinned to himself. It was an ironic contrast to the authenticity of Guild Hall exhibits and the zeal for accuracy that his occupation required. Hanging out here appealed to him.

Marcie set down his beer and a glass. "Tab?"

"No."

Ken paid for it and looked around to see if he could find a seat. From what he could see, the place was filled to capacity with a mixed crowd. Most of the people looked like older residents of the neighborhood, though not all. He suspected that the young man in the beard and the white turban was somehow affiliated with the World Headquarters of the Guild, and probably also the two middle-aged women speaking French. If they recognized him, though, they either respected his privacy or just didn't care.

Ken relaxed, comfortable with his solitude in the disinterested crowd.

"You promised me!" Sharon wailed, throwing her long arms up in exasperation. One hand accidentally knocked against a stack of cardboard boxes, and she turned to steady it.

Donna wiped her hands on her bright yellow sweatshirt and looked around her cluttered second bedroom. "Help me get this box into the closet, okay? It's full of books."

The taller woman nodded, and they both lifted a cardboard box of old paperbacks. Their feet shuffled awkwardly sideways through a layer of scattered magazines and old clothes as they carried it to the closet and set it down with a thump on a footlocker.

Sharon took a deep breath of relief. "Really, Donna."

Donna smiled impishly and looked around at the floor. "Instead of sorting this stuff, I really ought to throw it away."

"Come on, answer me. You actually offered to let him *stay* here?"

"It was a whim. Besides, I told him he'd be sleeping in the living room."

"Well . . . that's something. Why didn't you tell me before?"

"Just to see what you'd say." Donna shrugged, suppressing laughter.

"Thanks a lot. So why are we hefting your leftover flotsam and jetsam all over this room if he's going to sleep on the couch?"

"Well, *if* he accepts, since he hasn't yet, it would be nicer to offer him a room. Anyway, I've been meaning to clear this out for ages."

"Well, that much makes sense, at least. I just wish you knew what you were doing."

"I do, Sharon. And—" She stopped, hearing the phone beeping. "Maybe that's him." She hurried out of the living room to answer it. "Hello."

"Donna?" A familiar face filled the screen. "Hi."

"Tommy?" Donna blinked in surprise.

"It's Tom," he said exuberantly. "I'm downstairs at the security phone. Hi ya, kid."

"Uh—hi, Tommy. You're here?"

"Sure." He gave her a happy smile. "Didn't I just say so?"

"Well . . . I guess you can come up for a little bit—"

Sharon leaned over her shoulder and broke the connection. "Was that Tom Laney?"

"Sharon, that's rude. Tommy isn't that bad."

"He's a chubby little puppy dog who never understood that you broke up with him. Look, I'll get rid of him. That parasite will be just as happy to hassle me, except that I can get rid of him when I'm ready to. See ya later."

"Sharon, he came to see me—" Donna stopped, watching Sharon resolutely snatch up a couple of her belongings and march out the door. When it had closed, Donna let out a long breath and indulged in a wistful smile.

Ken returned to the Guild Hall after dinner, in a good mood. He had struck up several conversations at the Quay Hall that had been enjoyable for their very routine quality. The afternoon had convinced him that he had had enough of VIP treatment.

His head was throbbing by the time he got back to his suite. He sat down in the waning light of dusk to call Donna. When her face appeared on his screen, the light flickered against the darkness of the cavernous rooms. "Uh, Donna? It's Ken."

"*Hi*, Ken." She brushed hair out of her eyes.

"I, well, thought maybe I'd take you up on your offer of a place to stay."

"Sure, no problem. I'll come and get you at the Guild Hall."

"I'm being enough of a bother already. I'll find my way there if you'll give me the address."

She shook her head, and he could see the sweat shining on her face. "I've just been cleaning up around here. I think I would like a walk. Why don't you meet me in the lobby in about half an hour."

"Okay. Thank you."

Ken clicked off with a sudden fear that he had acted too hastily. Well, at least they would have a chance to get acquainted. He got up and started packing his one suitcase.

Donna was prompt. Ken lugged his luggage on the ten-minute walk, telling Donna about his excursion that afternoon. Much of the trip was sharply uphill. She led him to a white tower that spiraled up from the bluff overlooking the Guild Hall. He had glimpsed it before but had never really looked at it. While she unlocked the door, he craned his neck to look up at it from the base. The spiral effect came from an enclosed escalator that ran around the outside of the structure. Horizontal landings at each level led to individual doors or to an interior hallway.

"That must take forever." He set down the suitcase and flexed his aching fingers.

"Oh, that's just a gimmick. Nobody over the third floor uses it, usually, except that in case of fire, the power goes off and the stairs are a fire escape. There are elevators inside."

"Looks like a bad movie version of the Arabian Nights."

Donna smiled over her shoulder as she pushed the door open. "I think that's why it appealed to me."

She lived on the eighteenth floor. By the time she had led him down the hallway, he was shifting his suitcase from one hand to the other every few steps. Finally, she unlocked her door and held it as he tugged the suitcase around the corner, banging it on the doorjamb and the walls before dropping it. It fell over on its side in the foyer.

"Mind if I leave it here for a minute?"

"Of course not. Come on, I'll give you the tour."

"Sure." Ken looked around with interest. The place was bright and cheerful—white walls with yellow and lavender and green trim. They were the colors he had seen her wear.

"It's pretty basic. Kitchen there, little dining table, the living room, of course—"

"Fa Mulan." Ken nodded toward the painting of the Chinese warrior woman. "That's very well done. Where'd you get it?"

She waved for him to walk toward it with her. "My friend Sharon painted it. I'll tell her you like it. The armor's genuine and all, of course. I helped her with the research."

"That was nice of—say, that's you, isn't it?"

Her smile was an unguarded flash of delight. "I wanted to get you close enough to see the face. Yes, I model for her sometimes. She gave me this as a kind of appreciation, but she kept the publishing rights."

Ken stood back and admired it. The rounded lines came right out of traditional Chinese portraits, as did the stance of the figure and the colors. She stood proudly, legs somewhat in leftward profile, but turned from the waist to face just over the viewer's left shoulder. Silver brigandine armor gleamed from her shoulders and peaked out anywhere the white surcoat had flowed back. She held a halberd in her right hand, horizontal at the waist in the classic pose. Her face was framed by a heavy banded helmet and collar from which long black hair streamed; a red tassel flew back from the top of it.

"It's appropriate for you, isn't it?"

"I liked the idea." She put her hand over her heart. "I've been immortalized. Now, let's see. My couch, here, is where I spend most of my time at home, but there's plenty of room on it. Or you can sit on the chairs, or wherever you want. . . . I'm chattering, aren't I? A little nervous, I guess. Well, follow me."

"Lead on."

"Down this little tiny hallway, we have the bathroom, my bedroom, and the extra room. I've been cleaning it out, more or less, but it's got a ways to go. I've only emptied out one drawer of that dresser, but if you don't mind the junk, it'll be more private than the living room."

The room was clean, with a single bed neatly made under a colorful quilt, but boxes were stacked up against the walls. "This is fine. I don't have that much stuff with me, and when the rest of it arrives, I can store it at the Guild Hall."

"Why don't you get your suitcase and get settled in? I want to make some tea. Want some?"

"Sure."

Ken hauled his suitcase into the room and filled the empty drawer with clothes. Then he set his toilet articles out on top of it. The bed proved to be firm when he sat on it. With a shrug of satisfaction, he got up and strolled into the kitchen.

Donna was dropping tea leaves into a large Ming Dynasty style teapot. As he came in, she took one more pinch of the curled dry leaves from a tall can. He couldn't read the Chinese on the can, but he noticed the little painting, beneath the logo, of a monkey clinging to a tree branch.

"Say! Is that the, uh, the monkey stuff?"

Donna giggled. "If you mean monkey-picked tea, yes." She grimaced and poured hot water into the teapot, leaning away from the steam. "Have you ever had it before?"

"No, but I know it's expensive. I'm flattered." He raised one eyebrow. "It doesn't taste like monkeys, does it?"

"*No,* it doesn't taste like monkeys."

"They wash their little hands before they pick it, do they?"

"Oh, stop it. Let's go into the living room. I'll take the cups if you'll carry the teapot."

They sat on the couch, facing Donna's blank wall-screen.

She poured the tea, and Ken held his cup up so that he could smell the aroma.

"People have been talking about you ever since you won that tournament. You're from Detroit, right?"

"Sort of. I worked out of the Detroit Guild Hall, but I lived in Ann Arbor. It was an easy commute. I went to college there and just stayed on."

"I'm from Chicago. I moved here about three and a half years ago. I think you'll like it."

Ken grinned and sipped his tea. "I grew up here."

"Here? Really?" She stared at him over her cup.

"Sure. I was little when the World Headquarters moved here, to be in the middle of the country. It's made the city much more international than it used to be. I remember even in high school, we had kids moving into town every year from all over the world because their parents were involved with Guild HQ. Other people assumed I was one of them."

She smiled in acknowledgment. "People do that to me even now. They think I'm from Hong Kong or China usually. Sometimes other countries. Now that you're better known, I bet you don't have that problem anymore."

"Well . . . it's receding, I suppose. What did you do before you took up gaming?"

She blew on her tea for a moment. "Nothing in particular. I floated around. Had a few dead-end jobs. I wasted quite a few years not taking care of myself."

Warned away by her tone, Ken raised his cup toward the painting. "I'm really impressed by that. The style and colors are so accurate, it looks like a Chinese painting. I have one of Guan Gong in the same style. Even the same pose. The colors are different, though."

"Sharon's very good. But look—I didn't mean to make you change the subject. It's just that I'm not very proud of some of those years. That Donna Wong is gone."

"I didn't mean to pry—"

"I know you didn't. And I would like us to get acquainted."

"So would I. And remember, if you want me to leave, just say so. I'll go back to the Guild Hall if I don't have my own place yet."

"I'm not worried about that. In another week, I'm sure we'll be old friends."

CHAPTER *Five*

Ken slept well in his new accommodations, finding the room cozy and homey. He liked Donna and felt comfortable here, though he was concerned about overstaying his welcome. Nor did he want to dampen their new friendship by complaining to her about his concern over Richard.

When he had showered and dressed, he found Donna in the kitchen stirring the contents of a large pot on the stove.

"Morning," she said brightly. "You like this stuff, by any chance?"

Ken leaned carefully over the steaming pot and then raised his eyebrows at the rice gruel richly laden with chunks of ham and beef and peas. "Congee! It's my favorite breakfast. I don't usually make it, though, 'cause it takes too long."

"Great! If you'll make the tea, I'll dish this out."

"Sure. I'll clean up."

"I usually make a lot of this and then freeze it in smaller amounts. I thawed out two of them for us. When you live alone, it's a more efficient way to cook."

"Personally, I hate cooking, but I'll do all your dishes."

"Wow—you got a deal."

They shifted breakfast to the little round yellow table just off the kitchen. Ken settled into a seat and poured soy sauce into the congee. "After eating in restaurants and the Guild Hall, this is really special."

"I'm glad." She poured tea and spoke casually. "I enjoyed our talk last night. That was nice."

"Until I yawned in your face so often you told me to go to sleep."

"I just didn't want to keep you awake."

"This really is good." Ken sat back in his seat for a moment with his teacup. "Hey, you—last night I was so busy talking about, well, get-acquainted-type things that I forgot the big news."

"Oh?"

"Lou is contracting me to play the first game to come out of the Guild Act."

"What—*you forgot*?" In a mixture of laughter and astonishment, she stared at him and dropped her hands to the table. "You forgot to tell me you were doing that? I thought gaming was a master's whole life."

"Well . . . so did I." He shrugged. "I forgot. But maybe I was avoiding the unpleasant part. I'm going up against Richard."

"Richard Ross?"

He nodded.

"I've always heard he's very good. But he never won a tournament of the kind you did."

"Well." Ken shrugged again and returned to his breakfast. After a moment, he added, "I'll have to start a practice schedule. So I guess I'll be playing practice games and apartment hunting for a while."

"I don't want you to feel trapped," she said slowly, "but you don't have to rush the apartment hunting on my account. I think we'll get alone fine, and you still have the Guild Hall if you decide you can't stand my company. Look, I guess I've ambushed you, and I didn't mean to. I just want you to know it's okay."

"Thanks. I may just take you up on it." Ken caught her eye, and for a moment they looked at each other in the slanting morning sunlight.

Donna giggled suddenly and looked away.

"What's the matter?"

"Oh . . . nothing."

After breakfast they walked to the Guild Hall. In daylight it stood tall and proud beneath the bluff, its classical facade stately and bright. Donna tossed her hair once in the flower-scented breeze, smiling to herself. Even if Ken moved out tomorrow, she would enjoy telling Sharon that she had invited him to stay for a prolonged period, just to watch her scream.

In the lobby they split up, Ken going to check for messages at the reception desk and then to contact people about practice games. She thought it would be presumptuous to volunteer herself, and he had not asked her to play him. When he had gone to the desk, she walked to the public phone corner and slipped on a headset.

Sharon's reaction was disappointing. Instead of throwing a minor tantrum that Donna could laugh at, Sharon's face on the screen showed resignation and a reluctant smile.

"I don't know about you, kid. I harrass you like, I don't know, a fishwife or something and paint you as Fa Mulan, the warrior woman. Only you keep trying to become a cortesan instead."

Donna laughed. "He's staying in the other room, Sharon."

"Did you have a good visit last night, then?"

"Oh, yeah. Until he was so tired, I had to tell him to go to bed. And he can be really silly. He was teasing me about the monkey-picked tea."

"So he's not one of those swell-headed, temperamental celebrity types?"

"I don't think so. In fact, he's worried about this upcoming game he got against Richard Ross. He didn't say much, but I can tell."

"Just be careful, okay? Don't get all off-center over him, and don't let him get like Tommy."

"Tommy! Of course—what happened?"

"Nothing much. The poor slob isn't that particular who he

talks to. I let him whine at me for a while about how rotten his life is, then I said good-bye."

"Poor Tommy. I really should have let him come up to talk."

"He's a parasite. He's never meant anyone ill, but he's still a dependent kid looking for soft touch. And don't you let Ken lean on you, either."

"Ken isn't like that."

"Maybe not, but you attract that sort. Remember?"

"Yeah, you and I talked about that, but I keep telling you it was a long time ago. I don't want to lean on anyone, or let them lean on me. Besides, with you around, how can I forget?"

"I guess I've been lecturing you a lot the last few days, haven't I? Well, I'll let up. Promise. Look . . . have you got time this afternoon to sit for some sketches? I won't lecture at all."

"Sure. I'll meet you after lunch."

Donna clicked off feeling guilty for teasing her.

Ken was surprised to find a message from Richard waiting for him. It suggested that Ken come up to meet him in a certain room, with no other explanation. Aware that he could take a long time finding it on his own, Ken enlisted the aid of a reception clerk, who escorted him to the right door.

Ken knocked. Richard let him in and glanced up and down the corridor before closing the door again.

"Are the rules against fraternizing different at World Headquarters?" Ken asked with a sarcastic smirk.

"No." Richard laughed nervously. "It's a matter of tradition here, too, not a matter of rules. This project is a private concern of mine, though."

Ken turned to look. They were in a practice room, identical to the one in which they had played Tunis except for wires and electronic equipment littering the floor. "What's up?"

"Well, I know we shouldn't fraternize too much before we play each other, but I wanted to show you what I'm doing.

Since we've just signed, I figure our mutual prestige will squelch any complaints if I show you right away."

"That's if anybody finds out."

"Ha! That lousy native guide who let you up here is telling everyone this minute that we're together—wager on it."

"You think so?"

"He knows this room is on extended lease to me. But forget him and come over here."

Ken followed him to a pile of items he could not recognize, and several tangles of wires. "Since when are you into electronics?"

"Not too long. Can you guess what it's about?"

Ken looked over the jumble and managed to trace several wires up to the sensory band hanging by one of the gaming seats. The sensory band was much thicker than usual, with elaborate straps and pads that would cross the top of the wearer's head. It was almost a kind of helmet. "You refining the sensory bands or something?"

"Watch this." Richard sprang up into the seat and turned on the projector. The empty gaming field jumped to life with rolling green prairies and one tiny, lone human figure standing in the middle. Richard pulled the sensory band down into place over his eyes and ears. "Look at the guy down there."

Ken moved to the edge of the field, watching the holographic figure. Nothing was happening that he could see. He started to look up at Richard.

"No! Don't look away. Keep watching."

Ken looked back just in time to see the figure walk slowly toward him. "Yeah, so?"

"Up here."

Ken suddenly realized that Richard had never swung the keyboard up into place. He was sitting with both hands palm down on his thighs, concentrating his gaze on the field through the eyepieces of the sensory band. Ken turned back and saw the figure on the field turn and jog back the way he had come, zigzagging as he went.

Richard let out a long, deep breath and pulled the band off

his head. His face was flushed and sweaty with effort, despite the few moments he had actually been wearing it. He grinned and climbed down slowly.

"Is that what it looked like?" Ken asked quietly.

Richard nodded. "Gives me an incredible headache, though. Want to try it?"

"The headache? No, thanks. But, uh . . . what is it? How does it work?"

"This guy, an elderly retired scientist, brought it to me and asked me to help test it. It was some pet project of his; I don't think he even took it too seriously. Then he passed away and nobody ever came to get it, so I've continued working with it. That's practically all I know. He called it a neurofeedback system and said it works by reading the visual area of the brain. You picture what you want, and the band reads it. That's the hard part. Then the band orders the computer accordingly."

"So we could actually play without keyboards someday."

"That's the idea. I can use it in games to some extent, though. The simple version, here, is what I use for testing. Of course, real use is still a long way off. And, supposedly, it can be a little dangerous."

"Dangerous? How?"

"Some kind of feedback of energy. I've never had any trouble."

"Except that incredible headache. Maybe you ought to do this in the company of someone who understands the electronics a little better."

"Ha! Do I detect a little envy here?"

"Not hardly." Disgusted, Ken turned away. "When you have it perfected, let me know."

"Well . . . you have a point. Actually, the guy told me that it works better if you turn up this one dial. Only that increases the danger of causing some kind of cerebral overload . . . perhaps a coma."

"A *coma*? You're crazy to be doing this alone. This thing could kill you."

"I'm careful enough. Besides, these overloads have a regular pattern. If you go into coma, you should wake up within eight to twelve weeks once the overload is dissipated."

"Eight to twelve weeks? That's not exactly paltry."

"But it's reliable. For a coma, I hear that's rare. Anyhow, keep the danger to yourself, all right? I don't want it to ruin the publicity for this later on."

"All right. And like I said, once it's perfected, let me know. In the meantime, I have enough headaches, thank you."

Richard laughed and then winced. "You're starting to convince me. C'mon, let's go downstairs. I have to get something for my head."

Ken shook his head in mock wonder and led the way out.

CHAPTER Six

Ken started his practice schedule with no changes in his usual routine. He took the approach that this game was no different, at least on the gaming level, than any other. Even in the first few days, though, he found himself making simple mistakes and lapses of judgment that he had outgrown years ago. At first he blamed the problem on moving and having to store so many of his belongings in the Guild Hall, where he could not get at them easily. However, Donna was a flexible apartment mate, and he quickly grew comfortable with the arrangement. So the charade failed.

The light, breathy spring days matured into full summer. He did not care much for swimming, but he enjoyed relaxing by the outdoor pool at her building, and watching Donna dive, swim submerged like an otter, and then hoist herself out slick with chlorinated water in the June sunlight. He developed a routine of playing a practice game early in the morning, having lunch, and then playing a second one in the afternoon. Then he would meet her at the pool for several hours. The pastime helped him avoid thinking too much about the fact of his intimidation by Richard—at least enough to go back and practice again the next day.

As the weeks progressed, however, he found that his anxiety was translating into more and more blunders on the gaming field. They, in turn, drove him more often to the Quay

Hall, where he could stare in silence at nothing in particular and not worry Donna while he did it. At least he was not drinking any more than before; his wariness of what alcohol could do to his career remained at the fore.

The name of the Quay Hall and its poor excuse for a medieval decor were oddly refreshing. As he leaned back in his booth and gazed at the shields on the far wall, he found himself remembering the last game he had played before starting that long and exhausting elimination tournament. He hadn't been overconfident, exactly, but he hadn't given any real thought to his opponent, either.

For just a moment he missed the simplicity of the situation, though he had been hurting at that time for a different reason. A year and a half had passed since he had last seen Lydia, right after the game she had contracted him to play for her. Memories of her didn't hurt any more . . . perhaps Donna had something to do with that. Which battle had he fought for Lydia? Oh, yeah . . .

Ken pushed buttons on the arm of the gaming chair to adjust its position and looked down over the big white holographic playing field in front of him. The announcer had finished his introductions, and Ken had already tuned out the presence of thirty-five thousand excited, eager spectators packed into the stands around the Granicus Arena of the Detroit Guild Hall. Now he swung up the flat keyboard on a steel arm and worked it into exactly the right height and distance from him.

Ten meters away, across the playing field, his opponent finished maneuvering his own keyboard and raised one hand, signifying that the was ready. Ken centered his keyboard and made sure that the small video screen across the top row of keys was not obscured by any glare from the lights. Then he raised his hand.

An attendant seated on the left edge of the playing field pushed a button on his own keyboard. Instantly the blank field came alive with holographic terrain and miniature armies drawn up in battle formation. His keyboard screen read, "Culloden Moor, 1746. House of Stuart. Prince Charles Edward Stuart." A list of Victory Conditions followed.

Ken nodded to himself. Culloden? Yes. . . .

A month before, Ken had stood up behind his desk as his secretary brought in his next appointment. "Why didn't you just call me at home? I didn't know you were coming until I checked the calendar this morning." His heart started pounding.

The slender, honey-blonde woman stood by the closed door, across the room. "I'm here to see you professionally," she said coldly. She wore a simple dark blue dress that he remembered.

"As a client, then, please have a seat." Ken gestured toward the two padded armchairs in front of his desk.

"A *prospective* client." Clutching her purse in both hands, she walked primly forward and sat down. "I guess you know I wouldn't be here if I wasn't absolutely desperate."

Ken sat down behind his desk, intensely curious. "Yeah. I never expected that you, of all people, would volunteer your litigation for a Guild contract." He picked up a pen and nervously twirled it.

"Have you read about the case? It's been in the papers." She held herself stiffly erect.

"I saw some headlines. When I realized they were about you, I . . . quit reading." He smiled a little, self-consciously.

"I know you're good, and I know your fee. I'll pay you in full, of course." She opened her purse.

"You know it's customary to give discounts to friends—"

"I'd rather pay you in full." She pulled out a checkbook.

"Even so, you're premature with that. Don't worry. I don't intend to turn you down. When you're in trouble, I'll still do anything for you. Now. What's the case about?"

Lydia settled back in the chair slightly. "It's about Johnny AA9. Remember him?"

"Mm—isn't he classified? You never said much about him."

"He's our most successful artificial life-form. I can't tell you much more than that."

"You're covered under gamer-client privilege, you know."

"He's still classified. The main thing is, Carnehan-Chang Labs contracted us to conduct certain experiments, and Johnny AA9 resulted from one of them. We don't want to proceed any further because Carnehan-Chang won't commit themselves to full responsibility for him, and we don't want to give him up until we know he'll be taken care of properly." Lydia shook her head tightly. "The cell differentiation is . . . I can't tell you how advanced, but I can tell you we had to put the . . . put AA9 into cryogenic sleep when we first went to court. It's been six years and we're getting nowhere. So finally both sides agreed to a game."

Ken fought to keep his voice professional and not to feel the strong attraction he still had toward her. "So you're resolving a simple ownership issue? Does the winner of the game take ownership or relinquish it?"

"It's not that simple." Lydia's voice was almost a whisper. "Johnny's *human*, Ken. He—"

"What? I thought that was just a nickname or something."

"If he reaches full term, as we expect, he'll have all the human needs. But who's responsible for him? The bureaucracy of a corporation? And who's going to protect him from being experimented on constantly by that collective bureaucracy? For that matter, will he be a person under the law? Or an animal, which can be patented and owned by a corporation? We made him out of lab chemicals, not human gametes. I want some legal definitions before we go on, and the standard judicial process hasn't given me any."

"Well, as you so often told me, a game won't provide a legal precedent. So what are you asking if you win?"

"That the fetus—that Johnny stay in suspended animation until my lab gets all the legal decisions we're asking for."

"What does the other side want?"

"They want immediate full ownership and the total control that goes with it." Lydia forced an ironic, unpleasant smile.

"Why are you asking all these questions? Aren't you the one who said that playing wargames was independent of issues?"

"Well, that's true. As a gamer, I don't pass judgment on the controversy, but I do like to know the magnitude of the case." He shrugged, very slightly. "I know you still hate the Gaming Masters' Guild, not to mention me. If you didn't think this game was of extreme importance, I guess you wouldn't be here."

Lydia shook her head angrily. "Never! The system is terrible—it doesn't give us any justice based on the issues at all."

"But you're going to pay me for it, anyway." Ken couldn't help a little smile of his own.

"Well . . . all the new technology just keeps outstripping the laws on the books. We have to have something to go by, until society catches up with us."

Ken nodded. "Exactly. I'll take your case."

The day before the game, Ken had taken Lydia out for brunch. Giving one's client an encouraging talk before a game was part of the psychology of being a *master gamer*, and though he was uncomfortable with her, he wanted to be strictly professional. The conversation was awkwardly polite.

"I don't like to sound ungrateful," she said over her coffee, once the plates had been removed. "I know you'll do your best for me. I just wish we had laws that made the games unnecessary."

"I agree it would be better for everybody," said Ken with a shrug. "It's also impossible to rush the process. Science and technology are rolling right along, and the legislators have to be caught up before they can pass decent laws."

Lydia sighed and nodded. "So . . . how have you been?"

Ken remained motionless, looking down at the table in front of him for as long as he could. This was the last time he would be able to talk to her for a long time, and maybe ever. He decided to sacrifice pleasantry for honesty.

"I miss your daughter. Very badly."

"She's fine. She doesn't need you."

"I helped raise her for three years. And it's not as though she remembers her father or that he's around somewhere. I'd just like to see her sometimes. Take her places."

"She doesn't need you. It's not like you think."

"You don't know what I think," Ken said angrily. "You never let me tell you. Every time I tried to talk about her, you just told me I was wrong. After years of telling me you couldn't read my mind, you suddenly decided you could when it served your own selfish purposes. Thanks a lot."

"You're not her father, you know."

"Have you told her you won't let me see her?"

"She hasn't asked."

"So you're just letting her wait to see if I come to visit her, and letting her assume that when I don't, it's because I don't care about her? You don't even have the guts to tell her it's your decision, do you?"

"Forget it, Ken. Thanks for brunch." Lydia slid out of her chair and walked away quickly, slinging the strap of her bag over her shoulder.

The Battle of Culloden—that was where the House of Hanover, represented by the English and certain Scottish clans allied with them, defeated the Stuart heir and his rebel Scots and brought about the end of the traditional Highland way of life. Ken studied the disposition of his troops, just as the game activated. He played the role of Prince Charles and had most of the limitations imposed on him that the Bonnie Prince had endured. His only edge over the Prince was his own tactical ability, of which the Prince had had very little.

The Victory Conditions were simple enough. The rebel Scots had to destroy a certain number of English or drive them from the field. The English had to destroy a certain number of Scottish rebels, or kill the Scottish heir. If Ken withdrew with the Prince and his army intact, the game would be drawn and another one played. However, with the royal superiority in cavalry, the last possibility was too unlikely to consider.

Quickly Ken worked over the keyboard to correct certain

flaws in his order of battle that had been allowed by the Prince's incompetent Irish advisor, John William O'Sullivan. For instance, the left of his lines angled away from the enemy, so that they were farther from them than the right. It was nothing more than sloppy supervision, and he issued orders to have the clans there brought forward. They were anchored by the Macdonalds, a sullen lot who were angered over losing their position on the right, which had been theirs by tradition for many centuries. Ken could not move them there now. Nor could he do anything about the lack of food and sleep endured by his army prior to the time of the opening of the game or about the rain and sleet falling out of a nonexistent sky. Their physical and emotional condition would be considered by the computer as it resolved conflict.

Ken's opponent was in the role of the English Duke of Cumberland, and he gave the order for his artillery to fire. Ken gave a similar order and hurried to rearrange his right. He felt flushed now, and the sweat flowed freely down his face and back from the effort of concentration and from the tension. A flash of memory came to him—a quote from aged Lord Lovat, who had brought his Clan Fraser out for the Prince: "None but a mad fool would have fought that day."

A small stone house called Culwhiniac stood far to the right of the Prince's line. A long stone wall ran from the Prince's line all the way to the royal line. More stone walls ran from this wall to the right at perpendicular angles, making them excellent barriers against the royal army, but O'Sullivan had failed to defend them. Ken knew better and drew clans from his second line to hold the walls. He also sent his meager cavalry there, the Fitz-James Horse that was down to squadron strength and the half troop of Life Guards he still had. This was out of character for the Prince, since the Life Guards were acting as his personal bodyguard, but Ken had the prerogative.

He had no other cavalry, however, and he was outnumbered overall by about 8,800 to less than 5,000. A third of the rebels had drifted away recently, driven by starvation and lured by the nearness of their homes. Historically the House of Stuart had been routed in twenty-five minutes.

The royal lines began to advance.

Smoke, rain, sleet, and fog obscured the formations on the battlefield, but Ken could see that the royal artillery, with its light snapping sounds, was tearing viciously into the motionless rebel line. On the rebel right, English dragoons and the Clan Campbell were advancing to the first stone wall of Culwhiniac. The Campbells, afoot as classic Highlanders, began to dismantle the wall for the mounted dragoons. At the next wall, they would be met with a hail of fire from the rebel right.

Ken recalled breathlessly the kind of troops his Highlanders were, as the last feudal army to assemble in Britain. They wore kilts and plaids, and they carried muskets and claymores and dirks and targs. Their only effective tactic was the legendary charge of wild, screaming, furious clansmen down upon their enemy and the panic it sometimes caused.

It had not worked at the real battle.

The rebel artillery ceased firing. The Prince's guns had been in poor condition and his gunners inexperienced; they had silenced themselves early in the actual conflict, and the computer had silenced them again on that basis here. Ken gave the attack order to his restless warriors, keying in the cry, "Claymore!"

The first line of Scots rebels raced forward across the moor with cries that sounded in the arena's speaker system. A great roar of excitement rose from the spectators seated in the giant oval, even breaking through Ken's concentration as his fingers danced over the keys. Then, blinking sweat from his eyes, he suddenly saw a chance for advantage.

The computer had been programmed to include all the personalities who were known historically and for the behavior of them and of the ranks in general on the particular day in question. Also, of course, Ken's opponent would be using his own knowledge of the battle to strengthen his advantages, though in this case the royal victory had been quick and easy. He was probably not making any significant changes. On the rebel right, where the Fitz-James Horse and Life Guards were waiting behind a stone wall, Ken saw a chance to rewrite the conflict.

Historically the skewed angle of the rebel line had caused the charging Highlanders to run somewhat to the left, instead of straight at their enemies. The Macdonalds, on the left, had been slaughtered or driven back by artillery and musket fire even before they reached the enemy, because of the great distance they had to cross. Just to the right of center, however, the charging Frasers, Appin Stewarts, and Camerons had overcompensated by running too far to their right. This cut off the charge of their allied Atholl men, who were racing down the moor with one of the stone walls next to them, on the right wing of the line. They were driven into the wall by their Cameron fellows. There the enemy Campbells had turned the rebel flank, lined the stone wall, and fired their muskets point-blank into the blunted Atholl attack.

Ken had already straightened his line, and the Highland charge before his eyes was running straight, though the orderly musket fire and artillery fire from the royal lines sliced into it savagely. On the right, however, the Campbells were just beginning to line up along the stone wall. Afraid he was too late, Ken had the Prince send a messenger running to the rebel horse. Just in time, they too leaped their own wall and charged the Campbells and the English Dragoons.

To defend themselves, the Campbells turned to face forward, allowing the Atholl regiment, with the rest of the Highland line, to finish their great charge.

Now came a terrible moment for Ken, who was tense and nearly drained already, and still drawing on reserves of energy. Just like a real commander, he had made certain choices and given certain orders. Also like a real commander, he could only wait and watch as they were carried out, looking through the rain and smoke and fog for another order that might help.

On the left, the Macdonalds had closed with the royal

line, which they had never done historically. The battle was in the balance now. If the charge failed to break the royal line, the rebels had no other tactic.

In the center, Clan Chattan had closed with the English in the face of a furious fire of grapeshot and steady, disciplined, relentless volleys of English muskets. Even so, the Scots broke the first line and fell upon the second—upon their bayonets, which outfought the claymores when properly used. The English center held.

On the left, the Macdonalds simultaneously drove a shock wave into the English right, enduring the same murderously heavy fire and disciplined lines of English bayonets.

Ken raised his head to look through smoke toward the rear of his enemy. Historically, the Duke of Cumberland had sent the Kingston's Horse regiment and two regiments of infantry from his rear around his right flank to smash the Macdonalds. Yes, Ken could see them moving. He could do nothing about it.

Ken's only chance was on the right. The men of Atholl, led by the Prince's fine but disfavored general, Lord George Murray, had also pierced the front line of Barrel's regiment. That regiment was courageous, however, and was virtually the only one that had withstood the Highland charge in the last battle between these armies, the rebel victory at Falkirk. Yet the odds were now just uncertain enough to offer hope.

Breathing hard and fast, Ken ordered his second line to charge. This was a group of Lowland Scots, Irish, and dismounted cavalry regiments, the last because enough horses could not be found. In the real battle, they had been of no consequence, and the computer would not figure them to have great combat power. They charged, however, before the Macdonalds were smashed by the enemy cavalry, before the Campbells and Dragoons overwhelmed the weaker rebel horse and before the rebel center began to flee and obstruct the force of the second charge.

The Camerons and the Atholl men had driven the remnants of the royal front line back. Yet the royal lines stood three regiments deep, and the regiments of Semphill and Wolfe in the second line now poured their musket fire onto the clansmen.

Those Highlanders, however, rallied when their second line came charging down behind them. Again, the shock of the Highland charge drove back the English line with horrible casualties. If the rebels were to win, this was the spot that would bring victory.

Ken, still working fast over the keyboard, watched with clenched teeth as Kingston's Horse drove into the Macdonalds and scattered them. They fled, to be ridden down by the English. With grim satisfaction, however, Ken noted that Kington's Horse gave chase, as would the English infantry behind them. They would take themselves out of the battle.

On the rebel right, beyond the stone walls and away from the rest of the battle, the numbers of the Campbells and the numbers and discipline of the Dragoons broke the rebel horse. Ken sent the Prince out to rally his Life Guards, and then realized that no one could do so against those odds. With both flanks collapsing, Ken had nowhere to send the Prince except after the Atholl men, into the battle itself.

Finally, the improbable happened. The men of Atholl, still led by Lord Murray, burst around the right of Wolfe's regiment where it had been anchored against the stone wall. The Prince charged after them, calling stragglers forward still. With the right of the line broken, the clansmen all across the center ran forward again, enraged by the fever of battle and encouraged by the partial success.

Courage in a common soldier was always a variable and unpredictable quality. At Falkirk, Barrel's had been almost the only royal regiment to withstand the Highland charge; historically, at Culloden, they had all stood fast and carried the day. The computer calculated the fragility of human courage and either provided it or withdrew it according to its own complex judgment of the battle at any given stage.

Though the royal army had taken both flanks of the rebels, and the Dragoons on Ken's right were in position to return and fall upon the rear of his men and destroy them, the computer suddenly broke the morale of the royal flank, which had been turned. The men of Semphill's Border Scots and Wolfe's turned and fled yet another time from the triumphant, screaming Highlanders chasing after them. The royal army was still in the better position overall, but panic was contagious, and the royal lines collapsed like dominoes, in a repeat of Falkirk. Cumberland could not contact and control the widespread wings of his army, but the Prince was now riding with his own most successful troops and was able to keep them together.

As the royal formation collapsed, Cumberland withdrew. A moment later, the holograms all froze in place. Ken read on his keyboard screen, "Victory Conditions: House of Stuart."

Ken let out a long breath and slumped back in his seat. Exhaustion overtook him now that the game was ended. The crowd around him was cheering wildly. He closed his eyes, chest heaving, and indulged himself in a grin. Lydia would have her way, at least until the courts got to work.

A Guild attendant took Ken to the reception room in an electric cart, as was customary. Ken thanked him and hopped out, feigning more energy than he felt. As the crowd parted before him, waving and calling congratulations, he reflected that the bounce in his step resulted more from unsteady knees than from his exhilaration.

If he had lost, of course, he wouldn't have any bounce at all.

Ken made his way to the refreshment table, where a smiling young female attendant had a cup of red punch to hand him. He downed it quickly and then stood with his back to the table, accepting hand after hand of good cheer, all from privileged spectators whose position with the Guild had in some way gained them entrance to the private reception.

One hand suddenly thrust a sealed envelope into his. Ken looked up into Lydia's face.

"Thanks. I do appreciate it," she said quietly. "That's a check for the balance of your fee."

"I'm glad I could help. Really. Thank you." Ken was uncomfortably aware of the grinning strangers all around them.

"I still despise this method of reaching decisions. It proves nothing about the issues at hand. It's totally arbitrary." Lydia spun quickly and disappeared into the crowd.

"It's supposed to be arbitrary," Ken said lamely, after her. Then he looked around at the crowd of people surrounding him, waiting with big smiles for some snappy comeback from their idol.

"Well." He smiled and shrugged. "Justice is justice . . . isn't it?"

Ken smiled weakly at the memory, staring into the tall blue candle flame on the table in front of him. That last comment had sounded lame at the time, and it still did. Donna would not have thought more highly of that particular opinion, he guessed, than Lydia had.

The tournament that had followed had changed his life substantially. He had more victories, more prestige, a better position. He decided now, with ironic humor, not to meet any more clients for pregame lunches. Still, Lydia was normally gone from his thoughts, as well as his life, all to the good.

Ken sighed and got up to leave. The respite from practice still hadn't made him feel any better.

The day before the formal game, Ken played one last practice game. Normally, he took a rest the day before a formal game, but he just didn't have the confidence for that now. The game he played did not restore any of it. By the end of the game, his arms were stiff and weary as he punched the last sequence of keys. The move sent the scant remainder of his Arab army into retreat under General Ziyad ibn-Salih.

The game had been a disaster. Ken had been pressing too hard for a victory and again made amateurish mistakes. His opponent, playing the Tang Dynasty General Gao Xianzhi, had brilliantly escaped a pincer movement by Ken's Arabs and an army of Karluk Turks led by a computer-programmed personality. The retreat would give Victory Conditions to his opponent, but it would constitute a better performance than if he simply kept fighting until the Arabs were routed or slaughtered.

Through his sensory band Ken watched the lightly armed Arabs galloping away across the dusty hills, robes flying out behind them, with bows slung on their shoulders and bloody scimitars still in their hands. In July of 751, the Flame of Islam had met the Golden Age of China on the banks of the Talas River near Aulie-Ata. A huge conflict had decided, perhaps for all time, whether Central Asia would be part of the Islamic world or remain under the sway of Chinese culture. Historically, the Arabs had marched north and the Karluks had marched south to trap the immense Chinese host between them. They had destroyed the Chinese army and had taken thousands of prisoners on the wastes of Central Asia north of Sogdiana. Yet Ken's Arabs were in frantic flight.

Several seconds passed and the computer froze the field with "Victory Conditions: Tang Empire" written on Ken's keyboard screen. Shaken, he gave his opponent a quick congratulations and hurried away.

He was striding out of the lobby with his head down when he overheard Richard's name. Not wanting to listen, yet not able to resist, he paused long enough to hear one gamer tell another that in a practice game Richard, as King Roderick of the Goths, had actually fought the Arabs to a standstill at Wadi Bekka.

He had never heard of anyone doing that before; usually, the Gothic side had to accept a handicap from the Guild computer in order to compete.

That evening Ken went up to the roof of Donna's building to be alone for a while. He found a beat-up, rusted metal chair and sat down gingerly. The summer sun was still high, and the air was humid and heavy. The bugs were never bad up here, though, and from this height the city was pretty.

Ken propped his feet on an overturned paint can. In the distance, he could see the old Union Station, where Pretty

Boy Floyd had once had a shoot-out with federal agents. Beyond it, tall modern buildings gleamed in the sunlight. Ken leaned back and gazed at them, studying the lines of architecture, the flight of occasional birds, and the sweep of the billowing white clouds.

Time passed easily, and the slant of the sunlight grew sharper.

"Just sitting here?" Donna asked.

Ken jumped in surprise, then grinned. "Uh, yeah. Hi. I didn't hear you."

"I'm sorry to bother you. One of the neighbors said you came up here a long time ago, and I just wondered if you were here."

Ken squinted into the sunlight, looking up at her. The breeze was blowing her hair into her face, and she held it out with one hand. She was wearing a turquoise sleeveless T-shirt and white shorts that emphasized her tan. Her legs and feet were bare, and he made a point of looking away from them.

"Do you want to be alone?" She started to turn away.

"No! Not necessarily, I mean." Ken realized that he wanted her to stay. "Listen, did you ever see a movie called *The Golden Horde*? It's old. I saw it when I was a kid."

"No, I don't think so. Some epic about Mongol Russia?"

"Supposedly. It was no more accurate than most historical films. It suggested that the Mongols merely overwhelmed their enemies with numbers and never made any real military contributions."

Donna squatted Asian-style next to him. "That sounds like typical Hollywood. Why do you ask?"

"Oh . . . I've just been thinking about how I got to this point—being a master and getting to World Headquarters and all. It's a little frustrating, coming all this way and still carrying around an old childhood fear."

"It's awfully irrational, too." She smiled gently. "I guess you know that."

"Yeah." Ken nodded. "If you weren't a gamer, what would you be?"

Donna looked away and stood up. "I don't know. Not much, certainly."

Ken wished he and Donna were closer. He suddenly wanted a hug, but he could see that she had become leery of the conversation after his last question. He decided to change the subject a little. "I'm also trying to face the fact that I'm going to lose."

"Hey!" She put a fist on her hip in exaggerated disapproval. "You can't talk like that. You haven't even started playing yet. That's even more irrational than feeling intimidated by Richard. At least we all admit he's very good. But you can't just give up before you start."

Ken lowered his head. "Guess I just need moral support."

For a moment, neither of them spoke.

"You need a good dinner, too, and some rest." Donna took his arm and pulled him up, then let go. "It's late. Let's eat."

Ken followed her downstairs with a feeling of disappointment.

They heated up leftovers for dinner. Afterward, though, Ken could not sit still. He paced around the apartment and finally went for an extended walk just to burn up his nervous energy. This was the first time he had felt this tense before a game since his very first formal contest. Even the elimination tournament had not thrown him off his stride this much. In fact, his confidence had been a large part of his success there. Eventually, Ken decided he was tired enough to go to bed. "See you in the morning."

"All right." Donna looked up from her book as she sat on the couch with her feet drawn up beneath her. "Tell you what, I'll treat you to breakfast out tomorrow. Interested?"

Ken gave her a surprised, appreciative glance. "It's a date. Thanks."

Once Ken was in bed, however, he did not sleep well. In the darkness, his mind wandered on the verge of sleep, just beyond conscious control. Thundering hoofbeats and clanging swords accompanied the constant glow of blue and orange lines of battle, flexing and shifting across the sky.

Rivers flowed on the edge of battlefields, running red with blood instead of water. Inca warriors dressed in feathers and gold battled burnoosed Bedouin. Vikings in furs and leather assaulted the stone towers of Zimbabwe.

When he finally slept, he dreamed.

He dreamed that he walked the narrow ledge atop a winding castle wall that wandered in and out of the clouds. Howling winds threatened to carry him away, but he kept his balance. A full-length mirror appeared in front of him, reflecting his own slender frame, with slanted eyes and wind-tossed black hair.

What kind of career is this? he asked his image. *Even if it is for important issues, it's still a game.*

What's the difference between Varus and Verus? asked his reflection. What about Pax Sinica and bar sinister?

Around the mirror and himself a lavish baroque ballroom took shape, shining with gold leaf, marble statuary, and chandeliers.

Do you have to win all the time? *If you can't win, will you pout and go home*? *Where does your ego lie*? He asked the face in the mirror.

This room is ugly, said his reflection.

It vanished, to be replaced by the dry mountain walls of Tassili N'Ajjer in the Central Sahara. Paintings of cattle over eight millennia old listened to Ken say, *Winning is the glamorous side of these wars, but you can't have winners without losers.*

Can you tolerate being a loser? sneered his reflection. If you lose, it's desolation city.

The empty, wasted mountains grew forests and jutting crags. High, heavy walls of carefully cut stone sprang from the rocky soil. The thin, cold air of the Andes blew through ruined Machu Picchu.

Ken shivered. *It was cold, this business. You did your work all alone, despite the crowds and friends and colleagues. The real work went on in your head, where no one else could help. When game time came around, it was just you and the keyboard and the field.*

Is the Temple of the Moon really the Haram Bilkis, as Yemenis say? Who cares? Did Hui Shen and his monks really reach Teotihuacan? Does it really matter to anyone?

I don't have to win.

You do.

I'm not good enough to win.

That, of course, could be.

Thanks a lot.

Clouds roiled up around the dead bones of the Andean city. Ken's image in the mirror put on a gray cowboy hat and tipped it.

Good-bye.

The dream faded to a fitful sleep.

CHAPTER Seven

When the moment finally arrived, Ken found himself sitting in his game seat on the floor of the Guild Hall's formal Marathon Gaming Arena. On all four sides, spectators packed the rows of theater seats, up to a height far above him. A giant video screen was embedded in each wall over the highest row, so that if spectators could not follow the holograms clearly on their own, they could watch an overview close-up on the screen opposite them.

Ken waited patiently while an attendant adjusted the keyboard's position in front of him. Then he fitted the sensory band on and looked across the white playing field. Richard was also prepared.

The announcer's voice boomed over the loudspeakers as he introduced the case to the crowd: ". . . is the position of Warford Medical Supply Company. Their opponent, represented by Master Richard Ross, is LeHew Business Machines. Their claim in this dispute is as follows. . . ."

Cheers from the crowd rose up at the names of the principals, as well as the names of the masters. Those who followed the masters were usually pure fans of the game. Spectators interested in the principals normally had either wagers riding on the outcome or an interest in the welfare of the companies. At the moment, however, Ken just barely heard any of it as he composed himself.

The announcer finished. To Ken's left, seated on a high platform, another attendant waited for both masters to raise their hands. When Ken and Richard had both done so, he pushed a button. The playing field lit up with color.

Ken's keyboard screen read, "Bosworth Field. 1485. Richard III."

He felt a pang of disappointment, followed by a seizure of panic. Richard III. From what he knew about Bosworth, where the House of Plantagenet of England had come to an end with the death of Richard III, the best way to beat the role would be to get the King away from the battlefield alive, but the computer would not be impressed with a hapless retreat.

Since this was a formal game, they had only fifteen seconds of orientation before the game activated. Ken lost a few more seconds wiping his palms on his shirt. Then he studied the battlefield.

His army, led by him as Richard III, was divided into three sections. The units in the van, led by the Duke of Norfolk as a programmed personality, stood in position around the northwest slope of Ambion Hill. On the crest behind them, Richard III commanded the main body of his army. Altogether, the royal units represented 8,000 men. That included reserves of about 3,000 under the Earl of Northumberland, a mile to the rear.

The disposition of forces resembled a four-sided card game. Henry Tudor, the Lancastrian heir to the throne, advanced from the west with 3,000 French mercenaries and 2,000 Welsh supporters. His van, led by the Earl of Oxford as a programmed personality, advanced along Redmore Plain on their way to Ambion Hill, skirting the north side of a large marsh that separated the rebel and royal armies. Sir William Stanley, a supposed vassal of King Richard, held 2,000 mounted knights to the northwest. His brother, Lord Thomas Stanley, stood about a mile to the south with units of another 2,000 men. Ken, as Richard III, nominally had the combat power of 12,000 men ready to take the field against 5,000 in the rebel cause.

Ken's royal units also represented better fighting men than Tudor's mercenaries and had greater combat power in the computer as a result. However, the loyalty of both Stanleys, and also of Northumberland, was suspect. The Stanleys had prospered during the Wars of the Roses by keeping a careful eye on the main chance. Lord Stanley had changed sides six times in the preceding twenty years, always aligning himself just in time with the dominant side as the situation fluctuated. The Stanleys had neglected to challenge Tudor's entry into England from Wales through Stanley lands, neither joining him nor obstructing him. As the battle approached, they remained in neutral positions.

Thanks to Ken's childhood play and enthusiastic study, he had remembered the situation quickly. However, the field activated before he had figured out what to do. He doubted either his opponent, Richard, or his own historical role, Richard III, shared that problem.

Oxford led the rebel van resolutely forward. Ken made minor adjustments in his own van through orders sent from King Richard to the Earl of Norfolk. His van stretched in a line across the northwest slope, with the flank curving slightly forward in a pincer shape. Those flanks were chained serpentine guns—early cannon. The units of mounted knights waited some distance behind the guns in two wings. In the body of the line, units of longbowmen were clumped at intervals with handgunners and pikemen between them.

Ken keyed his sensory band on, to check its perspective. As King Richard, he instantly looked down the slope toward Norfolk's men. Their heavy plate-steel armor shone in the sun, blooming with the red badges of Norfolk's livery. This particular viewpoint offered no special advantage now, so he keyed off the band, aware that later he could be counting on it in crucial moments.

The rebel van advanced in a triangle, with its base forming a straight front line and the body of the triangle tapering to a point in the rear. Historically, Oxford's tactic had been to hurl every man forward as fast as possible. Since it had worked, Ken expected Richard would allow the tactic to stand.

Ken watched anxiously as the enemy units advanced. As they entered the range of Norfolk's field guns, he remembered a little rhyme from the day before the battle: "Jock of Norfolk, be not too bold, for Dickon thy master is bought and sold." The two Stanleys had agreed with Tudor to enter the battle on his side and Northumberland had agreed not to take the field at all. In the game, those three roles were programmed personalities whose decisions would be made by the computer.

Ken just had time to feel another wave of hopelessness and to wonder if Richard III had shared one. No, he realized with embarrassment—of course the King's despair had been much worse. He had been fighting for his life, his kingdom, and his house; Ken was playing a game.

Oxford's van cleared the marsh. The two sides exchanged cannon fire and then volleys of arrows. Holes opened in both front lines and were filled by the lines behind. Norfolk ordered his units to advance when the line of rebels started up the slope. The royal van eased forward at a trotting speed in close order, well disciplined. If necessary, Ken could still send new orders down.

Ken searched the field. The key to the battle was the action of the Stanleys. If they could somehow be induced to stay out of the battle, or come in for the King, then Ken's royal forces still outnumbered the rebel army.

The game program would include the secret agreement betraying the King, but also the Stanleys' instinct for self-preservation. The only small advantage Ken had was that his opponent Richard, in the position of Henry Tudor, could not totally trust the Stanleys, either.

Norfolk's center was wavering under the onslaught. The only response Ken could think of was to follow the example of Richard III. He sent units forward from the main body of the army to bolster the sagging center, in groups of one hundred men at a time. Yet if he continued to use the tactics of his predecessor, he was likely to suffer the same defeat. He had to think of something new and effective.

Ken sent more men forward in blocks of one hundred.

Richard III had been an experienced and highly successful general, as well as a ferocious fighter personally. Ken was not sure he could improve on the King's tactics. Again, now, he saw that he would have to imitate Richard III.

Ken's units on the hilltop were dwindling, and the time had come to call Northumberland and Lord Stanley forward. Ken sent out two messengers but did not waste one on Sir William Stanley.

Ken had one slight chance that either Lord Stanley or Northumberland would respond. It lay in the near impossibility of some blunder by his opponent that was known to the computer already but not yet apparent on the field. That was hardly likely, but Ken had to consider the possibility.

As the battle raged, holding Ken's career in the balance, he tried to anticipate the coming developments. The next logical step was an even greater jamming of the densely packed and quickly shifting units on the slope of Ambion Hill, as the two main bodies of troops pushed toward each other behind their front lines. That would begin the critical phase in which the entrance of the Stanleys and Northumberland on the royal side could crush the rebels.

That phase never fully developed. In one of the variations open to the computer, Lord Stanley decided to attack. His 2,000 men charged from the south, directly toward the left flank of the royal army.

Ken gasped quietly, angrily, and realized that his flank would probably be turned and possibly routed. He forgot his previous expectations and chose his last resort.

King Richard himself had always been a fine combatant, but in this battle he had been desperate. Ken sent in the royal unit, and keyed on his sensory band.

Suddenly Ken was looking out over the great, nodding head of White Surrey, the King's charger, as he led a thundering gallop of reserve knights in support of their own left flank. His lance angled out ahead, pennon fluttering. Ahead,

Stanley's men smashed into the royal line, driving it back and sideways. Seconds later, the King's lance shattered against the shield of some nameless Stanley knight. He cast the useless handle aside and unslung his huge, trusty axe. As White Surrey plunged and reared, with hooves flailing, the King swung his axe two-handed, furiously, in the crush of steel and bodies and horses.

The King's men surged around him. Those before him pressed on, rather than feel their fighting King close on their backs; those behind him shouted their battle cries and came on to join the fray. Ken's greatest asset was the King himself, but if he should fall in the fighting, Ken would lose instantly. That was the way of dynastic struggles.

Historically, Northumberland had not moved against the King's rear; too many of his northern men favored the King. Yet even if the computer repeated that abstention, King Richard alone could not save the left wing. Ken keyed off his sensory band and pulled the King out of combat, back up onto Ambion Hill.

The royal lines were crumbling. Any second, Sir William Stanley would order the killing blow. Ken felt that he shared a feeling of desperation with the real King, even if that was presumptuous.

Like the King, Ken wanted to win, not just to survive. In the real battle, King Richard had located his personal rival, Henry Tudor, observing the struggle from a small hill to the right and rear of his line. The King had gathered his household knights and other somber volunteers, over a hundred in all, for a charge to the standard of the Lancastrian heir. The danger: the charge would carry the royal contingent right in front of Sir William Stanley and his two hundred horse just to the north.

Historically, the King had fought his way through the surprised party around Tudor and, with great effort, reputedly even fought him hand-to-hand briefly. However, Sir William Stanley had seen the charge and its purpose. The Stanley knights had roared forward to protect Tudor. The force of their charge had swept the King from his rival; he had been unhorsed and killed. The royal force had fled, and the Lancastrian heir had founded the House of Tudor as Henry VII.

Ken had King Richard gather his household knights and call for volunteers. All of the royal party must have felt a special anger, Ken thought. If Northumberland or even one of the Stanleys had held to his oath of allegiance, the battle would have been very different.

Ken himself was outraged, watching the 5,000 men under Northumberland and Sir William Stanley who should have been fighting for the King. Tudor, at least, was an openly avowed enemy.

Ken's chance to win, like the King's had been at this point, now lay entirely in the possibility of killing Tudor himself. That figure still stood on the same hill where the real Tudor had stood; Ken's opponent had kept him there so he could observe the battle.

Ken keyed his sensory band back on. It looked hot there on Ambion Hill, with the blazing summer sun shining on their heavy plate-steel armor. The King sat high on White Surrey, his visor open, sweat running down into his eyes. His personal followers crowded around; if the sensory band had allowed it, they would have sent up the varied smells of horses, leather, blood, and sweat. The wounded slid off their mounts with help, others unbuckling their armor for them. Someone raised a bulging waterskin up to the King. He took two long drafts and handed back the empty skin. Then, when he took a new lance that was offered up, the knights around him, too, strengthened their resolve and grasped fresh lances.

King Richard turned White Surrey and waved for his axe. The charge they were about to make would finally end these long civil wars—the King wore a golden crown outside his helmet and would either die as a king or triumph as one. Then, as a party of more than a hundred knights gathered behind him, he made a sweeping arm gesture toward their goal: the red dragon banner of Wales, atop a distant hill behind the lines, ringed with a reserve bodyguard. Everyone could also see the formation of Stanley horse in the distance, in bright red jackets.

Suddenly Ken thought of an additional tactic. He directed one of his captains to withdraw another troop of knights from the struggling lines. The royal lines were about to break, anyway, but Tudor's death would give them the victory if the gamble worked.

Ken ordered that the second block of one hundred charge behind the royal contingent at an interval and farther out in a wing to the right, virtually beneath the Stanley banner of the white hart. Both maneuvers were likely to be suicidal, but if they succeeded, the battle was won.

This double wing had something in it of a betrayal itself, to the values of Richard III. He had asked only his household knights to join him, those sworn to the protection of his body and no others. The men of this second wing were simply following direct military orders.

The royal center was disintegrating. Ken could not wait longer. Blinking sweat away from his eyes, he led the charge down Ambion Hill.

The way was open; the right flank of the royal line held the rebel left committed, and the King's charge thundered around them. Ahead, Tudor's bodyguard saw the charge and prepared for the impact, jamming themselves around the person of their proclaimed king. King Richard's knights smashed into them, and Ken grit this teeth as he heard the splintering of lances and human screams in his sensory band. The action at close quarters was too fast for logical thought; all was reflexes, pressing forward, smashing and slashing, always toward Tudor himself. One by one, King Richard hacked away those who rose before him, swinging his axe with lethal abandon, eyes always on Tudor, who suddenly pulled away, behind his line. He was no fighter and simply turned on his charger and ran for his life, with a meager escort of two knights galloping behind him. Even his standard bearer was hemmed in by the furious fighting on the hilltop, and abandoned. King Richard held his breath, swinging his axe with both arms straight, chopping against the wall of flailing steel around him—and then, suddenly, the sensory band went off.

Ken sat away from the keyboard and looked at the field. The King was gone—dead.

Ken tried to blink sweat away, then had to wipe his eyes with one hand. He had been so involved in the scene . . . and now the game was lost. His screen read, "Victory Conditions: Lancaster."

Ken heard applause vaguely around him but did not react. He leaned toward the field again, still breathing heavily, to peer at the motionless figures. The position of forces at the end of the game was still visible.

Someone's hand plucked at his arm, but he shook it off. He located Tudor on the screen, a short distance from the hill where the King had fallen. Then he found the important information—behind the remains of the King's first contingent, whose survivors were scattered like confetti as the charge of the Stanley horse held motionless in mid-gallop. There Ken found his second wing of charging knights. They were scattered, also, their momentum smashed by the force of the Stanley sweep. However, from the positions still evident on the screen, Ken knew that the tactic had worked. It had partially broken the Stanley attack and delayed them very slightly. In the real battle, King Richard had been only seconds away from cutting down Tudor. Ken had found a way to gain those seconds. Even though he had failed to destroy the Lancastrian heir, his ploy had fulfilled its purpose.

Ken let out a long breath of relief and fell back into his seat. A moment later, an attendant came up to move aside his keyboard. The applause was continuing; Ken became aware for the first time just how enthusiastic it was.

The attendant helped him to his feet and down the steps to an electric cart. As Ken was being driven out, he looked around at the crowd and realized that many of the people in the audience were looking at him, applauding for him, as well as for Richard. Surprised, he smiled wryly.

Across the arena, Richard was also being driven out. Ken felt a cold pang in his stomach at seeing him. He hated losing, and he especially hated losing to Richard.

Donna was already waiting for him in the reception room, standing next to the long refreshment table with a cold glass of white wine for him.

"Ken? That was wonderful." Donna handed him the glass and knelt next to him. "It really was. And that finish was spectacular."

"Yeah, well, I still lost." Ken accepted the glass and hooked his other elbow around her neck to draw her close. He hesitated, first to gaze at her full, waiting lips and then, amused, to look at her eyes as she watched his own mouth. Then he kissed her.

"Consolation prize?" Richard's sardonic voice came from the other side of Ken's cart.

Ken and Donna both started laughing, and she stood up. He turned and extended his hand to Richard, whose own cart had pulled up alongside. "Congratulations."

"Thanks." Richard shook his hand briefly, chuckling with a sudden, embarrassed shake of his head. "You know, that final ploy of yours was incredibly ruthless—sending all those guys to certain death on that extra wing. Matter of fact, it was pretty sharp, too."

Ken shrugged. "Almost worked. Not quite, though."

"You may have a masterplay on your hands, there."

Ken looked at him sharply, ready to find Richard's edged sarcasm mocking him. Instead, he found Richard in his professional mood. "What did you say?"

"Well, it's not proven, but that wing tactic of yours just might turn out to be the masterplay for Bosworth. You created it, even if you didn't execute it properly. It'll have to be tested by other masters, but if it proves out, you're on record as devising it." Richard reached up to accept a glass of red wine from someone.

Ken felt a warm sense of accomplishment building in him, as Richard's appraisal sank in. Gradually, he realized what he had acquired since arriving here by shuttlecopter. He had Donna's friendship; he had honest praise from his old friend, a quality he had rarely received; he had, perhaps, a masterplay to his credit. All three were victories, despite the official outcome of the game.

Ken spoke quietly to Richard. "It *is* complicated, isn't it?"

Richard grinned and clinked his glass against Ken's. "Welcome to World Headquarters."

Ken and Donna stumbled crookedly down the hall toward the apartment with their arms around each other, giggling more from the giddiness of victory than from drinking, though Donna's face was glowing with an alcohol flush. He got his key out first and unlocked the door. As they went inside, he reached for the light switch, but she caught his wrist. The only light came from a security lamp outside the living room window, over the external walkway; it filtered through the curtains.

She tossed her purse onto a chair and turned to look up at him.

When she didn't speak, he searched for something to say. "I remember that lavender dress. You look very elegant in it. You were wearing it the night we met."

"We've been together for hours, and you're just noticing it now?" She laughed.

"Uh—no, I noticed. I just, uh . . ."

"I wore it especially for your game. For luck."

"It worked." He bent down to kiss her again. It was the first time since just after the game, and just as impulsive. This time she slid her arms around his neck and he encircled her in his. She felt warm and small. After a moment, she pulled back and looked at him again, smiling and not saying anything.

Anywhere else, he would have asked her to come to bed

with him. Here, as a guest who had merely been offered a room, he was reluctant to do that. She seemed to sense that.

"Come on," she whispered, turning away. She led him, still holding his wrist, to her bedroom door. Then she glanced up impishly. "You don't know . . . but Sharon's gonna be *mad*."

CHAPTER Eight

Donna stopped in the silent hallway of one of the upper floors of the Gaming Masters' Guild and looked down all three corridors that converged there. She deliberated for a moment, trying to remember, and then started down one of them, reading all the doorplates as she went. The Chandragupta Maurya Room appeared before long, and she knocked softly. The door moved slightly with the impact, and she saw that the latch had been turned to a setting that kept it within the door.

She pushed the door open and stuck her head around the edge. "Hello?"

"Hi! Come on in." Ken grinned and waved her into the room. He was perched in the gaming seat near the door. Across the playing field in front of him, Richard Ross sat with military rigidity in the other seat.

Donna flipped the latch to its normal position and closed the door. "Hi, Richard," she called.

"Hi." The shy master, whom she had heard called a gaming genius by some, smiled slightly.

"You can sit over there if you like." Ken pointed to a padded recliner placed along one side of the field.

Donna looked at the jumble of black and pink cables running from a small silver box to each of the game seats. Another twist of colored wires ran from the silver box up at an angle over the field to a hole recently drilled into the ceiling, near the opening for the holographic projector. It was more elaborate than the testing equipment Ken had described seeing once before.

"Have you tried it?" she asked Ken.

"Just a little. I think it's great."

"May I?"

"Well, it's his contraption," said Ken.

"Sure, I guess." Richard shrugged again and leaned back in his seat. His long arms and legs were folded and looked cramped up there.

"Okay." With a cheerful grin, Ken swung sideways in his seat and jumped all the way to the floor.

Donna gasped in surprise, but Ken landed in a crouch with one hand on the floor and straightened up easily. He threw his arms around her and gave her a quick but enthusiastic kiss on the cheek.

Donna carefully placed the three-inch heels of her shoes on the steps and held the railing as she climbed into the seat. She felt she was too short to go around without the added boost. When she was seated, she swung the keyboard up on its arm and let it drop into position in front of her. "Is it really that different from the regular sensory band?"

"You'll see." Ken grinned. "The one on this side is, uh, turned down as far as it goes."

"What does that mean?"

"Uh—well, they're experimental, so there's an unknown factor. Richard's sensory band is turned up very high."

"Never mind; I don't get it." Donna looked across the way at Richard. "Ready?"

"Whenever you're ready," he said, sitting up. He pulled his own keyboard into place.

Donna keyed for the computer to select a game at random. A moment later her keyboard screen read, "Gettysburg. 1863. General Meade."

Donna's heart began pounding, as the seconds ticked off the brief orientation period. Here she was only an apprentice gamer, about to play against one of the finest gamers ever in the Guild, with the man she lived with looking on—but it was not really a game, not even a practice game. It was just a demonstration. She wanted to look capable without appearing too aggressive. Trying to prove herself in a friendly setting would mark her as an amateur for sure. If she was really one of them, she would be as casual as they were.

On the playing field in front of her, projected from above, a motionless hologram had taken shape. The Army of the Potomac was stretched across a wide front as it marched across the fields of Pennsylvania, measuring roughly forty miles from end to end. Donna had never seen a holographic game map on such a large scale before. The Army of Northern Virginia was also on the move, west of Gettysburg. Worst of all, though, was that Donna knew relatively little about the details of Gettysburg.

The Gaming Masters' Guild had always had a cutoff date of 1750. The armies in most of the significant battles before 1750, and admittedly a number of them after, had been not only commanded but also effectively led by one particular individual. That person's role could be taken by a *master gamer*. In the more complex battles of recent centuries, crucial decisions were made by more individuals all over the sprawling fields of battle. A gamer working on a keyboard had enough to do in the simpler games. Yet other battles were available in the computer for leisure such as this.

Donna looked over the field. She had two brigades of Union cavalry posted on a ridge west of the town, across the Cashtown Road, on the lookout for Confederates. Supposedly, she was in the role of General Meade, and Richard was Robert E. Lee. Both men were a long way from that ridge, though, when the game activated and a triple line of Confederate skirmishers entered the holographic field, approaching the bridge over Willoughby Run on their way toward Gettysburg.

Donna didn't remember what unit that would be, but she knew the skirmishers would be preceding a regular column.

"Put on the sensory band," said Ken.

She should have been wearing it already, but in her nervousness over trying it, she had forgotten. She gave Ken a self-conscious smile as he reached up to press it into her hand. Then she slipped it on.

"Remember what we discussed," Ken said. "Pick a window."

Donna hit a sequence of keys. Suddenly she was in the midst of the little holographic figures, from the viewpoint of the Union commander in Gettysburg itself.

"You're General John Buford," said Ken, with amusement in his voice. "I brushed up on the battle this morning."

Donna, as General Buford, had two brigades of cavalry. In this age, cavalry alone was not considered the equal of infantry in direct combat, but Donna knew the overall pattern of Gettysburg—the Confederates had arrived in greater numbers first and should be slowed down if possible. She ordered her brigades to dismount and line the ridge. With another sequence of keys, she ordered her battery of six guns to set up in the line.

The sensory band was so far working normally. Donna watched her cavalrymen in blue scatter along the ridge behind trees, fences, and any other cover, while one man in every four stood to the rear holding horses. They looked out across green pastures and wheat fields toward the approaching skirmishers. In the distance, roiling dust marked the fast advance of Confederate guns pulled at a gallop. She turned and saw the Lutheran theological seminary on a nearby ridge and started toward it as the sound of rifle and carbine fire picked up. From the tower, she would see that the enemy infantry was coming on in strength and setting up more guns.

This perspective was available to her from the gamer's usual overview, but she was here for the sensory band, so—

Ken touched her arm and she jumped. She pushed up the band to look at him.

"There's a jack in the band," he said. "I'll plug this wire into it. Use the keyboard to change roles, and remember, Richard has the choice of taking a role to oppose you or of letting the computer play out your immediate opponent. If he does the latter, he can be fighting elsewhere—though right now I don't think there's any other combat available." He stepped back a little. "Just don't forget that the rest of the field continues, no matter which role you take."

Donna nodded and fitted the band on again.

"Imagine the orders you want to give. Actually say them to yourself in your mind. It works on a neurofeedback system."

Donna found herself in the belfry again. With effort, she imagined herself moving, picturing herself going down the stairs, watching her booted feet on the steps. It seemed to be working. Elsewhere, she reminded herself, the computer was allowing her troops to act as they had in the real battle, without her orders to the contrary.

Aides sat on their horses outside the seminary. As Buford, Donna gave them orders that she imagined she spoke, for them to ride fast for General John Reynolds. He was bringing up a corps from the south; fortunately, she didn't need to know its number. The aides turned and galloped away. According to what Ken had told her the evening before, the computer could read the aural center of her brain if she "heard" her own words in her mind. So the holographic aides had also heard her.

Donna felt a surge of excitement at this apparent success. Now for the fun part—she keyed for a change of role again and found herself to be General Reynolds, galloping ahead of his column up the road with the sound of artillery and infantry fire up ahead. Two aides came galloping this way in the distance; presently, they pulled up sharply, kicking dust into the air.

"General Buford reports rebel infantry present in strength, sir, just west of town." The aide seemed to say it; the computer had read her mental words and given them back to her through the speakers on the sensory band.

She galloped on ahead by picturing the scene that way; again, the computer read her optical center. As the three of them rode hard for the town, she became aware that she was smiling. This was fast and fun and simple, leaving her more free to think about the complexity of this huge and tangled battle. Yes, maybe this system could work—allow gamers to move around a large battlefield easily enough to stay involved. She and the aides turned west at the town and rode toward the seminary. Buford waved from the tower and leaned out—then all went blank, into darkness.

She shoved the sensory band up and looked at the field. It was an empty white square again, devoid of holograms. Ken was running along one sideline, toward Richard, who hung limp in his chair to one side, apparently unconscious.

Donna stared for a moment, disoriented by the sudden shift out of the game. Then, suddenly alarmed, she yanked the sensory band off her head, pulling her hair as she did so. With another glance at Richard, she climbed carefully down from the gaming seat. "Ken? What happened?"

"Call the front desk! The Guild keeps a paramedic team on call." Ken was already up on the steps, holding Richard under the arms, easing him down to the floor.

Donna went to the videphone on the wall and called, thinking, *That might have been me*.

Ken accompanied Richard to the hospital and gave Richard's identification and insurance cards to the desk as the paramedics wheeled Richard into the emergency room. He had already explained the situation as well as he could on the fast drive from the Guild Hall, but he had not had much to tell. Ken did not really understand the new sensory bands.

The woman at the desk inserted the insurance card into a slot on her console and frowned at the information it brought to her screen. "Just a moment, please."

"What?" Ken drew himself up, ready for an argument. "Is something wrong with the policy?"

"No, sir. Just a matter of procedure." She rose from her desk and disappeared into the back.

Ken paced impatiently in front of the desk. The air-conditioning was cold on the sweat he had generated out in the blazing sun and humidity of the July morning. The phone rang several times, then was apparently answered by someone out of sight. Several other people got in line behind him. He looked at his watch a number of times, once after an interval of less than a minute.

"Excuse me, sir. Are you the one who brought Mr. Ross in?"

Ken turned to see a short, round-faced man with a fringe of brown hair around his balding head. He stood with both hands in the outside pockets of his gray suit jacket.

"Yes, I'm Ken Li. What's going on?"

"Ah, yes. I've heard of you, of course. Congratulations on developing your masterplay in your last game. Come with me, will you?"

Ken followed him around a corner and into a small office behind the reception area. He sat down in a chair facing a modest wooden desk, rubbing his arms.

"I'm Dan Theel, insurance liaison." He sat down on one corner of his desk. "Are you a close friend of Mr. Ross?"

"Yes! Now quit stalling and tell me what's wrong." Ken folded his arms angrily.

"I will have to make my point my own way, Master Li. Bear with me. Now, Mr. Ross's condition appears to be serious. They'll continue tests, of course, but I checked on his condition before I came to see you. He may be unconscious for some time."

"Get to the point." Ken felt a sinking worry settle in his stomach.

"Mr. Ross has held a policy fairly common to *master gamers* for a number of years. Perhaps you have a similar one. He chose an option, however, requiring under certain conditions that he be placed into cryogenic sleep."

Ken sat up sharply. "*How long*? How long can he remain unconscious before that clause goes into effect?"

"It's not that simple, Master Li. If our medical staff feels he is making progress, perhaps by interpreting his brain scan—I'm no doctor, now—the clause will not come into effect at all. On the other hand, if at any time the staff feels certain that he cannot make any further progress, the freezing procedure must begin according to the terms of his policy."

"Look, I agreed not to tell anyone, but I think you'd better know . . ."

"Yes, Master Li?"

"I told Richard I wouldn't pass this on. He knew that those headsets of his, the neurofeedback arrangements, might cause this. He had cranked up the power in his to see how well it worked. The other one, which his opponent was using, was set very low, so she wouldn't be in any danger."

"Wait a minute. Didn't you tell the paramedics that you don't know much about this?"

"I don't, except what I just told you. One paramedic said he'd make sure the doctors knew Richard was involved with neurofeedback. But the important point is that Richard knew this could happen. And he told me that if it did, I shouldn't worry about it. He said he'd wake up on his own."

"How certain of this are you?"

"Completely."

"He should have checked with the Guild insurance people and altered his policy."

"Oh, *come on*—how often do people think about the details of their insurance policies in the course of a normal day? It just never occurred to him."

Theel looked down at his desk and started straightening items idly. He picked up an unpolished amethyst paperweight. "You're right, I suppose, but that doesn't help me any."

"What do you mean?' "

"Master Li, all I have to go on is his policy. I don't doubt your word, but you—and he—have no more medical credentials than I do. If the conditions for cryogenic sleep develop, then legally we will have to abide by the policy."

"But it doesn't—" Ken shut up abruptly, stifling his temper. This was a legal matter that left him on unknown ground. He should have a lawyer arguing for him. "All right, Mr. Theel. Look, the reason Richard took out that particular policy is that he doesn't have any surviving relatives to make the decision for him. And I'm the one to contact if his condition changes. You'll find that on the policy itself."

Theel nodded gravely. "With luck, the policy will never come into effect, anyway. I'll see you out."

Moments later, Ken stood outside the main entrance of the hospital in the late-morning sunlight, trying to organize his thoughts. Events had happened so fast since his initial panic and rush to the hospital that he had not had time to worry. His first order of business was to get an expert at work on that insurance policy.

The Guild Hall was a long walk from here. Ken had a lot of nervous energy to expend and set out down the sidewalk. More than anything, he hoped that Richard would simply wake up soon—very soon.

Ken rolled up the sleeves of his dress shirt and sweated freely as he strode along. The brilliant sunshine forced him to frown even more than he had been in the hospital, but he was too riled up to feel the heat. He tried to slow himself down, but whenever his thoughts returned to the issue at hand, he sped up again. His thoughts roiled continuously, madly, centering on two facts: Richard had been sure that his coma, or whatever it was, would end soon of its own accord . . . but if the hospital staff didn't believe that, they would put him into cryogenic sleep, leaving him frozen until some distant year when a future medical staff thought they could bring him out of his coma.

Donna sat on a couch in the lobby of the Guild Hall, surreptitiously gulping a margarita out of a coffee mug. A sympathetic security guard had smuggled it out of the Guild Club for her, since as an apprentice she could not go in without a host. Finally she was beginning to unwind.

After Ken had left with the ambulance, she had had to explain to Guild security what had happened. The security team had been polite and efficient, but she had felt out of her depth. Still, she had mustered the courage to demand that the practice room be sealed in case the settings and hookups on Richard's equipment might somehow be important in treating him.

Donna did not really know Richard, but she was concerned about Ken's worry for his old childhood friend and rival. When Ken burst into the lobby, his shirt drenched in sweat, she lifted the coffee mug and waved it slightly. She searched his face as he came over and collapsed onto the couch next to her, causing her liquid level to sway.

"Ken? What did they say?"

He shook his head brusquely. "They don't really know anything yet." He wiped his forehead on his sleeve. "If it's a coma or something like that, he's in real trouble."

Donna listened as Ken explained the pertinent clause in Richard's insurance policy. She had heard of such clauses but had never known anyone before who might have it invoked. More than anything, though, she watched Ken's face as he talked, gesturing broadly, looking anxiously all around the lobby, and speaking very fast. She had never seen him so upset.

"Is there anything you can do?" She asked.

"*I* don't know." He threw his arms out in a wild shrug, and she ducked away to avoid him. "Maybe the whole insurance thing is a false alarm. He might just wake up tomorrow morning all of a sudden. But I have to get a lawyer on this! Right away."

"If he's really not going to wake up, though, isn't it better to freeze him? Otherwise, he'll just grow older without having the chance to live his life."

Ken's head swiveled sharply toward her. Then, after a moment of hesitation, he sagged backward against the couch. "Uh—well, that's . . . that's the argument. I guess that's why he chose the option. That's why the companies offer it."

Aware of a shift in his manner, Donna said nothing.

"Look, he told me a few things in confidence about all this. I felt I had to say one of them to a guy at the hospital, but I'm . . . well, Richard asked me to keep it to myself, and here I've broken that trust already."

"It was an emergency. You don't have to tell me about it if you don't want to."

Since they had been living together, Donna had seen him in a variety of moods, ranging from cautious pride after his strong showing against Richard to laughing exuberance one weekend when they had gone to the Ozarks for a float trip. Yet he remained guarded most of the time, and he was withdrawing now, suddenly, in response to what she had thought was a simple, reasonable question.

She took another sip of her margarita. Most of the salt was gone from the rim now, and she didn't want the rest of it.

"Ken? Are you going to be okay?" she asked quietly. She wanted to be supportive but she felt shut out.

He nodded, looking down into his lap. "Yeah, I'll be okay. I just don't know if he will be."

CHAPTER Nine

A week later, little had changed. The beeping videphone woke up Donna one morning, and she reached for it while still groggy. She remembered to kill the live camera, though; her caller would see a pleasant still portrait of her, instead of her newly roused appearance.

"Hello. Is this Donna Wong?" The caller was a well-dressed woman with short, curly blonde hair and very large glasses that gave her a wide-eyed look. "I'm Ellen Breslow, a Guild contractor."

"Yes!" Donna was instantly awake. She threw off the covers and swung her legs over the edge of the bed as she sat up. "Yes, this is Donna Wong."

"Well, I guess I have good news. Your name has finally come into the draw for qualifying games. I—"

"Great! Finally!" Donna laughed delightedly. "Finally. Oh, what the hell." She hit a button on the phone that turned on her camera. "Sorry I look so frazzled. I just woke up. But here I am." She slept nude, but at this distance the camera would send a portrait transmission.

Ellen laughed. "I'm sorry to call you so early, but I wanted to catch you before you left home for the day. I'm on this month's rotation to handle qualifying games, and I'll be arranging your game with one of the masters. Right now, I just wanted to let you know that, and to make sure this was still your number. Well, you might want to start practicing if you haven't been. I should have a date for your qualifer nailed down in a few days at most."

"I have been practicing, sort of, but I'll get serious about it now. I'm really glad to hear from you."

"Why don't you take down my phone number? And my office is in the Guild Hall. Feel free to get in touch with me."

"Okay." Donna found a pen and scribbled down the information. When she had hung up, she fell back sideways on the bed, laughing. She had worked a long time to reach this point, and now she would have her chance to earn master status. To qualify, she would not have to win the game, but she would have to play well enough to earn recommendations from both the computer and also the master who played against her.

Even better, she like Ellen's manner. Ellen appeared to be in her late twenties or early thirties, and if she, as a younger contractor, happened to be taking on clients, Donna would be in a strong position to sign up with her . . . providing she qualified.

Sobered, Donna sat up and looked over her shoulder at the window to make sure Ken hadn't opened the curtains before he left. Two years before, she had gotten out of bed one morning before noticing that a work crew on a scaffold was resurfacing the exterior wall by her window. She had merely laughed and ducked out of the room, but still, she had glanced at the curtains nearly every morning before rising since then.

By the time she had showered and dressed, she was too excited to eat much breakfast. She forced down what she could of some leftover salmon loaf just to have something in her stomach. Then she hurried out, anxious to get her name up on the waiting list in the Guild Hall for impromptu practice games. After lying fallow, her ambition was back in full force.

She walked down the sidewalk in front of the Guild Hall toward the main entrance, smiling to herself in the bright morning sunlight. The Guild Hall was a tall, modern building with a classical stone facing. All along the first floor, between the high vertical windows, life-size statues of great generals stood in solemn dignity. She squinted against the sunlight to recognize some of them: Julius Caesar, Bayan of the Hundred Eyes, Napoleon, Dionysius, Pachacuti Inca, Ban Chao, Hannibal, Sagaman-dir, Tokugawa Ieyasu.... The ones on the far side of the entrance were too indistinct to identify.

She had seen them thousands of times, but hadn't really looked at them since the first few times she had come here. Now, with her qualifying game in mind, the Guild Hall seemed different. She could really belong here soon.

A couple of people were passing out leaflets at the foot of the front steps. Donna accepted a light blue sheet of paper quickly as she started up the stone steps. With one foot on the third step and one on the fourth, she stopped. The main doors were flanked by statues of Genghis Khan and Alexander the Great, on pedestals. She studied each of the grim, staring faces as though for the first time. Their history had been part of her education; she knew what each of them had accomplished. The statues were there for two reasons, both of which worked on her now: they inspired her and yet they reminded her—she was only a gamer.

She grinned and went on up the steps. Yeah, but she was going to be a ***master gamer***.

Donna had the run of all the Guild facilities except the Guild Club and the attached Lounge. She checked for messages at the reception desk and then hurried to the Xerxes Room, where apprentices could watch practice games going on elsewhere in the Guild Hall on the rows of screens that covered all four walls. She ignored the yelling, bustling crowd and punched in at the keyboard set into the wall just inside the door. Her name was sixteenth on the list, meaning that a master might page her today to play a practice game. If no one had called her by this afternoon, she would page one of the names ahead of her. Playing another apprentice was better than nothing, though she might not find a practice room free.

Meanwhile, she had to stay here. The impromptu list only applied to people paged in the building and was started fresh each day. She decided to go down to the exercise area, so as not to waste any time; she would hear the page there, if there was one.

The Guild locker room was the most luxurious one she had ever seen. It was carpeted in broad green and white stripes and had cushioned benches in the center of wide aisles. Donna kept several changes of clothes in her locker so that she could be ready for unexpected meetings or appointments that might come up.

She changed quickly into her red and white candy-striped leotard and went out to the floor. At this hour, the crowd was sparse. She sat down and started her series of stretching exercises.

Donna knew that her short, slender stature had affected her personality. She had learned to be formal and professional and reserved, as a way of forcing others to take her seriously. Aside from her high heels, her height did not occupy much of her conscious thoughts, except when she exercised. Here she felt little. She would never be a fast runner, with her short legs, or much of a swimmer, either; though she was in good condition, she was not going to out-muscle many women. So she had had to find something right for her body type.

Someone was on the uneven bars, so Donna went to the balance beam. When she got there, she found that she wasn't really in the mood for it. Right now, with the excitement still surging through her veins, she wanted to fly.

She returned to her stretching until the bars were free.

An hour later, happily breathless and sweaty, she walked back into the locker room. When she opened her locker, the blue leaflet she had been given drifted out and down to the floor. She picked it up and read, "Stop Legal Limbo—Repeal the Guild Act." A list of complaints was printed badly below, with an address and phone number of a group simply called "Citizens Against the Guild Act."

She folded it carefully and put it away. Then she went to shower.

As she was dressing, a page came over the loudspeaker: "Donna Wong, please meet Ken in the Guild Lounge." It was repeated twice.

Well, it wasn't what she was expecting, but that was all right. With a master as a host, she could relax in the Lounge for a bit. The freedom to go in alone, minor as it was, would be a genuine reward of master status.

Upstairs, Donna stopped just inside the lounge, left momentarily helpless by the darkness. All she could see were the tall white candles burning in high baroque candlesticks.

"Over there," said a woman behind the bar pleasantly.

Donna found Ken slumped down in his chair, staring fixedly into the candle flame before him. She didn't like talking to him when he was like this, but she wanted to help if she could. After a moment, she pulled out the chair across from him.

"Hi." She spoke lightly.

"Oh, hi. Didn't see you." Ken sat up. "I saw you'd signed on to practice, so I figured you were here somewhere."

"I got good news this morning." She said it tentatively, not sure if he was in the mood for it.

"Yeah?" He slid the candlestick aside so they could see each other.

"I'm finally up for my qualifer. A contractor named Ellen Breslow called and told me to start practicing."

"Great." Ken's face came to life for the first time since she had come in. He reached across the table to take her hand. "So that's why you signed up to practice, eh? Well, let's celebrate. Have a drink?"

Donna relaxed a little. "No, but I'll keep you company."

Once he had ordered, Ken frowned and shook his head. "I went to the hospital again this morning. I'm really not getting anywhere with those people. I've tried to convince them that they should keep waiting before they freeze Richard, but I don't have any leverage."

"What have you said to them?" Donna watched Ken's hands as he stroked one of hers. His hands weren't especially large, except in comparison to hers. He had long fingers, though, that could stretch across a keyboard where her small hands had to jump around. Then she realized that he hadn't answered her question. "Ken?"

He withdrew his hands and sat back in his chair, not looking at her.

Donna studied his face as the wavering candle flame sent yellowish light across it from below. The shadows exaggerated his features, making his brooding expression even more grim. She didn't know whether to speak or not.

When the drinks arrived, Ken roused himself to sign the check. Then he smiled slightly and clinked glasses with her. "Here's to your qualifying. Good luck."

"Thanks." Donna smiled with relief. What she needed to do was change the subject. "Ken, look at this leaflet I got. Did you get one? They were handing them out by the front steps." She fished the flyer out of her purse and offered it to him.

"I got one." Ken waved it away.

Donna looked at it again. "Citizens Against the Guild Act. Well, I've been one of those for some time now."

"You told me that the night we met. Remember?"

"Sure. I was a little uncertain about saying that to someone of your . . . stature."

Ken smiled at her, unguarded now. "You didn't sound uncertain. Are you going to get hold of them?"

"Yes, I think so. At least out of curiosity. What do you think?"

"I think you'll be the only gamer in the group. And if you qualify, you'll certainly be the only master."

"I'm not so sure, Ken. The Guild is awfully big, worldwide. I can't be the only one who's against the Guild Act for allowing people to be forced into accepting games."

He shrugged and tasted his drink.

"You don't think this movement has a chance, do you?"

"Well . . . I don't want to sound overconfident. But the Guild Act was just passed recently. The side fighting it lost. So why would they win now? Not until some time has passed, I would expect."

Donna frowned. "This is something I'm really serious about, Ken."

"I know. The trouble is, I am, too."

Donna smiled idly into the polished surface of the table. "Hmm?"

"Well, I've been wanting to ask you something, and I think I will. Ken, don't you feel like you're just a hired gun? Just a mercenary?"

He laughed. "Well, mercenaries have a long tradition in military history, so it fits right in."

"I'm serious. Doesn't it bother you? Wouldn't you rather play games for a side you believe in? So that you're fighting for a principle instead of just for the contract?"

He leaned forward into the light. "I've spent a long time trying to establish my career. I know you've been around gamers for a long time, but it's different when you're actually doing it. We're all self-employed and our pensions and other benefits all come from the percentage of our income that we pay into the Guild. So all the great deals we get are contingent on individual success. And I want to be successful. You can't be a master without being competitive."

"But you could be exactly the same person, except for screening the contracts you sign a little differently."

"You mean so that I played for less money but for the side I favored."

"Sure. I plan to do it that way. And sometimes your side will be the one to pay more."

"What if I don't have a side in a particular game?"

"Then it wouldn't matter. But at times it would." Donna leaned forward, close to him, matching his posture. "Concerning Richard, for instance—yes! What about this? Suppose you sued to have a game played over that insurance policy, to decide if Richard should be frozen or if the contract should be, I don't know, postponed or something. Wouldn't you really *like* to play for your side? Put your heart into it. For something you believe in."

Ken's eyes flickered down to the table once and then back up to her. "And exactly how would I get this game declared? Are *you* suggesting, of all people, that I sue under the provisions of the Guild Act and force the Guild to accept a game?"

Donna straightened, with a forced little smile. "Well, I . . . granted, I'd be against you. For all I know, freezing Richard is the best thing for him, anyway. And, no, I don't like to suggest the Guild Act as a solution for anything. But I'm asking how you feel. I can accept a difference of opinion between us."

"I can, too." Ken sipped his drink.

"So what do you think?"

"I'm not going to sue the Gaming Masters' Guild. The *Guild*? It's my livelihood, and yours, too."

Donna raised an eyebrow and gave him what she hoped was an insulting grin. "Scared?"

The flesh around Ken's eyes tightened, but otherwise his expression remained the same. "Loyal."

"*Oh,* you're loyal. What about your loyalty to your old friend?"

Ken looked off into the darkness over her left shoulder.

"I know what it is. You have too much at stake in the status quo. And the old ethnic problem—you're too responsive to authority."

"Are you kidding? It's the Cantonese who kept rebelling all the time! We're the troublemakers—" He stopped suddenly and grinned. "Yeah, okay—toying with my personal quirks, huh?"

"So make some trouble and take some risk. Look, Ken, I understand ambition. That's why I'm about to play a qualifying game. But you have one of the best reputations in the Guild. Your name is established. Now that you've proven yourself, you can afford to consider principles."

"Now, wait a minute. I'm not unprincipled. I've never done anything against my principles."

"But you've never taken a stand on a game you played."

"And I'm not going to take a stand I don't want. All right? Is that established?" He set his glass down hard.

"All right, Ken," Donna said quietly. She was not satisfied, but Richard was Ken's friend, and Ken would have to make the final decision regarding him.

"Look, I'm on edge because of Richard. That's all." His tone softened. "It's still early. I have to go up and see if Lou has any contracts on the horizon for me. What do you have on the schedule?"

"I just have to hang around here in the hope of getting a practice game." Donna relaxed a little, glad that they had changed the subject. She had wanted to ask if he could play a practice game or two with her before her game, but this was a bad time to ask for a favor. Besides, the protocol was awkward. Normally, an apprentice would simply not ask a master for this. They were personally very close, but she had no idea how he might take a blurring of their personal and professional lives.

She was also hoping he would make the offer himself.

"Okay," he said. "You know, while you're waiting, you could call those people on the leaflet. No sense wasting time while you're here."

It was an apology of sorts. Donna smiled, and reached across the table for his hand. "I might just do that."

Donna was able to get several practice games during the week that followed. Once she had made a habit of getting to the Guild Hall early each day, before the morning air became a steam bath, she was always at or near the top of the list. By reserving practice rooms herself, she was able to invite other apprentices from the list to play against her.

One day she attended a meeting of Citizens Against the Guild Act. She found the hall full of a broad cross section of people, angry and a bit rowdy, but all serious in their concern over the issue. Repeal seemed like a long, difficult political fight, though, and while she joined the group, she did not see any contribution she could make.

Donna and Ken did not see much of each other for a while, even just going in and out of the apartment. She knew that she had pressed Ken a little too hard about Richard, and practicing gave her a sound reason not to raise the matter for a while. He had not mentioned it, either, except to report every few days that Richard's condition was unchanged. In August, the roar of chirping crickets marked the final stage of summer, reminding her that every day that passed brought Richard closer to cryogenic sleep.

Ken was spending a lot of time with his contractor, with talk of another very important game in the wind. Lou was wining and dining European visitors who sometimes spoke fluent English and sometimes brought along interpreters. They were unusually important people, judging from the security teams that followed them, and Ken's celebrity status did good service at such functions. His natural reserve had been veneered over the years with a social grace he had had to learn as part of his success.

At least, Donna reflected, she already had that.

One evening, Sharon came over to sketch Donna. Sharon settled onto the couch with her pencils and a large pad and waved for Donna to turn slightly.

"This way."

Donna shifted to her right.

"Keep your feet where they were. Turn just a little at the waist. That's good."

Donna glanced down to get her pose clear in her mind, so she could repeat it, if necessary, after a break. Sharon occasionally asked Donna to pose either for preliminary sketches or for the paintings themselves. Now, Donna was standing nude in her living room with a bright light above her and just to the front, to cast the shadows Sharon wanted. It was a new kind of artists' bulb that was supposedly not as hot as previous ones, but she already felt warm.

"Where's Ken tonight?" Sharon asked as she sketched.

"He and Lou are out entertaining again. He invited me

along, but I've been practicing pretty hard. I said I was tired."

"So what do you do when you're not being an apprentice gamer?"

"I'm an artist's model in my spare time."

"Oh, you. I'm serious. Remember when we talked about hobbies, once, a long time ago?"

"Sure. But gaming is all-consuming. Once you really get into it, you live gaming. It's always at the back of your mind. All of life pertains to it—people and how they think, mainly. And you can't look at any land anywhere without imagining, almost as a reflex, how you would best deploy your forces."

Sharon shook her head without taking her eyes off her pad as she drew. "I guess I really don't get it. Everybody needs a vacation. How can you stand it? Or rather, how can masters who have been in the business for years stand it?"

"The really hard part is playing the games. Other than that, you might say we're on vacation all the time. So instead of trying to get away from it, we're always anticipating the next time."

"Mmm. Interesting way to look at it." Sharon looked up to study Donna for a moment, then returned to her pad. "Are you nervous about your qualifier?"

"A little." Donna started to nod, then caught herself. "I won't really get nervous till a day or so before game time. Everyone tells me that once the game gets going, you're too busy to be nervous."

Sharon stopped and glanced up. "Do you think that's true?"

"It has been for me in other games."

"And how long did you tell me you had left?"

"My qualifying game starts in four days, thirteen hours, and"—Donna shifted her eyes, but not her head, toward the wall clock—"twenty-two minutes."

"You have a lot of ambition, kid. I admire that a lot. What's the old saying? You got a lotta heart."

By the time Ken came home, Sharon had finished seven or

eight sketches and part of one complex line drawing. Donna was sitting on the couch in a short blue silk robe he had given her, pouring tea for Sharon. When she had filled Sharon's cup, she waved for him to walk over.

"Hi, come on in. How did it go?"

"All right, I guess. Hi, Sharon." Ken shucked off his suit coat in one smooth motion and tossed it like a rag onto a chair. "I'm sick of wearing this stuff." He yanked his tie loose and leaned down to hug Donna.

"Mmm." Donna kissed him and drew back to put down the teapot, which was getting heavy in her hand.

"Matter of fact, Lou signed me up for a game. It's—"

"He signed you up for a game, and you just say it went 'all right, I guess'?" Donna turned to Sharon. "That's the sign of being a master. So nonchalant."

"Now, wait a minute. Not exactly." Ken raised his hands, palms forward. "It's actually very exciting. The principals in this contract are two foreign governments."

"What?"

"Yeah. It's the first time, and it means real prestige for the Guild. Even more than usual. If this catches on, it could mean changes in diplomacy and all kinds of stuff."

"What's the dispute about?" Sharon asked.

"Shipping rights of some kind. It's between Portugal and Yugoslavia. I know that part isn't very earthshaking. But Lou says world attention will be focused on it."

"I would say so," said Sharon.

"If they actually set an example," said Ken, "other countries could follow. It's great to have the major powers talking instead of killing us all, but if these small countries set a precedent, we might eliminate brush wars and all completely. Masters could fight them on computers instead."

"You're the hottest master in town," said Donna proudly. "And that's in spite of losing to Richard."

Ken shrugged, but he was grinning. "Your qualifier is what, five days away?"

Donna caught Sharon's eye. "Four days, ten hours, and twelve minutes, now." They both laughed.

"I, uh, don't want to butt into your schedule, but . . . if I could help at all in a practice game or something, we could play."

Donna laughed delightedly. "I thought you'd never ask."

"Well, I had to get this promotional stuff off my mind, but it's under control now. Besides, I wasn't sure you'd want to."

"This will be a good climax to my practicing. Shall we do it the day before the game?"

Ken shook his head. "No, no—remember what I said? Always keep the last day free. Use it to rest your reflexes and rest your mind and get away from it for a day. If you're really ready, it won't matter; if you aren't, one more day won't help."

She also remembered that he had not taken his own advice before his game with Richard, but she knew better than to remind him. "So, the day before the day before."

"It's a date." Ken went into the bedroom, unbuttoning his dress shirt.

Donna gave Sharon a wide-eyed shrug. "I'm always off-guard," she whispered. "I never know what he's going to do."

Sharon smiled indulgently. "But you're still crazy about him."

CHAPTER
Ten

I must be crazy, Donna thought as she positioned the keyboard in front of herself. He's going to kill me in this game, and I'm going to play my qualifier with no confidence at all. So I could call if off but then I'd know I was a coward and I'd lose confidence all over again. So I'm actually going to play him for real. . . . I must be crazy.

Across the empty playing field, Ken signaled that he was ready. During most practice games, Donna and her opponent chose a specific battle that offered challenges they wanted to face. This time she wanted to simulate a formal game and take a random choice by the computer. She took a deep breath and keyed the computer to make a selection. And if I beat him—*ha!*—will that make me overconfident?

The screen across the top of her keyboard read, "Clontarf. 1014. High King Brian Boru."

Clontarf? She knew it, sort of. It was a fringe battle, so-called by the gamers because it did not involve a lot of tactical decisions. Her Irish force and small group of allied Manx Vikings were lined up to repulse an army of Leinstermen under King Maelmordha and Vikings under Jarl Sigurd of Orkney and Jarl Brodir of Man near Dublin.

At this time, Norse raids on much of Europe had secured land for the raiders; the nucleus of the Viking army was from Dublin, supported by Norse mercenaries from all of western Europe, including Normandy. They had been joined by Welsh, Flemings, and Bretons. Nearby in Dublin itself, which had been founded by the Norse, another division of Vikings remained with King Sigtrygg Silkybeard.

As the brief orientation period sped by, Donna's thoughts included one stray observation, born of her intensive study: earlier Western European conflicts of the Dark Ages had seen settled Celtic and Teutonic communities attacked by raiding Vikings. At Clontarf, the political conflict still ranged the Celtic Irish against the Norse invaders, but both sides numbered Celtic and Viking allies in their company. The battle represented a transition she found interesting.

On the other hand, she had little regard for either of these peoples as tacticians. They were emotional, spare of discipline, and relatively simple in their tactics. Much of this battle had been decided by the initial disposition of forces.

She looked out over the motionless hologram on the playing field. The opposing army was drawn up in seven divisions, with the Dublin Vikings on their left flank protected by the Liffey River, the Leinstermen in the center, and the mercenaries on their right flank, up against Dublin Bay, where their ships were moored.

Her own Irish were roughly equal in number and ranged across her side of the field in front of the enemy. Both sides wore little mail, though the Vikings had perhaps two thousand mail coats and also leather jerkins as protection. The Irish by this time had adopted some of the more efficient Viking weapons, such as long-handled axes and longer swords. They carried the larger Norse shields but did not wear much body protection.

But what, Donna thought frantically, is there for me to *do*?

The orientation light went out, and the field activated. Donna ordered a charge, which was probably superfluous for her emotional and martial Celts. Whoops and shouts went up from the speakers, and the two armies raced toward each other.

Her role, High King Brian Boru, stood behind the lines,

unarmed. Historically, he had been the first Irish king to unite his people, however shakily; his achievement had collapsed after his death at this very battle. He had taken no active part in it and had been killed by Jarl Brodir.

Donna could not think of any orders to give. She watched in frustration as the battle was joined. In the real conflict, the Leinstermen in the enemy center had routed the High King's center—but they had outrun their flanks. Their mercenaries had held long enough for the Leinstermen to rejoin them, but they were too disorganized to hold. The High King's Irish had routed and slaughtered them on the shores of Dublin Bay. On the other flank, the Dublin Vikings had withdrawn toward the single bridge into Dublin, but they had been cut down before they could cross to safety. A repeat of those events would give Donna a victory but very little practice.

She had no interest in the sensory band, understanding that this battle called for attention to the larger picture. As she expected, the Leinstermen in the center were driving back her own Irish. Ken was in the role of King Maelmordha, and his task was to restrain his men so that they would not advance to the point of breaking contact with his allied flanks.

She would have to do something. Setting her mouth hard, she ordered King Brian to call for his weapons and join the center. She did not want to bolster it, which would have been her aim in most battles. Instead, she called for withdrawal. Her roughly disciplined ranks first fell back slowly but quickly disintegrated into a rout.

The Leinstermen held. They did not break and pursue, as Ken must have successfully forced them to obey his orders. By holding steady, they allowed their allied flanks to stand fast, fighting toe-to-toe with the Irish flanks.

She had King Brian take a stand to rally his center. Slowly, the fleeing warriors began to gather around him, waving their spears and swords and axes with new enthusiasm. She was encouraged; a charge into the Leinstermen could smash the enemy center and give Ken a real shock. Maybe.

He didn't give her the time. Before her center had rallied in any numbers, the Leinstermen charged. Donna had to keep Brian Boru alive, and when he ran, his followers dispersed again in abject flight. Yet behind them she saw more reason for hope.

Now the Leinstermen did leave their flanks behind. Ken had had to risk this when he had seen that she might rally her center. She could not give more orders now, with her role running wildly from the enemy, but she watched as her flanks isolated the enemy flanks, just as in the real battle.

The Leinstermen were out of Ken's control, pursuing the Irish center. Behind them, to each side, the Irish were driving the Dublin Vikings back toward the city ridge and the mercenaries toward the Bay. The computer had control of the entire battle now, since both gamers' roles in the battle had lost command of their forces. With cautious relief, Donna watched the holographs struggle until the field froze.

In front of her, the screen on her keyboard read, "Stalemate; Advantage, High King."

Donna fell back in her seat, grinning to herself, on the verge of insane giggling. She had never seriously imagined she could play Ken to a stalemate. Of course, it was only a practice game and a fringe battle; that made a difference.

When she rose from the seat, she realized for the first time that she was soaked in sweat, flushed, and out of breath. She had concentrated to the fullest and had not noticed the strain until it was all over. Her knees quivered as she picked her way carefully down the stairs.

Ken was already coming down the side of the playing field, where the battle was still in place. She had forgotten to cancel it on her keyboard.

"Congratulations," Ken called. "That was great. And a good way to end your practice run, I'd say."

Donna smiled appreciatively and started back up the steps to shut off the projector.

"You even kept King Brian alive. And it's a tough battle to control. It's one of the fringe ones, so people say."

"I know." Donna hit a switch and the playing field became stark white again. As she descended the steps a second time, it occurred to her that Ken was bright and bouncy. He hadn't pushed himself the way she had.

At the bottom of the stairs, Ken gave her an enthusiastic hug. "Let's celebrate. Want to go out to dinner?"

"Dinner?" She looked in amazement at her watch. "I thought that only took, I don't know, half an hour."

"You were really giving it everything, then. It was closer to an hour and a quarter." Ken put his arm around her shoulders. "That's really good. I think you're ready."

"Did you forget about Sharon? She and a couple of friends invited me out tonight. I guess it's sort of a pep rally. In fact, I have to get ready now or I'll be late."

"Oh, that's right. Tell you what. You have a good time tonight, and tomorrow we'll break the pattern—do something to get your mind off all this nonsense. Okay?"

At this playful tone, she looked up with curiosity. "You sound like you have something in mind." She nudged him in the ribs.

"It'll be a surprise. We'll spend the day together, but remember—" He grinned and hit the light switch as they left the room. "You're in training. Don't break curfew."

Downstairs, Donna was relieved to leave him behind. She was not angry with him, but she was uncomfortable. He had been an opponent one moment, the terrifying master who was about to play for one government against another, who suddenly held power over her success in her chosen career. Now he was her friend and lover again. For the first few moments after the game, though, she had not felt affectionate. Experienced gamers must be used to this, but she was not. Not yet.

Sharon took her out to dinner with three other women they knew, but they were really Sharon's friends. In her daily routine, Donna saw Ken and Sharon often enough, but gaming had left her little time for anyone else. She found the situation acceptable.

The five of them went to an elegant Italian restaurant and consumed a considerable amount of wine long after they had finished the meal. Donna realized, giggling, that Ken had known what he was talking about when he told her to save one day, tomorrow, free of practice. That was part of her training, too.

Donna enjoyed herself, but the dinner was no escape from her growing anxiety over the game. For four hours at the restaurant, her companions assured her she would win, told her how impressed they were already, and guaranteed that she would qualify for master status. Every expression of well-intended encouragement seemed to prod arguments out of her subconscious: she could not possibly win; they only said they were impressed; she was certain to fail to qualify. Thankfully, by the time they returned her home at her self-imposed nine-o'clock curfew, she was too sleepy from the wine to dwell on her doubts. She was in bed very quickly, vaguely aware of amused, tender attentions from Ken.

Ken had arranged for them to spend the next day at the Guild Resort in the Ozark Mountains. It was a private retreat, and membership cost him a premium. Tucked away in the mountains of southern Missouri, the resort featured a luxury hotel, several excellent restaurants and bars, a private lake, and a gym. Outdoor whirlpools and swimming pools were covered and heated for use in cold weather. In addition, riding, canoeing, boating, swimming, and fishing were available in the surrounding country. During warm weather, flights left the city every morning and returned in the early evening. Other scheduling could be arranged for the half-hour flights.

Donna awakened clearheaded but sleepy and was content to let Ken lead her through the motions of the trip. She had been a guest at the resort twice before. This time, she didn't really wake up, she felt, until she was lying on a lounger in the sunlight by the pool, gazing at the forest-covered mountains just beyond the boundaries of the resort.

"The sun feels good. It's taking the aches away." She frowned down at herself, looking over her tan. It was good and not too dark, set off by her white bikini. Her gymnastics kept her well toned, but, she wondered again, maybe she looked too muscular.

"Sure is quiet here," said Ken, looking peacefully into the distance. "Resort's less crowded than usual."

Donna squinted into the sunlight toward him. His eyes were hidden behind dark glasses, but she had forgotten hers. "It's a wonderful place to relax. Thanks for bringing me."

"Sure."

"Ken? You know how you got a little nervous before your game against Richard?"

He grinned. "Yeah. I guess I panicked."

"Well . . . I think I'm starting to panic."

"Would it help to talk?"

"Couldn't hurt. Look—yesterday, during our game . . . Are you . . . did you go easy on me?"

"Me? What makes you think that?"

"I still don't think I could fight you to a stalemate. And let's face it, I was exhausted after the game. You weren't even breathing hard." She watched his face, afraid he would toss off her question with a joke.

Instead, he looked away again, toward the quiet green mountains. At this altitude, a few of the trees were already starting to turn yellow and red. "All right, look. If you mean, did I deliberately let you gain a stalemate and keep your role alive, the answer is no. If you mean, could I have played harder and maybe won if I had wanted—I would have played harder in a formal game, yes. Whether or not I would have won is an open question."

Suddenly Donna felt cold inside. She rubbed her arms in the light breeze. "I don't think I can do it." It came out in a whisper.

"I think that's normal. It's like opening-night jitters for

actors. Supposedly, even veterans get nervous before going out on the live stage in a new show. If I was upset, after all the games I've played, then why shouldn't you be a little nervous?"

"I'm terrified. And you know you're good; your record proves it. I don't have any record. Not at this level."

"Aw, Donna—"

"Wait a minute, Ken." Donna sat up and hitched the lounger into a chair position. "Do you remember asking me once what I would be if I wasn't a gamer?"

"Yes." Ken sat up also, respectful of her serious tone.

"This is the only thing I've done that was worth anything. I dropped out of college because it was dull, and I knocked around aimlessly for a long time. I survived on clerical jobs and lived with guys I was involved with . . . just drifting. Ken, if I can't do this, I can't do anything."

"You're not all that old, you know. And you have three chances to qualify for master status. If you think of it that way, not everything hinges on your game tomorrow."

"You don't panic before every game, though, do you? That last game was important because you were playing against Richard, and that would scare anybody. But normally?"

"No, I don't. I do get a certain charge of excitement, though. When you lose that, you're finished, I'd say."

"I didn't quit school because it was dull. I quit because I couldn't handle it."

"That was a long time ago."

"Ken, I flunked out."

"You didn't put any heart into it. That's all."

Donna smiled reluctantly. "No heart, huh?"

He grinned. "Yeah. Matter of fact, that's a little problem I've had over the years . . . till now."

"What do you man?"

"While you've been locked up in practice rooms day after day, and falling asleep at nine every night, I've been out chasing lawyers and rooting around in libraries." He paused, teasing her.

"And?" She prodded his leg with her bare foot.

"I filed suit under the Guild Act for a game to decide Richard's case."

"*Really*?" Donna leaned over and threw her arms around his neck, laughing. "I'm so glad. That's wonderful. It'll be wonderful for you."

"Well, you talked me into it. I had to find out what my chances would be, so I got into the research. I think, and my lawyer agrees, that I have a good chance of getting a game. Comas are still pretty mysterious to the medical community, and cryogenic sleep is considered a drastic step."

"That's great. It really is."

"Except that *you*, my persuasive compatriot, don't believe in the Guild Act. Isn't there a contradiction there?"

His voice was too teasing to challenge her, but she answered carefully. "I'm very happy that you've taken this step for yourself. It's important to you. As far as the Guild Act goes, I'm still against it, but I'm not against you making your own free choice. The Guild Act is law, so it's up to you."

Ken reached over to hold her hand. "I'm glad. This move has taken a burden off me. I have some hope, for the first time since the accident."

Donna felt tears stinging her eyes, despite her smile. She sniffled and turned away to wipe her eyes with her free hand.

"Hey, are you . . . What's the matter?"

Donna shook her head. She didn't want to say that no one had ever listened to her before, though it was barely an exaggeration. She had actually made a difference to Ken—made his life a tiny bit better, maybe. And he had freely given her credit for it.

It meant a lot, but sounded like so little that she just squeezed his hand without speaking.

"Donna—" He was understandably puzzled.

She leaned over to kiss him quickly and then jumped out of her chair to run toward the pool. The pavement was hot on her feet as she ran to the shallow end and kicked off into a smooth, careful dive that kept her off the bottom. The welcome cool shock of the water enveloped her, and she began to swim.

CHAPTER Eleven

The Marathon Gaming Arena was almost empty as Donna walked across the floor toward the gaming seat. Perhaps fifty people were in the stands, most of them in the lowest rows. The majority were apprentices who knew her and turned out to see if she would make it. Occasionally a few masters would attend a qualifying game, either to observe the potential competition or sometimes to watch the master playing against the apprentice. Finally, of course, Ellen Breslow was up there somewhere, and Ken would be as soon as he reached a seat. She had just barely felt the kiss for luck he had given her a moment before.

The hand Donna placed on the railing was quivering with nervousness as she walked up the steps to her gaming seat. She was aware that an attendant was watching her anxiously, but she reached the seat without trouble. After the game, though, she might be glad of the electric cart the attendant had standing by.

She didn't recognize the master taking his seat across from her. Sometimes playing an opponent one knew allowed a gamer to play against the personality of the opponent, as well as the enemy army, but she would not have that. She might glean something of his tendencies early in the game.

Her heart pounded hard as she prepared herself. Well, you're supposed to put your heart into it, she thought. She had meant it as a little joke with herself, but she was too nervous even to smile.

The announcer was reading her name and that of her opponent and explaining the requirements for qualifying to the crowd. It took only a moment, and most of them probably knew at it all already.

Her opponent across the blank playing field signaled to the attendant that he was ready. Donna did likewise, and the hologram came on. Her keyboard screen read, "Battle of Morat, 1476. Burgundy. Charles the Bold."

Donna felt an instant of relief, followed by a pang of disappointment. This was a very difficult role—her relief had come at recognizing the battle, but this . . .

Put your heart into it. All right.

Charles the Bold, Duke of Burgundy, had fought three major battles against the Swiss Confederation and its allies and had lost all three. This was the second one. What mistakes had he made, that she could correct?

She knew one fact that Charles had never understood, despite his creation of a multinational, permanent, professional army of many elite units that had become a model of European armies for over a century. It included the finest European fighters he could find, English and Welsh longbowmen, mercenary Italian horse lancers, infantry, and crossbowmen, a few German mercenaries, and Burgundian men-at arms, handgunners, and pikemen. Yet the citizens of the Swiss Confederation had developed an entirely new style of warfare in their use of pike and halberd squares. These Swiss pikes in squared formation more than matched a charge of heavy cavalry and returned infantry to a place of prominence in Europe it had not had since ancient times. Donna accepted this; Duke Charles never had.

She studied the motionless field below her.

The city of Morat lay on the east side of a lake. As Duke Charles, she was headquartered on a forested hill called the Bois de Domingue. The Duke had ordered fortifications built in the form of earthworks and palisades to run on a north-south road, as a defense against the Swiss advancing from the east. This fortification was called the Grünhag, and Charles had kept it manned for several days. After several false alarms of Swiss attack, however, he had ordered his army to return to camp, leaving only a garrison on the Grünhag of 2,000 archers and handgunners supported by 1,200 horse. He had concluded that the Swiss had sent out just a small column to draw him forward to the east.

This small garrison was all that defended the Grünhag when the entire Swiss Confederation army of 24,000 descended upon it in an encircling attack. Donna could correct that mistake to some extent; the computer would allow her to bring the army back to the Grünhag. The moment the warning light went out and the holographic armies began to move, she hit the one simple sequence of keys that would muster the entire encampment of the Burgundian army.

In the distance, her opponent was already sending his own army forward, hoping to strike before she could deploy her forces. She remembered, then, that she was not really playing just against her opponent. The Swiss Confederation had not given supreme command to any one person. A council of war had decided that the army would advance in echelon formation—the only time the Swiss Confederation army did so—and surround the Burgundian position.

According to Donna's screen, her opponent was in the role of Hans Waldmann, commanding the center and bulk of the Swiss army, numbering 12,000. The computer retained control of the Swiss van of 5,000 Bernese, Fribourger, and Schwyzer commanded by Hans von Hallwyl, of the Swiss horse under Duke Renatus of Lorraine and Duke von Theirstein, and of the Swiss rear of 7,000.

This arrangement prevented her, as well as Duke Charles originally, from playing against the tendencies of one person, if she had been able to detect some. Instead, she had to outthink an army that was like a creature without a head.

In the previous battle between Duke Charles and the Swiss, at Grandson, the Burgundians had been put to flight largely because Charles had mistaken the Swiss van for their entire army. However, the dearth of Swiss horse had allowed the Burgundians to escape with very slight casualties. Here at Morat, the Swiss had chosen their encircling movement to prevent another such escape. Meanwhile, Charles had learned from his first mistake and had been confident of victory by his own excellent army—until the attack caught him unprepared.

Donna's army seemed to deploy with agonizing slowness. Like any commander, she gave order after order for haste and discipline, then simply had to hope the order would be followed efficiently. The Burgundian army was well drilled, but they had a lot do and very little time.

The Swiss, of course, seemed to be racing westward in formation toward the Grünhag.

According to the Swiss council of war, the van was to engage the Grünhag garrison with handgun and crossbow fire. When the garrison was softened and the pikemen in the van close enough, a pike charge would attempt to break through the Grünhag. The center was following a short distance behind and to the left in support of it; the Swiss rear intended to sweep south of the Grünhag and the Burgundian camp to cut off retreat to the south. Retreat to the west was blocked for the Burgundians by Lake Morat and the city itself, which was still held by its Swiss citizens and garrison. To the north, separate Swiss contingents from Neuchâtel and Le Landeron were positioned to stop flight northward.

The Burgundian men-at-arms and English longbowmen on the Grünhag were ready for the assault. Their light artillery, longbows, and crossbows took a heavy toll of the Swiss. Donna looked to the reinforcements that were finally mounting the earthworks. They put up something of a fight. Reflexively, she looked to the south flank of the Grünhag, where in the real battle the Schwyzer under Landamman Dietrich had maneuvered past the fortifications and turned the garrison's flank.

With relief and then surging confidence, she saw that her garrison was no longer alone. Her Burgundian army was organized into twelve companies of one hundred "lances" each; each lance was comprised of nine men. She could see that one of her *diseniers,* so-called because Charles had adopted Italian terms, had led ten lances to the flank of the Grünhag in time to confront and throw back the Schwyzer maneuver.

And she understood, suddenly, her advantage. It was impossible to outthink a single opponent because she had none. Yet the Swiss battle plan had been decided the day before in council and could not now be changed—or even discussed—by the men now commanding units on different parts of the field. Her unity of command gave her a flexibility that the enemy did not have. The computer was fighting against her as the historical personages had fought against Charles—that was why the Schwyzer had attacked her flank even though the garrison was now heavily supported. If she could use this inflexibility of the Swiss somehow, she would have a chance.

Donna nodded to herself and turned her sensory band on. Instantly, she found herself on the Bois de Domingue, surrounded by holographic Burgundian household troops. A short distance away, her army was mounting the earthworks, more of them as each moment passed. The light culverin of the Swiss were volleying heavily into the palisade, and historically this and the turned flank had allowed the Swiss pike charge to ram through the Grünhag and sweep through the Duke's army. The Burgundians had not been able to deploy cohesively, and the mercenaries had panicked and fled. Nearly all had been slaughtered by the encircling Swiss. Here, Donna's Burgundians might be mounting the barricades in time.

Donna could see the Swiss pikemen forming a wedge to assault the palisade. She also knew that the most fragile part of her army was the motivation and discipline of her Italian and German mercenaries. Their confusion and panic had lost the battle of Grandson for Duke Charles and had been the last straw in the collapse at Morat. She knew how best to forestall a repeat of that.

She ordered her household troops and personal bodyguards to prepare to follow her. Duke Charles himself had led a charge of heavy cavalry at Grandson. All she would do here would be to ride up and down the rear of the Grünhag with a show of force that would boost morale along the earthworks.

The Duke's household troops numbered over 2,000 combatants, and his personal guards included four companies of mounted English archers of one hundred each. With the sensory band still on, she sent her hands racing and hopping over the keyboard. At the same time, she spurred her horse and led her personal contingent galloping down the slope of the Bois de Domingue toward the rear of the Grünhag where the Burgundian army was still taking positions.

She cantered quickly along the rear of the earthworks, shouting encouragement to the troops and orders to her lieutenants. The very sight of the Duke and his sizable retinue sharpened morale and boosted confidence all the way up the line. Then increased shouts and screams from one section of the Grünhag told her that the pike charge had commenced.

Donna switched off the sensory band and looked out over the battlefield. The forested caterpillar of pikes smashed into the palisade, where her own archers and handgunners had joined the Burgundian men-at-arms in hand-to-hand combat. Archers, crossbowmen, and handgunners from both sides poured their fire point-blank into the Swiss pikemen. The palisade was broken, smashed, and shoved aside, but more of the heavily armed Burgundians were in position to replace those who fell. Swords and axes were swung two-handed in the jammed section of the earthworks; when the Burgundians got inside the long forward thrust of the pikes, they had the advantage. Slowly, slowly, she saw the concerted energy of the pike charge dissipate and fall back. The fighting continued on both sides, but the Burgundians on the earthworks now dropped their weapons to pull up the palisade the best they could, protected by the bowmen and handgunners around them.

It would not be the last pike charge, but Donna let out one hesitant breath of relief. Defending the Grünhag had been her first priority; now she had another problem.

To the south, the Swiss center of 12,000 men was sweeping around the hamlet that anchored the south end of the Grünhag. Their path had taken them some distance and delayed them, but they were about to roll up the Burgundian line. The Swiss rear was a short distance behind them. Donna immediately took the Duke and his retinue south to meet them, ordering that artillery standing to the south be shifted toward the oncoming Swiss. She also ordered that units on the south of the Grünhag be alerted and turned.

She should have thought of this sooner. The transmission of the Duke's orders was delayed by the confusion around him as he rode behind the Grünhag. The turning of the artillery was painfully slow, and she now had to consider the Swiss contingents to the north, which could move down the left flank, and the Swiss garrison in the town of Morat, which could sally out to her rear. The Swiss had initially outnumbered the Burgundian army by about 2,000, but the Duke still had had a superiority in horse and artillery. She would have to consider the possibility of an orderly retreat.

Donna began to feel discouraged. The encirclement was still working, despite the stand on the Grünhag. Historically, 12,000 Burgundians had died, most cut down on the run or drowned in the lake where they had fled. Fewer than five hundred Swiss had died, most of those falling at the Grünhag. So far, she had done better than Duke Charles, but the elite Burgundian army was simply not the equal of the Swiss pikemen in strength and maneuverability.

The weakest part of the circle was to the north, both in numbers and in the fact that the enemy horse, of Alsace and Lorraine, were a long way off. They were covering the left of the Swiss van in front of the Grünhag where they could be neutralized by the Burgundian horse. Donna knew that in a retreat her mercenaries were almost certain to panic and rout. The rout would be contagious and break down her entire army. So orderly retreat was unlikely if not impossible, but she still might get out of here with an army.

She directed that the word be spread, that the Swiss were weakest to the north. Go north; go north.

The Grünhag was still holding, but another unit of Swiss pikes was preparing for a concerted charge. The Burgundian right was gradually turning to meet the Swiss center, rolling up from the south, but they were too few and too late.

Donna had Duke Charles order the retreat. Word would pass very fast through the army that the Duke himself was on the run. Historically, Charles had tried to rally his men at several different battles when they had broken, but she would not waste the effort.

She had one more ploy. The mounted retinue of the Duke would spearhead the flight north against the Swiss positioned there. It would be the only chance for her army to escape in significant numbers.

As the Duke cantered north at the head of his guards and householders, they left the Swiss center behind for the moment. Donna had him signal as forcefully and confidently as he could for other contingents of his army to follow in formation, while others ran after him in route step. The men on the Grünhag saw the retreat and peeled off the earthworks, starting at the south end and moving north. The artillery kept firing, to cover the withdrawal as long as possible.

In the real battle, the Fourth Burgundian corps under the Duke of Romont had not been involved in the early stages of the battle. They had been positioned northeast of Morat, behind the Grünhag and the conflict there. Romont had led them north against the Swiss of Neuchâtel and Le Landeron in a failed effort to break out of the ring. Now, in the game, Romont's corps joined that of Duke Charles on the drive to break out.

In Morat, to the west, Adrian von Bubenberg ordered the garrison out to engage the Milanese mercenaries under Anton of Burgundy. To the east, the Swiss pikes had burst through the palisade and their van was overrunning the Grünhag and swarming down the slope behind it. To the south, the Swiss center was rolling north and finding easy prey in the routed Burgundians fleeing the Grünhag. Even where complete chaos had been forestalled, the Burgundian army had broken down into individual units all over the field.

Donna watched the northwest corner of the field as she worked over the keyboard. The combined forces of Duke Charles and the Duke of Romont were still almost intact as they came into view of the Swiss waiting ahead of them. Donna ordered the Duke's personal retinue into a wedge formation, as he had used in the charge of lancers he had led at Grandson.

It was a risk, since losing the Duke's life would cost her the battle and the game for sure, but the battle was collapsing around her now, anyway. She would have to take the risk. The Duke prepared to lead a charge into the Swiss squares.

Donna turned on the sensory band again, and as Duke Charles, she looked north toward the oncoming Swiss. Two thousand men marched in formation, bristling with pikes and halberds like a giant hedgehog. Sunlight glinted off their heavy blades, their shining breastplates of Milanese steel, and their many different helmets—sallets, rondels, and kettles that the Burgundians themselves used. The Swiss banners, and especially their heraldry, came in many colors, but red stood out the strongest: red and black, red and gold, red and white, shown often on their surcoats and leggings, as well. Their drummers and pipers marched in the front rank; war horns called over the din of battle around them.

Donna signaled for the charge and cradled her lance. She spurred her charger and, with shouts and whoops filling the air, she galloped toward the Swiss line. On each side, the nobles close to the Duke galloped alongside, the rhythm of the horses and thundering hooves and flying pennons all bringing them closer and closer to the forest of pikes.

Ahead of them, the pikemen dug in and braced themselves to meet the charge. The long poles angled forward, far ahead of the men themselves. The ground before them shrank.

Donna grimaced as the line of lancers smashed into the pikes. The horses, with more sense than courage, reared and screamed despite their own heavy plate armor. The man on her left was out of his saddle; her own lance splintered, and she pulled up the mace hanging on the right of her saddle. Some of the pikes had shattered as well, and the front line of Swiss came forward with their swords and axes drawn, while their comrades still charged forward with their great pikes to the fore.

Donna turned off the sensory band to see the entire field again.

As the Burgundians followed Duke Charles to this front, they solidified his lines and began to push around the left corner of the Swiss square. As more handgunners and bowmen came up, the Swiss began to fall in greater numbers, but Donna knew that numbers here could be misleading. At the battle of St. Jacob-en-Birs in 1444, 1,500 Swiss had fought 40,000 Armagnacs for over five hours before dying to the last man. She did not have those numbers here, or any time to spare.

The massive Swiss center was clearing the field as it marched steadily up from the south.

The Duke and his men fought on savagely, jammed together facing the immovable pike squares. The Burgundians who were managing to outflank the Swiss were not continuing to fight, but fleeing; that judgment came from the computer. The Swiss showed no signs of falling back or collapsing—in fact, their record in this century was one of great courage and discipline. They were free men defending their homes from professional Burgundians, foreign mercenaries, and hereditary nobility. The difference in morale and motivation was crucial.

Donna would have to risk one last move. She pulled the Duke out of the fray and brought him somewhat to the rear. There, he and his bodyguards joined the general flight circling to the left of the Swiss squares. She watched anxiously as the routed Burgundians poured through a narrow space between the spines of Swiss pikes and a forested slope until the Duke himself galloped safely through and fled northward in the company of his men.

When she did not have Duke Charles attempt to rally his army, the computer judged that his control was gone. That meant the game was over. The holographic field froze in place.

Donna was caught off-guard. She had been concentrating so hard on the game that the abrupt end left her still hitting the deadened keyboard to no purpose. Then, realizing it was over, she held her breath and looked at her keyboard screen as she pulled off the sensory band.

It read, "Victory Conditions, Swiss Confederation. Status Recommendation: Master."

She had lost the battle and the game, but had earned what she had come to get. Her shriek of delight was cut short by the dryness in her throat. She leaped up and started down the steps, finally aware that some of her friends were cheering loudly for her, even if their few voices did not exactly fill the huge arena.

She stumbled, but the alert attendant at the bottom of the stairs caught her. Then Ken had his arms around her and eased her into the powered cart.

"You got it," he said with a grin. "Congratulations."

She clung to his arm, embarrassed by the tears she felt blurring her eyes. He sat down next to her on the cart and waved for the attendant to drive them out to the reception room.

"And *now,*" he said. "We'll go back to the Guild Resort for a real vacation. Want to?"

She smiled and placed her fingertips on her chest in an exaggerated theatrical gesture. "With all my heart, kind sir."

CHAPTER
Twelve

They returned from a week at the Guild Resort to business as usual. As summer waned into early fall, Donna signed on as a client with Ellen Breslow and nervously began awaiting her first professional contract. Ken once again began a rigid practice routine, this time in preparation for his international game. His suit to prevent Richard from being frozen entered the labyrinth of pertinent laws and legal precedents, with an emergency medical priority; at the least, a court injunction suspended any hospital decision until the court had acted.

In contrast to the dread Ken had felt as his last game had approached, he found himself rising eagerly each morning, rushing to the Guild Hall to take on the day's practice opponent. He had experienced a similar rush of confidence during the elimination tournament, when he had reeled off seven victories in a row against the world's top competition outside of World Headquarters itself. The very feeling itself was self-perpetuating.

If good luck generated more of the same, he was in great shape. He had realized even before signing the contract that he could not really lose in career terms. The game itself was in all the headlines, a professional coup that even surpassed his winning the tournament. The next best thing to winning this game would be losing it. That left him with very little to worry about.

That luck was still riding with him when the court turned in an early verdict and granted that a game be played over his lawsuit. He immediately set Lou to contracting it and returned to his practice games.

When the formal game finally arrived, it was anticlimactic: Ken played the role of Arturus Rex, the person upon whom King Arthur of legend was originally based, in the Battle of Mount Badon, and defeated the enemy Saxons in spectacular fashion.

Yugoslavia, the losing principal, began meeting its obligations under the game later the same week. Again, Ken was named in the news media worldwide as the implications of this development were discussed. Three weeks later, two more countries—small ones, admittedly—had agreed in principle to submit their economic dispute to a Guild game.

Ken remained emotionally high on that news well into the next month. Then the new ratings came out, and he found himself with the coveted number-one rating. Despite the work he had put into his career, this still felt like an impossibility, and when he wasn't giddy with excitement, he teased himself with the idea that a mistake had been made. His luck was still carrying him, and all he had to do now was wait for Lou to contract his game about Richard.

One morning after Donna had left their apartment right after breakfast to go to the Guild Hall, he switched the videphone to the open speaker to call Lou. The small, opaque blue screen flickered twice as it bypassed Lou's receptionist; Ken grinned, still amused after all this time. Lou's clients numbered several older masters who still had not been given the private line, despite more years with him.

"Yeah?" Lou's full, scowling face appeared on the screen, then relaxed. "Oh, hi, Ken." He looked away, at someone off-camera. "Excuse me for five minutes, will you? Thanks."

"Lou? I can call back." Ken reached for the phone.

"Nonsense! That's what I gave you this number for in the first place. What do you have in mind?"

"I just wanted to ask if you'd heard anything new about my game. I mean, the one the court—"

Lou laughed. "I know which one, Ken. I'm your contractor, remember? If I had signed you up to play another game, I'd know it."

"Sorry, Lou. I've never been a principal before. The idea of sponsoring a game is new to me."

"It's new to everyone, bucko, and that's part of the problem. If you had sued for a game before you established a masterplay against your friend Richard, you'd have masters all over town clamoring for a game against you. Now, though, everyone knows you're going to play for your side in this game—hire yourself, so to speak—and you're scaring them off."

"They can't all be scared, Lou. These are masters we're talking about, working at World Headquarters."

"Well, granted, a lot of them are contracted at any given time." Lou stuck a pencil sideways in his teeth and talked around it. "And some of them are booked up a long way in advance." He grinned behind the pencil. "Some of them have heavier financial obligations than you do, for instance, and they're afraid not to sign up as many contracts as they can."

Ken felt a flush of anger. "So what's the Guild Act good for, if I sue for a game and the court awards it, but no one contracts to play me? I just give up?"

"Settle down, bucko. Consider it this way. You came to town as the new hotshot, after winning that tournament. In your first game here, you almost defeated Richard Ross, the most feared master in the history of the Gaming Masters' Guild, and you apparently developed a masterplay in the process. In your second game, you just finished playing for the first contract ever to decide a dispute between two governments, establishing a landmark not just in Guild history, but in international relations, and you won an overwhelming victory. *Now* word is out that you've filed suit under the Guild Act against the Gaming Masters' Guild itself, through its medical insurance, exhibiting substantial courage, and that you intend to play this game yourself because it is personally very important to you—and you wonder why other masters are wary of you?"

Ken grinned sheepishly. "When you put it that way, I do sound impressive. I don't feel like it, though."

"You are, Kenny, believe me. Now, then. I started at the top, to get you the best matchup I could, but no one's biting. So I'm figuring now to locate a newcomer, someone hot to make a rep playing you even if they lose."

"Whatever it takes. I just want this game played."

"All right. I've already posted a new ad on Signal Flare. Just remember, a master with nothing to lose can be unpredictable. No pushover is going to sign up against you."

"Just get me someone. Thanks, Lou." Ken clicked off and leaned back in his chair, remembering something Richard had said to him long ago, when he had first arrived here at World Headquarters: "Our esteemed colleagues have the souls of circling buzzards."

Donna picked up a guest badge for Sharon at the reception desk and handed it to her. "Thanks for coming over. I really need to talk to someone."

"Nothing to it." Sharon smiled down at Donna, then frowned at the lapel of her brown corduroy jacket as she clipped the badge to it. The jacket shifted momentarily around her broad, slender shoulders, and she shrugged it back into place. "Besides, it's a free lunch in the Guild Club, isn't it? After all these years of your telling me about it, I can finally see it for myself."

Donna laughed. "I couldn't take anyone there until I became a master. This will be my first time as a host instead of as a guest."

They started down a long hallway. A roar of voices from a room up ahead grew as they approached it. Sharon hesitated at the doorway, leaning sightly to peek inside.

"That's the Xerxes Room, for apprentices. Would you like to go in for a minute?"

Sharon turned in delighted surprise. "Can I?"

"Sure. Come on."

It was a large rectangular lounge with a high ceiling. The carpet, as in every part of the Guild Hall, was thick and springy; the decor featured browns, greens, and white. Heavily padded sofas and easy chairs were arranged throughout the center of the room with tables between them, all positioned to face the walls. Medium-sized spectator screens, a meter square, had been installed side by side into every space of every wall. Apprentice gamers were perched, sprawled, and propped against all the furniture, laughing and cheering and yelling in a variety of languages at the screens and at each other.

Sharon gazed at the walls, taking in one screen after another.

Donna stood on tiptoe and leaned on Sharon's shoulder to speak into her ear. "These screens are monitoring practice games going on here in the Guild Hall. They're played upstairs."

"Really? I thought those were private."

"Both gamers have to give their permission for the monitoring. And no one ever knows which gamers are playing, unless they tell people themselves. That's frowned on. It's all supposed to be confidential, like you said."

"You know, it's funny. We've known each other all this time but always socially. You really are a *master gamer,* aren't you?"

"I guess." Donna laughed.

"And everybody's having such a great time." Sharon looked around at the crowd.

"It's a lot of fun, really. For one thing, you don't even know what battle you're watching, unless you can figure it out from the terrain and the armies. It's good training for an apprentice, just like watching the maneuvers." Donna pointed to a nearby screen. "Can you tell me what that is?"

"Can *I*?" Sharon laughed. "No. I've seen plenty of games live, but watching on these screens is different."

"I can tell those are medieval archers slaughtering

mounted knights bogged down in a marsh. Beyond that, I'd have to sit and watch for a while."

"I think I still prefer watching the games in person, with the holograms on a full-sized field. The 3-D makes it seem so realistic." She turned. "Well, I guess I'm holding us up, huh?"

"Oh, look at that one." Donna pointed to a screen high on the wall opposite them. "That one's interesting. It's the Battle of Caishr, in 1161. General Yu Yun-wen of the Sung Empire—China, that is—used explosives made with gunpowder. They're fighting the kingdom of Jin . . . uh, a kingdom ruled by Jurchen Tungus descended from Manchurian tribes."

Laughing, Sharon took Donna's arm and steered her out of the room. "Maybe I'm not the one keeping us here, after all. Let's eat, kiddo."

Donna knew that the staff in the Guild Club was required to recognize all the masters working out of World Headquarters, but she was still surprised when the maître d' merely nodded formally to her and led them to a table without any questions.

"Wow," said Sharon, taking in the decor of the Club as she sat down. "This place is really fancy. And that guy didn't blink an eye when you asked for a table for two. You *are* in, aren't you?"

"Well, not exactly." Donna was still feeling pleased and excited. "I'm not assigned to World Headquarters. Technically I'm an *adjunct master*, because I qualified after doing my apprenticeship here. I can play here for a while, but I have to keep applying for regular status at any opening at any Guild Hall, no matter where." She wrinkled her nose in distaste. "I could wind up anywhere in the world for my first assignment. The worst places have the most openings, of course."

"Of course. Every career is like that in some way. But, uh, how long will they let you stay here as an *adjunct*?"

"As long as I keep applying for regular status whenever I

can, I can probably stay indefinitely. Once you're a master, the Guild really pampers you."

Sharon rolled her eyes. "So I see."

After they had ordered, Donna took a deep breath and started folding and unfolding the linen napkin in her lap. "I have a real problem. And if I don't take care of it just right, I stand to lose a lot. I really do."

"Is it a personal thing or a career thing?"

"Both."

"Uh-oh. What is it? Something about Ken?"

Donna nodded. "My contractor, Ellen, called me late this morning and said she's sure she can get me my first game contract."

"That's *great*. Congratulations."

"Thanks, but uh . . . I'd have to play against Ken."

"*What*?"

"Do you remember when I told you that Ken had sued for a game to be played, that he would play for his side? Well, no one wants to play against Ken. The other side is still open and Ellen found it posted on Signal Flare, the contractor's net. She's sure I can get it."

"Can you do that? Play against someone you're, well, very close to? I would think they'd have a rule about it or something."

"There's nothing formal. Most people avoid it because the public thinks it looks bad, but sometimes it happens. Anyhow, this case is really unusual."

"What do you mean?"

"The Guild's medical staff has decided that Richard Ross has been in a coma long enough to be put into cryogenic sleep. Ken is sure that he'll wake up on his own and is trying to stop the Guild."

"Does he have any medical authority backing him up?"

"Sort of. Some doctors gave depositions saying that comas are unpredictable and that no one can tell if Richard will wake up or just go on getting older."

Sharon frowned. "Wow. That is a tough one."

"So if I sign to play against Ken, I'm also playing to have Richard frozen. Or at least, he'll see it that way."

"What if you didn't have any personal stake in this? Which side would you choose on merit?"

"I've been thinking about that all morning. To be honest, I think the medical information is more or less even. Nobody really knows much about comas in general. But the insurance policy was Richard's own idea. He didn't have to sign it. So I would have to say that on merit, I would support the Guild against Ken."

"Say, wait a minute. Doesn't the Guild have its own master to represent it in cases like this?" Sharon paused to take a drink of water. "It seems ridiculous that the Gaming Masters' Guild can't find anyone to play its own side."

"Traditionally, the master with the current number-one rating acts as the Guild's champion. The trouble is—"

"Oh, no . . ." Sharon covered her smile with the fingertips of one hand. "And Ken is the current number-one. That must make the Guild mad, huh?"

"Privately, maybe. Officially, everything's okay. Ellen told me that the Guild Executive Committee formally asked several other masters to represent them, but they all declined. After that, the opening was posted on Signal Flare like a regular game."

Sharon looked at her askance. "And no one has come forward?"

"No, for a variety of reasons."

"Didn't you tell me once that anyone can be beaten?"

"Yes, that's true. But some masters are still better than others. Now that Richard's incapacitated, anyone who defeats Ken will be scoring quite an upset."

"I really want to see you do well, Donna. And I don't mean to be discouraging . . . but why does your contractor want you to play him? The chances of . . . of a newcomer beating him aren't too good, are they?"

"No." Donna smiled self-consciously and looked back down at her napkin. "But playing in a prestigious game could be good for someone just starting out, even if you lose. If I do well against Ken, I can start building a good reputation. And right now I don't have any reputation to ruin."

"Take it, Donna." Sharon leaned forward earnestly, picking up her silverware in both hands. "Think about it. After this, people will always say that you, the beginner, were the only one who stood up to Ken. It'll be *great*."

"That's funny," said Donna, not quite suppressing a smile. She looked up and saw the waiter in tails approaching with their lunches. "That's exactly what Ellen said."

After lunch, Sharon left and Donna relaxed in the Xerxes Room, watching whatever games came on the screens in front of her. A master was not expected to benefit much by mere observation, but Donna still felt more like an apprentice than a master, despite her official status. Besides, occasionally a situation would develop or a maneuver might be used that would enlighten anyone. Donna also found that watching the screens offered a welcome escape from the day's worries.

When an hour had passed, Donna took the elevator down to the second basement of the Guild Hall, where the spa, gymnasium, and indoor courts for various games were located. She was talked out now and avoided any more conversation than a quick greeting to those she knew. In the locker room, she changed quickly into her leotard, colored in a purple and white swirl pattern. She had bought it for herself in celebration of qualifying as a master.

The floor was moderately crowded. Donna sat down on an open mat to do her stretching. Her favorite exercise was on the uneven bars, but that required concentration. Right now she was still occupied with thoughts of the game contract.

The stretching was a pleasant routine, a ritual that reaffirmed her self-discipline as well as making her more limber. Gradually the rhythm and repetition cleared her mind. It was a relief not to be dwelling on the game, though she would still have to decide one way or the other...

Suddenly she gathered her legs underneath her and sprang

up. She had done enough stalling. Carefully, she jogged across the floor, weaving around the exercise machines and the other people to a house phone on the wall. She punched in her contractor's number and waited.

The screen on this phone was very small and set deep into the wall as a precaution against accidents. After a moment, Ellen's receptionist appeared.

"Hello . . . Donna. I think she's free; just a moment."

Several seconds later, Ellen appeared on the little screen, but she was not sitting at her desk where the videphone camera would catch her in a portrait shot. Instead the camera had been turned to show her lounging on a couch in her office, dressed in a formal gray suit and a white blouse with a ruffled front and cuffs. She also wore a pair of large, fluffy gray slippers with koala bear faces on them, complete with floppy ears and sharp black eyes.

"Hi, Donna. Have you made a decision?"

"Yes. I want it."

"Great. I know it may be awkward for you, but it will be a very important move for you to make. I'll call Lou Crandall right away. Is that the spa in the background?"

"Yes, I'm downstairs."

"All right. Come up before you leave the Guild Hall and I'll try to have everything for you to sign. Bye."

"Bye!" Donna clicked off, grinning, with a sudden burst of relief and enthusiasm. She turned and jumped onto the track that ran the perimeter of the area and swung into her jogging speed. That would do until the uneven bars were free.

CHAPTER Thirteen

A short time later, Ken rode down the elevator in the Guild Hall in a fit of anger. When Lou had told him that a master had agreed to sign to play his game, he had felt a wave of elation. Then he had been amazed to learn it was Donna. At the very least, he thought she might have discussed the matter with him. He had no power, however, to stop her from signing. The relationship between the Guild and the master who played their side was strictly between them.

Ken was wearing his black trench coat, unbuttoned with the ends of the belt hanging loosely on each side. It was still wet from the cold, light rain outside, which would become snow soon. He walked into the warm spa area feeling out of place, bundled in his street clothes and raincoat in the midst of light, scant, brightly colored exercise outfits. From the doorway, he could see Donna on the uneven bars that kept her so trim, swinging high, flipping, swinging again, whirling and catching. Her short, compact form was taut and muscular, the reward of her dedication.

With his hands in his coat pockets, he threaded his way through the floor and waited near the bars, standing just away from Donna's spotters. After a few more moments, she did a simple dismount and one of her spotters tossed her a towel. Donna caught it with a smile of thanks, started wiping off the sweat, and then saw Ken.

Her expression froze, then changed to one of worry. She frowned, turning her head away as she wiped the back of her neck with the towel. When she looked up again, her face was a polite mask.

Ken was still angry, but that look of worry he had seen disarmed him somewhat. "Why didn't you tell me?" He kept his voice carefully controlled.

"I didn't want you to talk me out of it," she said quietly.

Above them and to one side, another woman started a routine on the bars.

"You could have found out what I thought, at least. I mean, we are living together." Ken's voice had an edge.

"That's a personal matter. This is business."

"Even business can include common courtesy, you know." He became aware that other people were moving away from them. This was no place for an argument. "Were you that desperate for a game? So you had to play to freeze Richard?"

"I'm playing to save him, if you must know! You just want to let him go on aging in a coma? Besides, I'm doing you a favor, getting this game under way when no one else would sign up. You ought to thank me." She pushed past him and spoke more easily. "See you at home, later."

Ken turned to watch her go. Her hair was tied back and bounced over the tight purple and white leotard as she jogged toward the women's locker room. *She doesn't know,* he realized. *I guess I never told her. No, I never did.*

How long had it been? Four, five months had passed since Richard had entered his coma. It seemed like a long time, and Richard had said he would awaken before this. Ken could hardly blame the Guild for believing that putting Richard into cryogenic sleep now was the right move. Still, if Richard was going to wake up spontaneously before much more time had passed, then freezing him for an indefinite period was a terrible mistake.

And what if Richard was wrong? He was no doctor, after

all. The thought came to Ken unbidden, and unwelcome. If Donna was going to play for her conscience, he would play for his.

As Ken walked back to the elevator, he decided not to tell Donna about his private conversation with Richard now, either. He wanted the game played and the issue decided, one way or another. If he talked her out of playing, he might have trouble getting anyone else, as she had suggested.

As usual, Ken was admitted directly into Lou's office up on one of the middle floors of the Guild Hall. Lou closed the door behind him and waved a hand at the expansive office.

"Sit anywhere, Kenny. Drink?" He walked to the bar built into one wall.

"No, thanks." Ken shucked his coat and hung it on a standing wooden coatrack with brass trim. He glanced around, always impressed by Lou's office, even after many visits. Usually, he spoke with Lou on the phone.

The chairs facing the desk were comfortably padded and matched the wheat weave of the couch against one wall. The carpet was a deep brown that matched the mahogany walls. Lou had a rotating file of hard copy set into one wall, mostly signed contracts and other legal documents. The other walls were covered with autographed pictures of Lou with various masters. Some had been taken at fancy restaurants or other social functions, but most had been taken after an important game, sometimes with both gamers present, but always with the victor.

Lou poured a drink for himself and gestured toward the couch. "You weren't too happy when I told you Donna wanted to sign the contract. Have you spoken with her?"

"Yeah." Ken sat down on the end of the couch opposite Lou. "She's pretty determined, so I didn't really object all that hard."

"Ah! Glad to hear it. I was a little afraid that, uh, well . . ." Lou paused to sip his drink.

"It's settled. We're going to play against each other." Ken shrugged. "Who knows? Her lack of experience could give me an edge."

"Or make you overconfident. Also, I don't want you having any thoughts of mercy toward her. Don't even think about going easy on her. She'll be playing as hard as she can, knowing she's the underdog. And she's a master, just like you, and she's capable of beating you. For all we know, the computer just may select a game that she played recently and you haven't seen in years."

"Don't worry about me. In this game, I'm playing for Richard. If she loses, her career will still benefit, unless she does a truly terrible job, and that's not likely. If I lose, Richard may wake up generations from now with all his friends dead of old age, in a society that's totally foreign to him. That's more serious, I'd say."

"Good! Keep that motive in mind. I repeat, though, don't get overconfident. Now. We also have a new problem with this situation."

"The public reaction?"

"Exactly. Ellen agrees with me on this, so the only question is what you and Donna decide." He swirled the ice in his drink for a moment. "Look, this is going to sound a little rough, but here are the choices. The first is, you can move out until after the game. We'll publicize the move as a demonstration of personal integrity and sacrifice on the part of both of you."

"No." Ken shook his head emphatically. "I don't like it at all. Donna and I still have to work out some awkward, uh, some awkwardness about this. Moving out is likely to contribute to misunderstanding between us. What else do you have in mind?"

Lou looked at him carefully. "The only other choice is for the two of you to do a media blitz together, to tell everybody that you're serious about your careers separately but still very close personally. The message is the same either way."

"I like that one better. If it's okay with Donna, that's my choice. Does it matter to you?"

"No. What's important is taking the initiative with the public, telling them what the score is before anyone thinks to ask. Tell you what. You talk to Donna about it. I'll notify

Ellen of your choice as a courtesy, and we'll take it from there. All right?"

"All right. Thanks, Lou." Ken rose.

"And starting tomorrow you'll be back on the practice games."

"My schedule is my department, Lou. Talk to you tomorrow."

Ken grinned as he walked down the hall, cinching the belt of the trenchcoat around his waist. This morning Lou had been telling him what a great and fearsome gamer he was, and now the man was chiding him to practice as though he was still an apprentice. Ken would set and play his own schedule.

By the time Ken got home, he had gotten used to the idea of playing against Donna. Now he just wanted the preparation time to go smoothly. When he came in, Donna was sorting laundry in the bedroom. Ken hung up his coat and joined her.

"So," he said lightly. "Are you all signed up?"

"Yep." She didn't look up.

"I'm sorry I got upset. I just thought we could have talked about it first."

"I didn't feel like it. I'm not obligated, you know." She finished folding one of his T-shirts and tossed it onto a pile of them.

"Yes, I know. It's okay." Ken picked up a pair of jeans and started folding them.

"You sure?"

"Yeah." He dropped the jeans, folded, and slid his arm around her shoulders. "I guess I wanted you to be proud of what I was doing. Before, you kept telling me I was just a hired gun with no beliefs. So now I've gone out and filed for a game myself, and I'm going to play it myself because it's important to me . . . and you're on the opposite side."

She put down the clothes she was holding and turned to face him. "I am proud of that. You're finally playing for something you believe in. I'm not against that; I'm all for it."

"But you can't cheer for me when we're opponents." Ken grinned and nudged her playfully.

Donna smiled reluctantly. "No, not very well. I would have liked having you help me prepare for my first game as a master, too."

"I don't blame you for taking it. You believe in the Guild's position, and the game will be good for you. Especially if you beat me." He kissed her lightly.

She poked him in the ribs. "Surely you don't admit to that possibility, do you?"

"Of course. The best way to keep my killer instinct is to stay insecure."

She sobered. "Ken, those aren't the only reasons."

"What do you mean?"

"I just can't afford to consider anyone else's concerns right now. I told you how I was drifting until I became an apprentice, with no plans, no direction, nothing. You told me once that gaming was your whole life, didn't you?"

"It used to be. You're the one who changed that."

She looked at him, smiling, without speaking.

"And, in addition to entering my life personally, I seem to recall you saying that a normal person should have a whole life, not just a one-dimensional one. That was on our vacation at the Guild Resort, after you qualified. Remember?" Ken sat down on the bed, in the midst of the clothes, and pulled her down next to him.

"Well, yeah." She nodded against his shoulder. "Only, I'm in a different position. Your career is all set up. I'm still getting mine off the ground. And how often does a new master get a chance to play for the Guild and against the current number-one in her very first game?"

"I see what you mean."

"So it's really okay?"

He grinned. "Yeah. It's really okay."

She laughed and put her arms around his neck. "Well, it better be, buster, 'cause that's the way it's going to stay."

They rolled over the clothes, laughing.

At mid-morning the next day, Ken was doing a handstand on the pommel horse, counting the seconds and waiting for his arms to quiver. The pommel horse was his favorite gymnastic choice, and one that had always come naturally to him. He loved watching Donna flying around on the uneven bars, but he was personally cool to any routine conducted at a high altitude over the floor.

"Uh . . . Ken?" One of the other masters leaned down close, his face upside down in Ken's vision. "Sorry to bother you, but you have a call on the spa phone."

"Know who it is?"

"It's Lou Crandall."

"Oh. Yeah. Thanks a lot." Ignoring his normal dismount, Ken lowered himself carefully to the floor and hurried to the phone on the wall. "Hi, Lou."

Lou grinned broadly, his face filling the little screen. "Morning, bucko. You ready for this? I've got a talk show lined up for you and Donna. Ellen and I arranged it and Donna's already agreed; she was in Ellen's office."

"Yeah?" Ken was delighted. He had done a few media shows but not many. "Which show is it?"

"It's Dorothy Clough's audience participation show. It's perfect for us. The show goes all over the country; she's a fair, decent interviewer, and with this publicity, you and Donna won't have to do any more. I'll handle the rest of the PR through press releases and my own jabbering. That way, you can both concentrate on your practicing."

"Dorothy Clough?" Ken was impressed. "That's great. I watch her myself, sometimes. When do we go on?"

"She wants to do it live, so people can call in as well as talk from the audience in the studio. I want you to go on as soon as possible."

"Now, wait a minute. I don't want any distractions in the middle of my schedule."

"It's the best I can do, Ken. If we don't do this now, we'll have to do a bunch of smaller ones, and that'll mean more distractions."

"Well, do we have a date?"

"No, not yet."

"I want to do this just a day or so before the game."

"Hold it, bucko. The whole reason behind this is to promote the game. We don't gain anything by waiting that long." Lou shook his head. "If we kick off with this, I can play it up between now and game time."

"Do the reverse," said Ken. He rarely gave Lou direct instructions; the gamer-contractor relationship relied on cooperation. However, he always kept firm control of his practice schedule. "Get the show for the day before the game, and play it up between now and then. You can forestall the criticism by telling everybody that all questions will be answered on the show."

Lou looked at him gravely for a moment, then glanced away. Ken could tell he was doing something at his desk off-camera, probably scribbling a note. Then he looked back at Ken and nodded soberly. "All right. I can arrange that, though it won't be quite as effective. Tell you what, though. If we get a lot of hassle, I may still have to schedule more shows during your practice period."

"It'll work out, Lou. Thanks." Ken clicked off and turned. A semicircle of his colleagues was standing nearby, straightening their socks, toweling off sweat, and eavesdropping. He grinned at them all and jogged back to the pommel horse.

In the weeks that followed, Ken was glad to find that he and Donna were able to keep their professional and private lives separate. The only obvious change in their routine was that by tacit agreement they no longer discussed games or military history at all, even in casual conversation with others. Ken spent more time than usual at the Guild Hall before and after practice games, talking shop with other masters and, sometimes, grateful apprentices.

As the winter holidays came on, his practice games produced a normal variety of results. Sometimes he played straight, as though it was a formal game, and more often he experimented with new tactics or even old ones that were considered out of date, just to see what happened. These experiments were usually very successful or totally disastrous. He suffered through a miserable defeat at Tannenberg in 1410 as the leader of the Teutonic Knights, beaten by Poles and Bohemian mercenaries supported by Russians and Mongols; then as Alfonse VIII of Castile, united with Navarre and Leon, he ended Almohade power in Spain at Las Navas de Tolosa in 1212. He fought against the Khmer Jayavarman VII in the twelfth century as a Cham king and led an army in Peru as Pachacuti Inca in the fifteenth century. He felt sharp.

Donna left town for the holidays to meet family obligations. Ken was relieved and suspected that she was just as glad not to spend the time with him. As their game date approached, talking with each other became more and more awkward. He would be glad when they could return to normal with each other.

After the new year began, Ken began to spend more time at the Quay Hall. They both knew that it was a form of maintaining privacy, so she did not complain. Even the brief ride on the Overhead seemed to settle his nerves as it glided smoothly through the city, so that when he stepped out, he felt that he was really free of gaming for a while. His visits had quickly taught him that the crowd in the Quay Hall frowned on shimmersuits and other flashy styles, and he fit in now that he wore whatever he happened to have on.

On his final day of practice, he made one more trip to the river bottoms. This time, instead of striking up a conversation with the acquaintances he had made there, he went straight to a table in the back, where the light was dimmest. He had come to get some thoughts straight.

He loved Donna very much. He didn't express that very

well or often; the shadow of his experience with Lydia had left him more reserved than he used to be. With all the tension surrounding the game and Richard and the Guild Act, their relationship was sort of on hold now, anyway.

Marcie lit the candle on his table and took his order for a Kirin. He leaned back in the cushioned booth and gazed at the tall, slender blue flame. The voices of the other patrons were a quiet murmur up by the bar in front.

Donna was the sort of woman he had always wanted to know—pleasant, very attractive, and most importantly, a gamer. This lifestyle was too intense and unusual to mix easily with more ordinary habits. Just being a gamer proved her other strengths of self-motivation and intelligence.

Of course, he reflected with amusement, his celebrity status had helped catch her eye; that had been obvious enough. Their disagreement over the Guild Act did not seem important, with the mutual respect they showed for each other's position. Again, the comparison to Lydia favored Donna.

No one had affected him as much as Donna, not just personally, but also in career terms. He knew very well that he felt different about his upcoming game because of his personal commitment. In fact, he felt considerable pride in the fact that he possessed the skills necessary to represent his side well.

Marcie set down his beer in front of him, where the candlelight illuminated the stylized Asian unicorn on the fancy label. He made no move to reach for it; often, he rented space here by paying a tab for drinks he never touched. The kirin, as the mythical beast was called in Japanese, was a sign of good luck. Perhaps it had been the secret to his success all this time.

The public outcry Lou feared had been fairly mild in its objection to Ken and Donna playing against each other. A more vocal opposition was raised to the Guild Act itself, fueled by the fact that Ken had filed his suit under its provisions. Ken had declined to do any shows other than the

Clough program tomorrow, however, and Lou had not pressed the matter.

The only danger he could see in the game was the one Lou had mentioned, of overconfidence. It was true that Donna, in her first formal game, could not match him for experience and accumulated knowledge. Several other points would keep him clearheaded, however. One was the random selection of the game by the computer which, as Lou had said, might pick one that played to her strengths. Also, he knew that her reputation would not suffer if she lost in a good effort, so he had no need to be lenient. Finally, of course, he had to keep Richard out of cryogenic sleep. As long as he kept repeating those facts to himself, he would keep the right attitude.

CHAPTER Fourteen

Dorothy Clough was a slender woman in her mid-thirties. While Ken and Donna sat in comfortable chairs onstage waiting for the show to start, Dorothy walked among the studio audience, joking and getting acquainted, swaying long, straight brown hair down her back.

Lou had explained that the show would appear on mainstream broadcasts as well as on gaming networks because the Guild itself was one of the principals. That made it news. Radio would carry the discussion also, and some of the 3-D transmissions. The publicity would be good for both of them, but would especially give Donna's career an unusual boost.

Ken was brought out of his reverie by Dorothy's voice, suddenly clear and formal from where she stood in the audience. The show had started.

". . . today are Master Ken Li and Master Donna Wong of the Gaming Masters' Guild. They are opponents in a very important upcoming game, and yet they are also living together. What's it like to be lovers at home and opponents on the job? Call in with your questions at this number. . . ."

Ken exchanged amused glances with Donna. He was nervous, but in a good way, as he welcomed the challenge of the show. Donna had never done this before, but she seemed composed.

"Master Li, I'd like to start with you." Dorothy walked gracefully down to the base of the stage, followed by an overhead mike. She looked up at him. "Can you summarize the game for us? What's it about?"

Ken gave a brief explanation of Richard's condition and the legal arrangements that had led to the game. He had been ready for that one.

Dorothy turned to Donna. "Master Wong, do you agree with that assessment?"

"Yes, I do." Donna smiled pleasantly and nodded.

"May I call you Donna?

"Sure."

"Donna, it sounds to me like you both agree that the life of this man Richard depends on the two of you. Do you really believe a man's life should depend on the outcome of a game?"

Ken looked sharply at Donna, surprised. Dorothy wanted to talk about the Guild Act, not about their personal lives.

"No," Donna said firmly. "I don't."

The audience erupted into applause. "Master Li." Dorothy called over the applause. "May I call you Ken?"

"Yes, of course."

"Do you believe a man's life should depend on a game?"

"Well . . ." Ken didn't have an answer to the question, phrased as it was. "In this case, I'm glad the Guild Act is in effect."

Several people in the audience booed, but not many.

"Why?" Dorothy asked.

"The reason I sued the Guild is that if they freeze Richard, he will lose the chance to come out of his coma spontaneously, as I explained. Now that the Guild Act is in effect, I was able to get a game to decide the issue. Without the Guild Act, allowing me to sue for a game to be played, I would have no chance to fight for this side."

"Thank you." Dorothy turned. "Do we have any questions in the audience?"

A number of hands went up. Ken cleared his throat and found it dry.

"You, sir. Please stand." Dorothy pointed to a burly fellow in a maroon sweater.

The man appeared to be in his early forties. He stood up and shoved his hands into his pockets. "Ah've bin a fan o' the games for many years, and Ah can see a lot o' luck involved. If that's true, then Ah don't believe these games are any decent way to make any decisions. Is it true, from your point of view?"

Dorothy turned. "Donna, what do you think?"

"I think that's exactly right. The games do involve some luck. And even where the skill of the gamers is involved, the games have nothing to do whatsoever with the legal issue over which the game is being played."

"Donna, let me ask you something else." Dorothy looked up at her carefully. "Are you actually saying you're against the Guild Act?

"Yes, that's right."

The audience applauded again, enthusiastically. Ken sat rigidly.

"Isn't that an ironic position for a master? It seems to me that you want to put yourself out of business."

"No, not really. Originally, before the Guild Act was passed, any two people could have their dispute decided by a game if they wanted to. I'm not against that at all. I just think we should go back to that system."

"And we have a caller. What's your question?"

The voice of an elderly woman came over the speaker system. "I want to know why these people think their games are so important that they can decide what happens to the rest of us. I think games ought to be for fun, not for important things. Why should anybody have to abide by a game if they don't want to?"

"Ken? Will you answer that one?"

Ken grinned, knowing he could not satisfy a questioner whose mind was probably made up already. "We have legal issues nowadays that are just too complicated for the laws we have on the books. Our technology has been developing so fast that it has created problems our laws just aren't designed for. We have to have some procedure for making decisions instead of just wading through court battles that take years and years to reach a conclusion."

A skeptical undercurrent of talk rippled through the audience.

"Isn't that better than trial by combat?" the elderly woman asked. "No matter how long it takes, we would have a real verdict. One that means something."

Ken shook his head. "Games don't prevent the passing of new laws, which are what we really need. And they don't set any binding precedent, either."

"Thank you for calling," said Dorothy. "Donna, how do you feel about this?"

"Well, playing games doesn't *have* to stop the passing of new laws, but in reality they do cause a lot of complicated issued to be ignored, I think. If we had to fight through long court cases all the time, certain people in power might be forced to pass new laws we need to cover new social developments. As long as we have the games as a substitute, they can take the easy way out and pass the buck."

Dorothy turned back to the audience."Sir, what's your question?"

A young, slender man in his twenties stood up. "I don't have a question. I just wanted to say that all these decisions we keep putting off are going to catch up with us someday. And the longer we wait, the worse it's going to be." He flung himself back into his seat and folded hs arms.

The applause was sharp and loud, punctuated by shouts of agreement. Ken glanced at Donna, who shrugged at him apologetically but could not help smiling at the show of support. He felt hot and was sweating freely.

"Ken," said Dorothy. "Before we go on, let me remind our audience of another concern with the Guild. Some months ago, you represented the government of Portugal in a game against the government of Yugoslavia. At that time, and shortly after, many people hoped that this would become a common diplomatic solution to international disputes. Do I have that right?"

"Yes."

"Were you hopeful that perhaps someday these games could even take the place of real warfare?"

"Well . . ." Ken shook his head in resignation. "That's a little farfetched. I do hope that occasionally they might take the place of some border disputes or small wars."

"How do you feel about the fact that earlier this week Yugoslavia violated the commitments it accepted after the result of your game?"

"Uh—I didn't know that."

"Ken, is there any way to require the government that loses a Guild game to abide by its agreements?"

"No, I don't think so."

She turned to the audience. "Do you have any questions about this issue? Yes, in the red."

A heavyset woman in a bright red dress stood up in the front row. "I have a question for Master Li?"

Ken smiled. "Sure."

"Well, um, do you agree with Master Wong that the games have a certain amount of luck? I mean, in addition to the skill and knowledge it takes to be a *master gamer*. I don't deny that."

Ken caught Dorothy's eye with an amused glance. The Guild Act still had everyone's attention. "Yes, the programs have been made as realistic as possible. That means some unpredictable factors are involved."

"Um, do these unpredictable factors sometimes shift the balance of the game? Regardless of the skill of the gamers?"

"Yes, it's been known to happen. I would say it's not very often."

"But even so . . . do you really feel your friend's life should be decided that way? Isn't it like flipping a coin?

The audience laughed, but Ken saw that the woman was not smiling. She was serious and sincere.

"Actually, I'm glad I'm able to handle this matter in this way. You know, the courts have been known to be equally capricious at times or even corrupt. And some court decisions have turned on legal technicalities that had no more to do with the principles involved than one of our games."

Dorothy started to interrupt, but the woman continued.

"But if we didn't have the games through the Guild Act, you still could have sued the Guild the normal way. If the case was decided on merit and set a precedent, all of society would benefit."

"I did that. Under the Guild Act, you have to start by bringing a normal suit. If the court judges that the case involves issues that can't be decided on merit, like the status of Richard's coma, they can grant a game to decide it. The Guild Act only comes into effect when a decision can't be reached on merit."

"Thank you," Dorothy said quickly. "Donna, do you agree with that?"

"No, not really. A decision can always be reached on merit. I know these cases can be awfully complicated—and courts aren't perfect, like Ken said. But I think we have to try."

Dorothy nodded. "Now let me get this straight for all of us. Your position is that if both sides want to have a game played, that's okay, but if only one side wants it, the other should not be forced into it?"

"Yes, that's exactly my position."

"Ken, you disagree?"

"I . . . yes, I guess so."

Dorothy smiled broadly. "Well! These are the underlying issues in the upcoming game between you. Now let's move on. What *is* it like, living together and yet preparing to play against one another?"

The rest of the show went the way Ken had expected, and he was comfortable with it. The questions and answers were respectful and not too personal. At the end, though, Dorothy asked for a show of hands in the audience to see how many of them agreed with Donna or Ken regarding the Guild Act. The response overwhelmingly favored her side.

CHAPTER Fifteen

Donna went home after the show, which ended in mid-afternoon. Ken, after assuring her that he was not upset by facing that audience, chose to be alone for a while. The game was tomorrow, and his practicing was over. He simply wanted to find his resolve.

Ken stood motionless on the sidewalk in front of his old elementary school, looking at it through a chain-link fence. School was just out; children from six to twelve years old were streaming past him, bundled in their caps and coats against the cold and clear winter air. The facilities and methods of teaching inside the old school had changed over the years, but the building looked the same, and the kids seemed eternal.

The school was built of red brick. It was in the shape of a rectangle, with a little courtyard in the middle, on the plan of a castle. Varying shades of red in the brick revealed alterations in the architecture over the years. Ken had noticed them even as a child. The two-story rectangle sprawled enough to handle over a thousand young students. A broad asphalt playground surrounded it on four sides, with kickball diamonds and markings for other games painted in bright yellow. Jungle gyms and swing sets shone a dull silver in the afternoon sunlight.

When most of the children had left, Ken entered the playground. A glance at the foundation of the building gave him a rough measure of passing time to his historian's eye: the asphalt reached almost to the top of the foundation of white stone upon which the red brick walls rested. When he had played on this side of the building, in the third and fourth grades, most of the white stone had still been visible. He smiled, thinking of the layers of asphalt that had been laid during the years since then. Hordes of small feet would wear away the tar of each layer but leave the white gravel, so that when the playground was resurfaced, it was just a little higher each time. It would make a curious digging for some archaeologist in the far future.

At one corner, Ken located the cornerstone he remembered, with "1939" carved into it. As a child, he had thought the year impossibly old. Now, with his awareness of history, it was hardly more than yesterday.

Ken walked slowly through the playground, surrounded by a crowd of childhood ghosts. Here, at one kickball diamond, he had first spoken to Richard. Neither of them had liked organized games, but the teacher had had the entire class playing together that day, so they had had no choice. He laughed aloud, remembering. Richard had always claimed that they had met a year earlier, in the second grade, also on the playground. Ken still maintained that they had met in the third grade, but neither of them considered the point important. It was just a historical dispute, of a sort, that was all their own.

To one side of the school, a short slope led up to a large athletic field. It had softball diamonds at the four corners, with backstops, and it was also used as part of the playground. The grass was worn and sparse, trampled by many energetic feet.

Ken stopped near the closest backstop and gazed out over the empty grounds. Field days had been held here. Richard had been a fast runner, though not otherwise athletically inclined. Ken had been a slow runner, but he had learned to pitch a softball one year. For them, though, the field had not been one for athletic competition so much as a battleground for historical conflicts that only they could see.

The memories were fuzzy now but still numerous. On the far side of the field, he recalled playing the American Revolution; he and Richard had been followers of the Swamp Fox, Francis Marion, or sometimes Green Mountain Boys up north. Richard had liked to pretend he was freezing at Valley Forge, too, while Ken had been partial to sniping at Redcoats from behind trees and hacking at them with swords while they reloaded their flintlocks. Ken laughed aloud again and turned to survey the big playground below him.

Toward the left, they had pretended they were buccaneers or sometimes privateers. On the far side of the building, they had carried shields and swords on the First Crusade, somehow passing through Byzantium to besiege Antioch and Jerusalem, all within a few hundred square feet. In front of the school, where Ken had just walked, they had fought Gettysburg and gone home to Shiloh.

Ken started walking across the deserted field. All around him, imaginary children from his childhood played at recess. A few had recognizable faces; most were a vague, half-forgotten mass.

The city of Troy had loomed here once in Ken's imagination, as it had separately, but simultaneously, in Richard's. As the other kids had played normal children's games, young Ken had envisioned himself in the back of a Trojan chariot, heaving spears at Greeks. He would hop off at intervals to trade sword-on-shield blows with the enemy, but always ran for it when some Olympian god favoring the other side appeared in the sky. Richard, with a tendency toward defeatism, kept facing such gods, and throwing himself down in the dirt, would yell his announcement that his chariot had just been blasted to flinders.

"I got up," he once announced, "just in time to see Paris shoot Achilles in the heel with an arrow."

"Must've made him mad," Ken had commented, momentarily dropping out of character. His arm was still upraised, lifting an imaginary shield against Greek blows.

Other kids, playing kickback, surged past them yelling, in pursuit of a kickball.

"Killed him," said Richard. "That's how he died."

"Poisoned arrow, huh?"

"No, the Achilles' heel is fatal. That's why they named it after him."

"But pirates had their legs amputated sometimes. It can't be fatal. The arrow had to be poisoned." Ken drew an invisible sword and started whacking Achaeans again.

Richard collapsed under an illusory blow to his head, and so it went until recess ended.

Richard's strange self-defined identity as an underdog had somehow turned into a supreme arrogance as a *master gamer*. Sometimes the two merged, as in the end of the game of Bosworth Field they had played against each other. Richard had won at the last moment by having the pragmatic humility to send his lead role, Henry of Richmond, into abject flight away from conflict, nearly alone and unprotected.

"Anyone else playing my side probably would have been afraid to run," he had told Ken once after the game.

Ken, gazing across the quiet field, smiled with an affection he felt only for his memories of childhood war-play. It had been so long ago—and yet it had never really ended. He was still playing.

Whenever these memories consumed him, he felt most keenly that he missed his old friend. That was followed, as now, with disappointment and a flash of competitive anger. He didn't just want Richard back. He wanted to play him again in a formal game and defeat him soundly.

Ken raised his head and let the breeze toss his hair. It sent a prickling chill down his back that had little do to with the weather. If Richard was put into cryogenic sleep, and Ken lived out his normal life, they had already spoken to each other for the last time. He looked at the big red empty building, feeling determination swell inside him. A battle was coming, and he would be flush and angry.

CHAPTER Sixteen

The next morning, Donna rose early and was out before Ken got up. They had not laid any ground rules, but he was relieved not to see her just before the game. He prepared himself for the day at his normal pace and arrived at the Guild Hall on time.

The Marathon Gaming Arena was packed with a tense, excited crowd. For the third game in a row, Ken Li was playing a game that broke new ground in the profession. They were also thinking that this new celebrity who had one masterplay to his credit might score another, and Lou's promotional expertise had hyped the game outside the profession, among the general public. Finally, the gossip had intensified the talk: the Guild's top-rated master was playing against the Guild itself, in the person of the woman he lived with, for the life of his best friend. The tabloids loved it. In an unusual concession, the Guild was even allowing media cameras inside the arena to transmit the image of the gamers during the contest. Usually, they only carried the image of the game.

Ken walked across the floor, aware of the cheers and applause from the spectators nearest him. He did not acknowledge them, feeling it would be unprofessional, though some masters eagerly hammed it up when given such an opportunity. People were still finding their seats in the bowl-shaped tiers that rose over the floor and enclosed it. The arena buzzed with voices.

Grinning with excitement himself, Ken climbed up the steps to his game seat and waited while an attendant adjusted the keyboard's position in front of him. Then he fitted the sensory band over his eyes to make sure it fit properly. Across the white holographic field, Donna was sitting primly in her seat, her sensory band pushed up on top of her head. Satisfied with his, Ken did likewise.

The announcer introduced the game to the crowd. A roar of cheers rose up in response to Ken's name and to Richard's; another wave of cheers answered Donna's name. When the issue at risk was explained, scattered boos cascaded upon the mention of the Guild Act.

Ken took the moment to look at the media equipment and the people staffing it. They were perched on high seats like his own just inside the floor, near the four corners of the field. Their cameras were light and compact, resting on tall tripods. No wires were necessary.

Then the introduction was over. Donna and he both raised their hands, signifying to the game attendant seated at a platform along one side of the field that they were ready. The playing field bloomed into a colorful holographic scene, and Ken's keyboard screen read, "Kadesh. 1285 B.C. Ramses II." The fifteen-second orientation period began to tick away.

Ken searched his memory for the details of this battle and was not pleased with what he remembered.

This struggle outside the walls of the ancient city of Kadesh was the earliest battle for which historians had detailed tactical knowledge. The Egyptian Pharaoh Ramses II had invaded the territory of the Hittite King Metella. From the arrangement of units motionless now on the holographic terrain, Ken could see exactly where in the historical sequence of events the game would begin.

Ramses had been fooled by false information given to his camp by the enemy. He was convinced that King Metella had retreated far northward with his Hittites, vassal kings, and mercenaries. However, unknown to Ramses, Metella had simply pulled his host of 18,500 behind the city of Kadesh itself, out of sight.

Kadesh was on the west side of the Orontes River, and the El-Mukadiyeh Brook flowed into the river north of the city. The Egyptian army, of about 20,000, was approaching from the south in four divisions: Amon, Re, Ptah, and Sutekh, plus an independent smaller division coming eastward from the Mediterranean coast. Ramses was in personal command of Amon, in the van.

When Ramses had heard that his enemy was in retreat, he had pursued, stringing out his army behind him for eight to ten miles. As he approached, however, Metella moved his army east of Kadesh, still out of sight, and prepared an ambush.

Ken understood the opening position of his side. As Ramses, he had set up the Egyptian camp for the day just west of Kadesh with his Amon division, while Re still approached. As the game opened, he had just been informed that Metella's 3,500 chariots and 8,000 men in infantry were in position for a classic flank attack.

The screen began to move.

Ken worked frantically, like the real Pharaoh had, even risking mistakes on the keyboard. He sent messengers to Ptah, commanding their advance at top speed, and to Sutekh, almost hopelessly far away. Then he gathered his officers for an emergency war council. The real Ramses had been confident that the Re division was close enough to draw up in formation. Ken knew better, but still he lost time waiting for his messengers to reach Re.

Donna lost no time. As Ken had expected, she imitated the real Metella and sent the Hittite chariotry south from behind Kadesh to ford the river westward. They delivered a devastating charge against the flank of Re. Still in marching order, the Egyptian division shattered.

Ken, as Ramses, could not aid Re. He continued to prepare the defenses of the camp, but watched helplessly as the lines of Re broke apart. Those south of the Hittite charge scattered.

Ken remembered that chariots in this age were not armored and did not attack directly. Two-man vehicles driven by charioteers, they would pass by and around the ranks of the enemy while the warrior aboard released his arrows. Warriors also carried spears, scimitars, and throwing sticks for direct combat. However, once the enemy formation was broken—as Re was now—the chariots were ideal for pursuit. Donna's Hittites ignored the Egyptians fleeing southward in order to chase the routed remnants of Re who ran north toward Ramses's camp.

By this time, Ken had rallied the heavy infantry guard of the Pharaoh, who accepted the survivors of Re and repulsed the pursuing Hittites. Behind them, however, nearly 2,500 enemy chariots were on their way. In the real battle, Ramses had been able to salvage a tactical stalemate out of the situation by great personal valor, holding his own until reinforcements arrived. However, the real Metella had kept his infantry inactive east of the river; Donna was not required to do so.

Hittite chariots were gradually surrounding the Amon camp. Ken tried to rally the division, but it was totally unprepared. The officers were still with Ramses, not throughout the camp where they could transmit orders, and the soldiers were in a state of relaxation after a day of marching. The Ramses unit gathered the householders, officers, and the nearest soldiers. Then Ken slipped the sensory band down over his eyes and moved into the scene of tiny figures.

Ramses, flamboyant and impulsive, leaped into his chariot and slapped his charioteer on his back. The charioteer lashed the two horses, and they took off. The rallied troops gave a roar of shouts and charged after them. Ramses extended his arm, bow in hand, and drew back the string. Sweat shone on hard muscles in the sunlight as the great triangular shape of his bow and string stretched to a diamond shape and snapped back, again and again, as he loosed his arrows. From behind him, more Egyptian arrows flew forward from the chariots rolling forward and fanning out. Hoofbeats pounded into the dry earth, kicking up dust. Hittite charioteers fell, leaving their warriors to grab the reins or crash; when warriors fell, the charioteers withdrew in search of Hittite warriors who had fallen but still lived—all according to odds figured and resolved by the computer.

Suddenly Ramses broke through the Hittites, into the clear on the west, but the situation there could not be held. More enemy chariots were coming on in overwhelming numbers. Ken retired the unit back into his own camp and shoved the sensory band up on his head again.

Ken was in a tough spot, and he admitted it to himself frankly. The computer had selected a game in which Donna had a number of early advantages; if he hung on long enough, the advantages would shift to him, balancing their opportunities overall. She was playing well, like the master she was, and overconfidence would certainly be no problem for Ken today.

Toward the bottom of the screen, far to the south, the Ptah division was drawing itself into renewed marching formation after emerging from the forest and crossing a bend in the river. They were moving north quickly but still had open ground to cover. Amon was surrounded.

Ken knew what to look for. As in the real battle, the surrounding Hittite line had formed last to the east, on the riverbank. Ramses ordered his chariot about, called upon his followers once more, and charged east, where the Hittite line was still gathering. Beyond the enemy line, across the river, Metella waited with his chariot reserve and his infantry of 8,000.

Ramses attacked a line that included a brother of Metella, the chief of his bodyguard, his charioteers, and a number of his officers. Ken pressed the charge furiously, concentrating attack power and driving quickly. The Hittite chariots, attempting to maintain a cohesive line, fell back. Seeing progress, Ramses renewed the charges in series. The repetitive sequences on the keyboard were easy to hit quickly. Ken maintained the pressure. The enemy chariots backed again and bogged down in the mud of the riverbank, where the tight Egyptian line began slaughtering them.

Ken was also carefully watching the events behind Ramses, where he would lose in an instant if Donna could enforce military discipline on her Hittites. The sweep of her chariots from the west overran the Amon camp and annihilated the disorganized Egyptians there. Instead of racing through the camp after Ramses, however, as Donna would have ordered, the Hittites succumbed to an order of the computer. Based on the knowledge of Hittite behavior, the computer dictated that the Hittite chariotry stop to plunder the camp. Ramses had broken the enemy on the east and now had the river protecting him on one side. The failure of Hittite pursuit from the west freed the Pharaoh and his guard to fight southward toward Ptah, while the enemy to the north regrouped at the captured camp. The position was still secure.

Donna sent Metella's 1,000 reserve chariots across the river to smash Amon before Ptah entered combat.

Ramses and most of his guard were charging southward, circling, and charging again. The Hittite chariots before him suddenly faded back, to make way for their reserve fording the river. The fresh chariots charged toward the Egyptian line. Ken, knowing that only the person of the Pharaoh kept Amon together, could not risk losing that unit. He withdrew Amon fast, toward the captured camp.

Ken realized, as he worked over the keyboard, that this game would continue to be as tough as any he had ever played. He had not been lax, nor was the selection of the game unfair or unusual. Donna was simply playing her role flawlessly.

The Pharaoh knew by now that the Hittites were plundering the camp. His withdrawal was not strictly a retreat. The enemy in camp was off-guard and unprepared; Ramses and his personal troop fell upon them easily, though the enemy reserve was close behind them.

Suddenly, as the Egyptians rallied in their camp, more units appeared on the left side of the screen. Ken stared at them blankly, confused. For a moment, he sat idle over the keyboard, watching them advance. Even the sensory band would not help, since it gave him a close-up of Ramses's field of vision and these units were out of Ramses's sight.

Ken stiffened suddenly and sent his hands racing across the keys again. Those new units were his, and Ramses should send a message for them to make all haste. They were the Egyptian division coming from the Mediterranean coast, on schedule.

Too busy to curse himself, Ken sought out the Ramses unit and pulled him toward the reinforcements. Donna had not stopped playing during those critical seconds, and her reserve chariots had nearly wiped out the guard around Ramses while Ken had sat motionless. Ramses just reached the new units, before the heavy rush of the enemy behind him, but the Egyptians had not recovered from their loss of their position and morale following Ken's lapse.

The odds looked close—too close? If the combat was very intense with even odds, Ken could be taking a dangerous risk here. To the south, Ptah had finally arrived to engage the rest of the Hittite chariots, but if Ramses fell, the battle was over.

"Anyone else playing my side probably would have been afraid to run. . . ." Richard's voice out of the past spoke in Ken's memory.

Without time to deliberate, Ken took the memory as a warning from his subconscious. He sent Ramses fleeing to the southwest, with units behind him. The pursuing chariots cut down the Egyptians in large numbers, but the sacrifice distracted the enemy enough for Ken to get Ramses away.

The headlong flight of the Pharaoh took him around the west flank of the struggle between the main body of Hittite chariots and Ptah. The pursuing enemy joined their comrades, and when Ramses reached Ptah, the Egyptian morale factor soared.

Historically, the battle had taken a different turn. The Egyptians from the coast had destroyed the Hittites plundering the camp, and when Ptah had arrived, the two Egyptian lines had crushed the enemy chariots between them. Metella had held his infantry out of the battle, and both sides had retired with an indecisive encounter.

Ken could see Donna's next move. Ptah now outnumbered the remaining Hittite chariots by far, and the enemy was about to break. Ken would carry the field—unless Donna sent in her infantry.

She sent her infantry south on the other side of the river. Now that Ptah was committed, she was going to move against them. Even if Sutekh arrived in time to meet the maneuver, she would hold a numerical advantage of nearly eight to five.

It was also her turn to gamble. Instead of assaulting the Ptah right, where her troops would have an immediate effect but would enter combat still hampered by the water, she was marching some 4,000 infantry south past the engaged lines. They began to cross behind the Ptah line. She was gambling that her chariots would hold Ptah committed long enough for her to catch the Egyptians on two sides at once.

Ken clenched his teeth and refused the temptation to try splitting his line without having it break. His experience told him that maneuver was too complex. He allowed her infantry to ford the river and deploy without harassment, instead pressing his attack on the enemy chariots remaining to the north. Tense moments passed, until they broke and fled. They made for the safety of the gates of Kadesh.

Ken indulged in a quick, grim smile. Now he hit the keys that brought Ramses to his officers of Ptah. Under his orders, the computer began to realign Ptah to meet the enemy infantry behind them.

Donna had lost her gamble. Though she now had more troops on the field, and fresh ones, they were in danger of being trapped if Sutekh came on fast enough. Yet Sutekh would be tired from a forced march of eight to ten miles. Meanwhile, Metella waited across the river with his final 4,000 infantry.

Ken had Ramses gather his chariots. Their mobility might make up for their numerical disadvantage. He ordered them forward and slipped the sensory band down over his eyes again.

The light, two-wheeled chariots rolled forward in the late afternoon sunlight. They were made of wood, secured and decorated with leather and metal. Without armor, they were not prepared for direct attack, but every chariot warrior carried a spear that could be thrown, and a bow and arrows, as well as a shield. The Hittite infantry had no defense against the mobility and arrows of the Egyptian chariots.

Ramses led the way in his royal regalia, crisscrossing and falling back from the advancing enemy, loosing arrows. They raised their shields, but a rain of arrows continued from the racing Egyptian chariots, and many found holographic flesh. The Hittites yelled and waved their spears and swords in the bright, hot sunlight, but they knew better than to break ranks against the chariots that made pass after pass in front of them. Ken was certain that Donna was pushing them forward quickly; in any case, they advanced, anxious to close with the Egyptian lines, where they would have a fair chance to fight.

Ramses's charioteer wheeled their vehicle about one more time, throwing up dust. Ramses could see that he and his chariots had been backed up nearly to the fore of their own line of infantry, where the Egyptian standard stood tall over each company of two hundred and fifty men. They, too, were hot-blooded now and shouting at the Hittites as they came on. They held their spears and shields, their narrow-bladed battle axes, and their early scimitars, which still had much of the shape of the sickles from which they had been derived. Ramses gave the order to retire the chariots and led the way westward, out from between the two closing lines of infantry. As the chariots thundered away, the two opposing lines broke toward each other, heaving spears and throwing sticks through the air.

Ken shoved the sensory band up on his head again and surveyed the whole scene. He had Ramses rally his chariots and then charge again, harassing the enemy flank and throwing it into some disarray. With this advantage the

Egyptian infantry began to turn that flank and drive the Hittites back and sideways into their own comrades.

For a time, the struggle progressed without elaborate moves on the keyboard. Both gamers had committed their troops in the manner they wished. The computer tallied combat and the conflict remained in the balance.

Gradually, the shape of the battle began to change. The Hittite flank, turned by the Egyptians, began to collapse into its own ranks under heavy pressure. The confusion began to roll up the Hittite line and suddenly they broke, fleeing toward the river.

The Egyptian chariots raced forward in slashing, bloody pursuit, but their infantry did not break ranks. Ken ordered them to hold fast and the computer judged that they would, with Metella's final 4,000 still visible right across the river.

Ramses drew up the ranks of Ptah along the river as the routed Hittites threw their waiting reserves into momentary confusion. Ken was tempted to pursue them but did not. The enemy had crossed the river in flank attacks, when the Egyptians had not been prepared. Now, with the enemy waiting in expectation, the water would make the attackers vulnerable.

Donna brought the Hittites into order once more and held them steady. She apparently had the same reservations about attacking across the river, now that the Egyptians were ready—especially with Sutekh visible to the south. The two armies faced each other for a time without movement, except for the advance of Sutekh.

Suddenly Ken realized that it was over. Neither of them had chosen to make any moves for several moments. The outcome was very close—possibly a stalemate.

Ken could not find any new attack that was not irresponsible. Neither he, nor she, would grow reckless at this stage.

Finally the screen froze. Terrified of what he might see, Ken closed his eyes and collapsed back in his seat. He took one deep breath, held it in, and opened his eyes. "Victory Conditions: Egypt."

Ken let out his breath and closed his eyes again. Frowning, he sat up and searched the details of the overlay of game results. No, Donna had not conceded. The computer judged that Metella, with 4,000 infantry and no chariots, could not press the day. Ramses, with 4,000 men and substantial chariots, had a significant tactical advantage. The strategic situation was not part of the game. As a result, Ken had truly won a very close match.

Richard would live—and awaken.

Donna.

Ken swiveled in his seat and started down the steps to the arena floor. Now, for the first time, he heard the din of applause, cheers, and shouting from the crowd, echoing in the huge bowl of seats. As he shifted his weight, however, his wobbly knees buckled from exhaustion and threw him downward, into the waiting arms of a burly attendant. The man eased Ken into a cart with a friendly grin.

"That way," Ken shouted into the roar of sound, waving toward Donna. He doubted the man could hear him, but the gesture was enough. They drove along the edge of the playing field, toward the steps Donna was carefully descending, as she gripped the railing with both hands.

Ken was relieved to see that she was smiling. He jumped up at the base of the steps and managed to control his quivering legs. The attendant waiting for Donna stepped aside, smiling, and Ken reached up to grab her around the waist. He tried to lift her down, but the two of them fell, laughing, backward into both the attendants, who caught them.

Ken and Donna found their feet and embraced without speaking.

Then Donna pulled away. "Congratulations," she said loudly, still smiling up at him.

Ken shook his head. "You did great. Never made a single mistake. You practically beat me several times. You were *great*."

Donna threw her arms around his neck again. Ken held her tightly, closing his eyes, aware that the media cameras were aimed at them, aware that he enjoyed the deafening echo of cheers and applause from all sides, aware that their embracing image was being transmitted all over the world.

"You're right," he whispered into her ear.

She gripped him more tightly in response; she understood.

Donna was right: This was a silly and terrible way to reach an important decision. The course of Richard's life had rested on the vagaries of a complex game, including the possibility of human failure in reflexes, memory, and judgment—not only theirs but of people who had lived millennia ago.

Richard was saved, but she was right.

CHAPTER Seventeen

Ken's normal flush of victory was moderate this time. He attributed that to his need not to gloat in front of Donna. She was justifiably ecstatic about her own showing, however, and during the following week, her contractor began fielding a number of offers for more games. When word arrived nine days later from the hospital that Richard had indeed awakened from his coma, she hugged Ken in celebration.

He had never known a master so resilient after losing.

Ken was elated about Richard, even though the hospital told him that Richard would have to wait several more days before receiving visitors. Richard's coma had actually lasted much longer than Ken had expected, so a few more days now meant nothing. Ken's position in the lawsuit had been validated. Yet that victory still seemed emotionally empty.

One night, Ken lay in bed on his back with his eyes closed. A thin shaft of light slanted in from the hallway, where Donna was arranging the items in her briefcase for tomorrow. He felt cold, despite the warmth of the blankets, and relaxed—too relaxed, since he should not have been tired. It was a sign of depression that he recognized.

"I'll be right in," Donna said from the hallway.

It's coming to an end, Ken thought to himself. *I can't continue my career much longer, feeling as I do—and I can't keep Donna's affection as a quitter or a . . .* He felt a twinge of amusement. A laggard, she might have called him in medieval England, though people named Li and Wong had been scarce there.

What am I going to do?

Donna turned out the hall light and came into the room. Faint light from the constant urban glow outside filtered through the curtains. Ken heard her slide her nightgown up over her head and felt the mattress shift as her weight eased onto it. She moved over to him, bringing the scent of the sandalwood perfume he liked.

"Tired?" She ran a small, warm hand across his chest and rested her head on his shoulder.

"Dunno." It came out in a low, uncertain rumble that even he barely heard.

"Hmm?"

Even his breath was slight and shallow, as though he was dozing already, but his mind was wide awake. He put out more effort. "I guess I'm tired."

She lay motionless for a moment.

He wanted her to stay where she was, but he couldn't speak. For as long as they had known each other, he had remained a celebrity in their field and a mentor to her. Now, no matter what he did, that would fundamentally change.

"Do you want to do anything?" She asked with clear puzzlement in her voice.

"I guess not," he said quietly.

She hesitated, then began to draw away.

He knew he should embrace her, bring her back, but he could not. He wished she would stay and hold him of her own accord. Asking would destroy that chance, though that would be better than not asking . . . but now she had moved back to her side and rolled over. The moment was gone.

Ken's thoughts, oddly detached from what was happening, turned to his dilemma. For all his adult life, he had been aspiring to be, working toward, and earning a living as a *master gamer*. Playing wargames for hire was all he had ever wanted to do. Right now, as the gamer rated number one in the Guild, he commanded the highest fees in his profession.

Donna, however, had gradually rearranged all his feelings about what he was doing.

The first step had been simple enough. She had convinced him to play for Richard's life because he believed in his own cause. The second step had been harder. As a result of that last game he had come to agree that the Guild Act was wrong—but announcing his opposition to it would make him an outcast among his fellow gamers and an opponent of the Guild itself.

Feeling cold, discouraged, and rejected, he drifted off to sleep.

That first step had been simple enough.

When Ken woke up, he was surprised to find Donna out of the apartment so early. She was not contracted for a game right now, so she would not need any practice games, and he did not recall her mentioning any morning appointments. Well, it didn't matter. He had his own appointment to keep.

In the hospital, Ken walked down the corridor briskly, following a blue line on the floor. He tried not to take furtive peeks of curiosity into the rooms as he passed them. When he reached Richard's room, he stopped in the doorway and lifted his hand to knock. Then he grinned, lowered his hand, and walked in.

Richard had a sizable room all to himself, and special equipment had been brought in. He lay with his bed cranked up, playing a computer game on a portable keyboard with the addiction of any *master gamer*. Across the room from him, connected by a signal from the antenna bead on the keyboard, a meter-square video monitor had been set up. He was playing a game against the Guild computer through a remote hookup. Ken could not be sure without more time to watch, but he thought the battle on the screen was Crécy, the first classic victory by the English longbow over French chivalry. He hesitated, not sure if he should interrupt. Then he walked quietly into the room and waited patiently.

Richard's blond hair was lank and short, and his face so emaciated that his nose seemed much too prominent. He had always been slender, but the arms extending now from the hospital gown were so thin that Ken thought he could encircle them with his thumb and forefinger. Richard's eyes were quick and intent, though, as he watched the screen, and his fingers moved across the keyboard in a rhythm that was steady, if slow.

"Haven't you won yet?" Ken said casually.

Richard smiled without looking away and froze the screen where it was. Then he turned, still leaning back on his pillows. "Hello."

Ken laid his coat across a chair and sat down in another one alongside the bed. "Hi. You, uh . . . you're really set up here."

"Yeah. The fallen warrior has to retrain, you know."

"Must have been expensive."

"I figured it was worth it. In fact, I actually made money while I was out of it."

"What? How?"

"I had full coverage for my hospitalization through the Guild insurance policy, and my home expenses were minimal—just utilities and other monthly payments. Meanwhile, my regular investments were paying off as usual, only I wasn't spending it as soon as it came in."

"It makes sense when you put it that way."

"By the way, thanks for taking care of my place during that time."

"No problem."

Richard looked up at the motionless screen. "To be honest, I don't really have my energy back. The result is a little embarrassing."

"It's also a flat screen. Wait till you get back in the practice rooms with the full holographic playing field. You don't even have a sensory band here. Besides, you're still recuperating."

"I, uh, read up on the game you played. To keep me out of cryogenic sleep. Thanks."

"Sure. It was more exciting than taking care of your place; I can tell you that."

"I should think so. Would you accept your standard fee from me? I'm the actual principal in the case."

"I'd . . . rather not. I had my own stake in this. Anyway, I made the choice to sue for a game and play it. I can't stick you for the bill when it was my decision."

Richard shrugged, with an awkward smile of acquiescence.

Ken cast about for a new subject. He found he was not ready to tell Richard about his new position toward the Guild Act. Richard did not share it, and this was no time for an argument.

"Anything interesting happen while I was out of it?" Richard waved a hand at the keyboard. "I've caught up some on world news through the Guild library, but what about the Guild itself?"

"Games are still coming and going. There's a movement out to repeal the Guild Act."

"The same crowd that lost when it was passed. Harmless, I'd say." Richard frowned at his screen again and the unnamed battle still in suspended play. "Too bad we don't have a second keyboard or we could play."

Ken forced a faint smile. "I'm not sure I want to play you. I haven't gotten over that licking you gave me before."

Richard snickered, showing some of his old spark. "Which time?"

"The only time we played a formal game, remember?"

"Bosworth Field. I won, all right, but you created a masterplay, as I recall. No mean feat at all."

"So far, I guess it's my high point." If Ken was going to give up his career, that masterplay might be his one lasting achievement. "Of course, the game wasn't very long ago by gaming standards. It may turn out not to be a masterplay. Maybe someone will find a way to counter it."

"I don't see how. I won that game because you had never tried it before, and your timing was slightly off. Next time the gamer's timing will be precise and the move irresistible."

"All it really means is that people will play the whole battle in a different way," said Ken. "Any gamer playing

Henry Tudor will try to avoid having the right circumstances develop. No masterplay means anything if the situation doesn't arise so you can use it."

"Sure. And if someone does find a way to counter the maneuver directly, then it wasn't a masterplay to start with."

"If someone does find a way, I hope it doesn't happen for a long time. I'd like to have the credit for this, at least for a while."

Richard flicked his hand up toward the screen. "Would you mind watching for a bit? I just started."

"Go 'head." Ken decided to voice his guess. "Crécy. 1346. Edward III, England."

Richard nodded as he set the keyboard on his lap and activated the screen. He was playing the role of Edward III, who stood on a hill directing his troops. They were fighting in France and seriously outnumbered. Lines of English longbowmen stood waiting as French knights approached along a road from a forest.

"Here they come," Richard said mildly. He obviously wasn't taking this too seriously.

In the game, the mounted knights were the most powerful in direct combat, especially in a concerted charge of heavy lance. However, they were harmless at long range and easily hampered by woods, hills, and marshes. The longbows were lethal within their range of flight, but the archers were virtually helpless if the knights reached them. The men on foot had a medium combat power.

"Look at that," said Richard. "This computer may be altogether too intelligent."

Ken grinned at the lighthearted comment. It was unlike his competitive friend to take any game less than seriously, but Ken understood that he was self-conscious about his debilitated condition. "I've played Crécy in practice games, but never against the computer."

"It seems to me that it's been programmed to play well, instead of the way the French really fought." Richard kept his eyes on the screen as he tapped the keyboard.

The French chivalry was approaching along a road

through a forest and assembling in a limited open space. They did not have much room before they would come into the range of the English longbows. Ken recalled that Edward III had chosen this site precisely because it tempted the French knights to do what they liked best: charge right at the hated English invaders. Historically, they had done so as soon as they had emerged from the forest, galloping toward the doughty archers in small, tight clusters that made perfect targets. They had expected the outnumbered English knights to gallop toward them in the old style and be slaughtered by the superior numbers of the French. Instead, the volleys of English arrows had slaughtered the piecemeal attack.

"Well, well. Look at that," said Richard.

"The French knights are assembling in order in the clearing." Ken nodded in approval.

The French charged together. Richard's longbowmen shot their arrows in fuzzy streaks on the screen.

The French fell in heavy numbers, and the first line faltered. The line behind it still came on, though, and many of the arrows fell harmlessly in the spaces between the oncoming knights. The third line caught up to the second and merged with it. Together, though much fewer, those knights smashed into the lines of the English. Far behind them, more French were still pouring out of the woods and forming carefully into widely spaced lines.

"This could be fairly short," Richard said gloomily.

The English archers fell back, and the English knights and men-at-arms clashed with the French in long, straggly lines. The French continued to charge and to fall heavily to English arrows. Still, they reached the English lines in substantial numbers, and the English began to fall back.

The struggle altered gradually, but steadily, and always favoring the French. The French charged into the hail of English arrows in such long, open lines that the archers' effectiveness was diminished.

"Imagine," said Ken, to break the silence. "There's the King of England up there, claiming the crown of France. When the French arrive, they see his standard—he's quartered the English banner with the Fleur-de-lis of the French king. They must have been enraged."

Richard nodded. "The French are still losing a lot of men, but they're going to win, I think."

The French had pressed the English back into a tight, defensive formation on the ridge. The computer was forcing Richard into a distasteful choice: whether to surrender or to risk a retreat that might become a rout. The French had fallen in great numbers to earn this developing victory, but historically they had lost even more in defeat.

"I've had enough of this." Richard hit a key that shut off the game. "Oh, I suppose I'll get back to normal eventually. I just don't like discovering just how far I have to go."

Ken said nothing, but he knew that Richard normally would have put up a much greater fight and probably would have tried some innovations in even a losing cause—or, perhaps, especially in one.

He was clearly tired now, so Ken said good-bye. His visit with Richard had been reassuring. Despite his friend's condition, he could see that Richard was on the way to recovery.

CHAPTER Eighteen

Donna had risen early, not wanting to talk to Ken after his odd behavior the night before. She took the Overhead south one stop to Westport and walked through the morning rush-hour crowd to Sharon's apartment. It was on the second floor of an old building, over a neighborhood restaurant and a bicycle shop.

The door was in the back of the restaurant near the delivery entrance. She pressed the buzzer, aware that she was interrupting Sharon's painting time. This morning she didn't care.

Finally she heard footsteps inside. Through the dirty, stained window in the door, she could see Sharon descending the stairs in a long, light green nightgown. Sharon looked through the glass, and her face brightened with surprise before she opened the door.

"I'm really sorry to bother you," Donna said. "If it's inconvenient—"

"Come in. It's nice to see you. Come on up."

Sharon led the way up the creaky wooden stairs, holding her nightgown up out of the way. She was barefoot. Donna could see smears and streaks of paint all over the nightgown, and also tears and loose thread on the lace yoke. It clung to her angular frame as she moved.

The door at the top of the stairs was standing open. Donna

followed Sharon inside and closed the door. She had been here many times, but not recently, and Sharon changed things around often.

Sharon's studio was a large rectangular room with a kitchen at the far end, defined by a breakfast counter and a bathroom and closet to the side. An old double bed, unmade, stood against the interior wall opposite an outside wall that featured floor-to-ceiling windows. The hardwood floor shone in the morning light with a random display of streaks and splotches of every color Sharon had dropped or splattered since she had been here. Paintings and sketches covered the walls, and more paintings were propped against the wall beneath those. The easel stood facing the windows, where Sharon had obviously been painting just now.

"Coffee's hot," said Sharon. "Want some?"

"Sure." Donna walked to the kitchen behind her, gazing at the paintings that she passed. She accepted coffee from Sharon and turned to look around the studio. "What happened to your curtains?"

"I took them down because they still blocked some light, even when they were open. I hang a sheet over the middle ones at night. See those big nails?" She stirred her coffee and dropped the spoon into the sink. "What's up?"

Donna started to pace. Her footsteps were loud on the wooden floor. She went to the windows and shaded her eyes with one hand as she looked down at the busy sidewalk below. Then she turned and saw the painting on Sharon's easel.

It was a painting of a woman's leg and foot, against a plain white background. The leg and foot were entirely blocked in, with the foot painted in detail, complete with a white ankle-strap high heel and red toenails. The detail faded out along the ankle, where the paint was still wet.

Donna smiled with a twinge of amusement. "What are you going to do at the upper end?"

"Don't know yet." Sharon patted her thigh. "It's mine. Just a thought I had. Sort of a partial self-portrait."

"Well . . . you have nice long legs. Not like mine." Donna

took a deep breath and went on before she could reconsider. "Ken was acting really odd last night."

"You mean you had a fight?"

"No, I don't think so."

"You don't think so? What the hell is that supposed to mean?"

"He acted like he was mad at me. He wouldn't talk or . . . anything. But we hadn't argued. Nothing like that."

"Something must have happened."

"No!" Donna's vehemence surprised her, and she looked down to see that she spilled coffee on the floor.

"Leave it there," Sharon said casually. "I always do."

"He's been kind of quiet, I guess, but he's a reserved guy. Then, just as I got into bed last night, he became totally withdrawn. He would hardly even *talk* to me." Her voice cracked, and she stopped.

"You've been living together some time now," Sharon said calmly. "But how well do you know him?"

"Pretty well, I think. I said he was reserved, but he's not made of stone. Why didn't he *say* something?" Donna wailed.

"Well, why didn't you demand an answer?"

"I asked him—"

"Not firmly enough. Did you?"

Donna was quivering with frustration. She hadn't realized, last night, how upset she had been. "I've messed up a lot in my time, but I haven't done anything now. I'm sure of it."

"Don't waste it on me. Go ask him again. And don't back off this time."

"I mean, before, I was too young. Emotionally. I went overboard for a guy and then I'd cling, or I'd run out too soon, or . . . or . . ." She waved her hands helplessly. More coffee spilled and broke the mood.

Sharon took her cup with a sympathetic look. "You'll feel better if you get it over with."

Donna finally caught up with Ken in the Guild Hall, after trying at home and at the hospital. She was striding down the hall to Lou's office when he and Ken came out. "Lou," she called out firmly. "May we use your conference room for a moment?"

"Hi," said Ken, with a tentative glance at both of them.

"I guess so," said Lou. "Well, of course; what am I saying? Come on in."

"What's going on?" Ken asked.

"I'll tell you," Donna said briskly, following Lou into the outer office.

"My office is more comfortable. Go on in. And take your time. I'll hang around out here and pester my secretaries."

"Thanks, Lou." Donna fixed Ken with a determined look as she held the inner office door for him. When he finally accepted the invitation and came inside, she slammed it behind him. "What was wrong with you last night?" she demanded.

Ken froze, studying her face warily. She recognized that look; he surveyed the playing field in a game with the same expression. Then he looked away and shrugged.

"We should get this out in the open. It's not fair to make me guess."

"I know." It was the same husky, resigned voice she had heard last night for the first time.

She watched him pace, hands in pockets, through the shafts of light from the windows. He stopped at the far wall, the one covered with photos and other memorabilia of Lou's career. She felt her temper flare again.

"If you expect me to just be a quiet little Asian girl, forget it."

He whirled. "I never said anything like that and you know it."

"Well, *say something*, will you?"

He offered a bitter smile; really to himself, she thought.

"I asked you once," he said, "a long time ago, what you would have been if you hadn't been a gamer."

"I remember. You were in some silly panic before your game with Richard. Don't tell me you're going to start that again. I'm getting sick of it."

Ken's jaw clenched and the flesh around his eyes tightened. She realized that she had made him withdraw even more, and she softened her tone. "Just tell me what's wrong."

"I guess I'm going to be a quitter. What do you think of that?"

"What do you mean?"

"I can't go on with my career the way I feel now. So I've decided to make a big change in my life—just this minute."

It was Donna's turn to freeze. She waited for him to say that their relationship was over, that he was moving out. When he didn't speak, she said, "You decided just now?"

He nodded. "I came up here to talk to Lou about it, but I still wasn't sure. Now I am. Look, I'm sorry about last night. It's really a business matter. I just had to figure something out."

Donna relaxed and let out a long breath.

"Will you bear with me till tomorrow? It'll all come clear." He was still gazing at the floor, looking uncertain and vulnerable.

She didn't know if she should approach him, embrace him, encourage him—or leave him alone. With last night in mind, she just shrugged.

"Sure. I can wait that long."

He nodded slowly and shifted his weight. "Give me a few minutes with Lou, will you?"

"Sure. I have errands to run, anyway. See you at home."

"All right."

She hesitated, then left without going to him.

Ken stood where he was, disappointed that she had not kissed him good-bye, but knowing that he had brought it on himself. Then Lou came in and closed the door.

"So, bucko. She said you wanted to see me." He walked around his desk and lounged back in the chair. Absently, he picked a small gray eraser and started chewing on it.

"I want a press conference tomorrow at ten A.M."

"Whoa, bucko. What for?"

"Not now, Lou. Tomorrow."

"Hey, wait a minute. I'm your contractor, remember? Your interests are my interests. And I can handle it better if I know what you're going to do."

"Not this time, Lou."

Lou studied his face, and Ken could see that he was torn between his own powerful personality, which took refusals poorly if at all, and his understanding that Ken had rarely refused him anything during their prosperous period as contractor and client. Ken waited, trusting that Lou would respect this demand.

"All right." Lou spat out the eraser. "Where?"

"The Guild Hall is fine."

Lou nodded. "See you then."

Ken's spirits were high all day. When he returned home, he ignored his depression of the night before and insisted that Donna come to his press conference. He would not tell her what he was going to say, either, but he teased her all evening, and she laughed and tickled him to make him talk. When that didn't work, she finally agreed to come.

At 9:50 the next morning, Ken was pleasantly amazed to find the Inalchik Conference Room of the Guild Hall packed and overflowing with reporters. He had expected some interest, but nothing like this, especially when he was not even under contract right now. Cameras began to click or whir as he edged into the room, and Donna followed him closely. He was always glad in moments like this that the bright flood lamps and flashes he remembered from his childhood were no longer necessary.

Lou was waiting for him at a long table positioned at the far end of the room. He had a chair there for Donna, too. When Ken and Donna had worked their way up to the table, Ken sat down between them.

He tapped the microphone to see if it was on, and the room became quiet. He looked up in surprise, then glanced self-consciously at Lou.

"Well," said Ken, "I'll get right to the point. I wish to

announce my new position against the provisions of the Guild Act and in favor of the movement to repeal it."

Lou's grunt of surprise was nearly drowned out by the startled murmurs and cries from the crowd. Ken felt Donna, on his other side, grasp his elbow affectionately. Reporters were shouting questions at him, but when the noise had subsided somewhat, he spoke again.

"I have reached this decision partly through my own experience in games and partly through the persuasion of Donna Wong here, my friend and colleague. Now, I'm willing to answer questions, but I'd like to stay organized. I'm, uh, new at this."

Lou took over picking hands out of the crowd. The questions were fairly easy to answer, probably because no one was prepared for his statement. They asked him when he had made his decision; he said it had been over a long period of time. They also asked if his most recent game, against Donna, was the deciding factor; he told them it had been the clinching experience, but that he had formed his opinion with his entire career in mind and with what he had learned about the Guild Act and its effects. One reporter asked if he had been influenced by the collapse of the agreement following his international game and the realization that no enforcement existed over national governments. He said no.

When the questions wound down to routine information, such as when and if he would sign his next contract, Ken had Lou end the conference. They waited at the table for the crowd to file out of the room.

"I ought to punch you right in the face," said Lou, with no discernible tone of jest. "You could have warned me, at least. Haven't we had a decent association together? Huh?"

"You wouldn't have come." Ken grinned.

"Of course not! I love the Guild Act. Anyhow, this is your career you're playing around with. I should have had a chance to talk you out of it."

"Sorry about ambushing you, Lou, but the fact is, I don't want to be talked out of it. And from now on, I only want to sign contracts when both principals have come to the games willingly. No more Guild Act cases."

Lou shook his head. "I figured that was next. Come on—up to my office, bucko. We got stuff to talk over."

Just before Ken stood, Donna reached over and gave him a hug. "Don't let him talk you out of anything."

In Lou's office, Ken unwound on a couch with Donna next to him. A great burden of tension had lifted from him, now that he had made his announcement. He was feeling some of that same excitement and challenge that he had experienced when he had first come here to World Headquarters; in fact, Donna was smiling at him with much that same glow she had had then.

Lou glowered down at Donna as he handed them both drinks. "I don't need a confession to know I have you to thank you for this disaster."

She met his gaze firmly. "Ken thinks for himself. You know that."

"Hmph! I wonder." Lou turned back to the bar for his own drink. "You know, my first impulse was to drop you as a client."

Ken felt Donna stiffen beside him, but he wasn't worried. He had grown familiar with Lou's style of speech and knew that if Lou had wanted to drop him, he would have said so by now.

Lou swirled ice in his glass, standing with his other hand in his pocket, studying Ken's face. He apparently was hoping for some kind of demonstrative reaction.

Just to be ornery, Ken decided not to give him one. He held his drink, untouched.

"Yeah, well, I guess I'm stupid, too." Lou shook his head. "I like excitement myself. You know, being your contractor has been rather smooth so far—nothing but unmitigated success. Now I get to watch you turn into a lightning rod."

Ken lifted his glass in salute. Before he could speak, though, Lou's phone began emitting "The Ride of the Valkyries." It continued until Lou sat down on the edge of his desk and answered it.

"That's new," Ken said to Donna. "I like that." He started humming the tune until Donna, laughing, put her hand over his mouth.

"It's for you." Lou grinned pointedly at Ken and moved away from the desk. "Your first bolt of lightning."

"Nobody knew I was coming here. It was on the spur of the moment." Puzzled, Ken moved to Lou's desk chair and found himself looking at the grave, distingushed face of Kirk Emerald. "Hello, sir."

"Hello, Ken. I'm glad to find you here; it saves me some looking, since you weren't home. I . . . have been getting calls and visits from reporters constantly for the last ten or fifteen minutes."

Ken couldn't help grinning. "I guess that's my fault."

"I guess it is. Are they telling me the truth?"

"Yes, sir. I would suppose so."

Director Emerald was too courteous to object strenuously. "Master Li, have you thought this out carefully? You do understand that you are the first master of prestige to take this stand, and of course you are in opposition to Guild policy."

"Yes, I do."

Left unsaid was the personal welcome Emerald had given Ken when he had first landed atop the Guild Hall heliport.

Emerald nodded. "I only ask that you continue to think about this issue. In the long run, you might reconsider. Will you do that for me?"

"I'm always open to new arguments," Ken said slowly. "But in all honesty, I've taken quite a long time to reach this position. It's not likely to change."

"I understand. Good-bye." The videphone screen blanked.

Ken stood up and realized only then that he had been quite nervous. A personal call from the Director was a rare event for any master.

"Welcome to the thunderstorm," Lou said gravely. "That's only the beginning."

"We'll see you, Lou. Thanks for the drink."

Lou nodded, but Donna had to set down her glass in surprise and jump up to follow Ken out. Distracted, he paused in the hallway for her.

"Sorry," he said as they walked down the empty corridor. "I'm a little jumpy. Too much nervous energy, I guess."

"What's wrong?"

"Noth— Well, everything. I have to fight to keep my rating in the Guild, but I have to do it by selecting my games carefully. I also have to do it while betraying the kindness of Kirk Emerald in the past and everything the Guild has given me so far. And now all my colleagues are going to attack me for taking a stand they don't like."

"All your colleagues except me." She took his arm. "I think it's silly for you to feel guilty. You're joining the side of conscience."

She didn't seem to understand, or perhaps care, how selecting his games according to principle could lower the number of important games available and cause a drop in his rating. And the nagging awareness that she was most proud of and affectionate toward him when he was riding high in success, prestige, and attention . . . he chose not to think about right now.

"You want to work off some of that nervous energy?" She tugged on his arm as they stopped at the elevator and gave him a playful smile.

"Uh—" He couldn't help grinning. "Now?"

"No, we should go home first, silly. What's the use of having a *master gamer*'s flexible schedule, if you don't use it occasionally?"

Ken laughed, remembering their awkward silence two nights before. "Good point. Now that you're a *master gamer*, I'll have to start taking your advice."

CHAPTER Nineteen

The rest of Ken's week was spent fielding and avoiding reporters' questions. It was hectic but allowed him to submerge his concern over the depth of Donna's feelings for him. The questions themselves still were not difficult, since his new position was simple to express. He found himself on the local news the first day, then the national and international news for several days thereafter. As near as he could tell, he was just repeating the same comments every time, but the journalists seemed to say he was elaborating his position. More than likely, he realized, they wanted the audience to think so; apparently, the Guild Act still held the public's interest. Other masters were quoted, attacking his position.

After a week, Ken wanted to escape the attention. When the questions began delving into his family background, childhood, and social life, he decided the public had grown weary of the Guild Act, after all. When he complained about this to Richard over the phone, his friend told him that he was being sent down to the Guild Resort in the Ozark Mountains for physical therapy, and Ken arranged to meet him there.

The greatest asset of the Resort was its variety. In addition to the enclosed complex, guests could enjoy the surrounding mountains and rivers, as well. Just getting there improved

Ken's spirits, as he was able to tell Lou, Donna, and the Resort staff that he was only to be contacted for emergencies.

Ken was surprised, as he walked into the lobby with his suitcase, to find Richard dressed and sitting comfortably on a couch, waiting for him. Richard was still underweight but otherwise looking well.

"I thought they'd bring you down here on a stretcher or something," said Ken. "You're coming along pretty fast, huh?"

"So I've been told. Matter of fact, they're force-feeding me a strict diet, and my exercise is also rigidly controlled. The crazy part is, I'm paying them to put me through this."

"You mean you're rushing your convalescence?" Ken set down his suitcase and flexed his hand.

"I'm not suited to sloth; I want to get back in the saddle. Speaking of which, one of the few unsupervised things I'm allowed to do is to ride horseback. How's that sound?"

"Fine. Just let me check in and change."

Half an hour later, Ken found himself bundled in longjohns, flannel, and a heavily padded jacket, riding ahead of Richard. They threaded through a thick forest that was brown with heavy trunks and bare, jagged branches reaching into the sky, varied by white patches of lingering snow and evergreens in large stands from time to time. The horse knew the trail, since he did little else in life but take inexperienced riders around and around the same couple of routes. Ken more or less let him have his head. Richard was allowed to ride, but only at a walk.

"I saw you on the news last week." Richard brought his horse up alongside Ken.

Ken kept his gaze forward and his voice neutral. "I guess a lot of people did."

"You trying to become an apostate master?" Richard's voice was sarcastic, but he eyed Ken carefully.

"No, I'm not trying to, but I'm convinced the Guild Act is a bad move." Ken had said something similar in most of the media interviews.

"You used to agree with me, that we offer a public service. Surely you can't think protracted lawsuits going on for years are good for anybody!"

Startled by Richard's vehemence, Ken was able to look away by ducking under a low tree branch. He had expected Richard to disagree, but he didn't want to argue.

Richard fell back as they went around a bend.

"I'm not against the Guild," said Ken. "I'm against the Guild Act. If both sides want a game played to decide their argument, fine. I just don't think they should be forced to accept one."

"We went all through this when the Act was first passed —and you agreed with me then! The Guild Act increases the number of games played and correspondingly decreases the number of cases clogging the court system."

"I've also come to realize that some issues should be decided the hard way."

Richard kicked his horse to come up alongside again. "Do I have to remind you that you sued for a game yourself under the Guild Act? And that if you hadn't, I'd probably be in cryogenic sleep now, never to see anyone I knew again?"

"That's a perfect example!" Ken whirled on him in his saddle. "Have you watched the tape of that game I played against Donna?"

"No. I haven't had a chance."

"You should. You have no idea just how close it was. I slipped badly at least once and just barely got through a couple of other times. The real fault lay in the insurance policy *you* signed—and your lack of precautions with those experimental gadgets of yours."

"A little ironic, isn't it? Without your help, I'd be as good as dead for who knows how many years, and you're saying that help was a mistake!"

Ken smiled in appreciation of the contradiction and spoke more calmly. "No, it wasn't a mistake. As Donna said to me, I was using the means I had available. But it was awfully chancy. Look—how many different battles are in the Guild system now?"

"Two hundred and forty were in the complete pool last time I checked—but only a hundred were on rotation any one time; everyone knows that. Did that change while I was—"

"No, the computer still randomly picks one game out of a hundred. But that's not my point. Have you considered the odds on repeating games, or playing one you've never seen before? After all the years I've been a master, I've never played a lot of our battles at all, but I've played several of them more than once. In my game against Donna, what if she had been fresh and familiar with Kadesh and I had just barely remembered it at all? That would have decided your fate more than our relative skill."

"True, but that's an inherent part of gaming. I accept that."

"It is inherent; that's why games should not be forced on people. And then there's the role of individuals—some of them controlled by the computer and some of them handled by us—whose unpredictable behavior can make or break an entire battle."

"Of course! They give the games their realism. Individuals have always dictated the success of tactical decisions. The uncertainty of the single crucial soldier on the field has been the heart of the games." Richard was puffing hard, short of breath already.

Ken looked at him with concern. His face was flushed and sweaty in the crisp, cold air. It was no place for a convalescent to get excited. He turned away and they rode on silently.

Altogether, Ken spent four days at the Resort with Richard, glad to be free of the reporters. Donna took the same opportunity to visit friends out of town, and Lou did not bother him, so he had nothing to do but lounge in the sun, read, and talk to his old childhood friend.

He only raised questions about the Guild Act one more time, over dinner. They realized that they were not going to agree and dropped the matter. Both of them were committed to their positions.

Richard's recovery seemed remarkable to Ken, who had not kept up with medical advances beyond an occasional item in the news. The progress Richard made resulted from no single discovery, but from a wealth of new information regarding individual body chemistry and nutritional needs, combined with carefully tailored exercises and his now considerable will. By the time Ken left for home, Richard was jogging, swimming short distances, and galloping on horseback. He still slept more than usual, but his weight was almost normal.

Ken took the shuttle out of the mountains, aware that his old friend—and old nemesis—was again alive and well.

The shuttlecopter touched down on the roof of the Guild Hall in mid-afternoon. Ken hefted his suitcase onto the belt that would carry it down to the reception desk in the front lobby and went down to Lou's office to see what was new.

He found Lou in a foul mood. When the big contractor had yanked him into the inner office by the arm and slammed the door on his secretary, Lou jammed both hands into his pants and pockets and glowered at Ken like a bull contemplating a charge.

"Bucko, you sure picked the right four days to leave town. The only reason I didn't call you is that everything moved too fast. And I would have joined you in hiding, but I had to keep track of developments."

"What are you talking about? I just took a couple of days in the Ozarks; that's all. What's been happening here?"

Lou threw up his arms and started pacing angrily. "What hasn't? Only, it was that darling announcement of yours that kicked everything into motion."

"Like what?" Ken demanded. "Get to the point."

"The *point* is, this reform group, these citizens—what's their name, Citizens Against the Guild Act?—have filed suit to force the Guild to stop having games played under the Act."

"Can they do that? No, wait a minute. The Guild Act is a

federal law, based on a constitutional amendment. You can't just file a civil suit like that, can you?"

"You're not listening, bucko. They found the route for a flank attack, as you masters might say. They are filing suit to stop the Guild, a private organization, from sponsoring the government's games."

"I . . . see." Ken felt excitement well up in him. There was no one else to sponsor these games. "If the Guild was prevented from holding games under the Guild Act, the Act would be meaningless. And the movement might get it repealed before some kind of government game system could be set up."

"Right. Now, there has been some talk of passing a law that would incorporate the Guild wholesale into the judicial system, but the red tape involved is unimaginable. It won't happen anytime soon. However—"

"What?"

"You're right in the middle."

"I am? How?" Ken folded his arms.

"First, they decided to file suit because of your announcement."

"You said that, but I don't get it. Why?"

"The Guild wants the matter resolved immediately. Kirk is sure that any games played under a cloud will have a taint in the public eye, and he doesn't want confidence in the Guild undermined. So—the court has made this suit a top priority. Everyone is postponing all the scheduled games until after this issue is resolved. And everyone's best guess is that the court is going to pass this one right back to the Guild and decree that a game be played."

Ken stared at him, stifling a laugh. "They'd have the guts to do that—declare a game over a suit involving the Guild's right to sponsor games?"

"It's not official yet, but it fits the pattern—this case is complex, has no legal precedent, and is urgent. I'm sure a game will have to be played."

"The Guild Act hinging on one game. Poetic justice, maybe."

"But that's why Citizens Against the Guild Act filed suit when you made your announcement. They assume you'll play for their side."

Ken straightened slightly. "That's presumptuous of them."

"They've been calling me constantly for a couple of days. I insisted that you were out of touch, but they want to meet with you right away."

"I can do that. Anyhow, there is no game so far."

"You're the top-rated gamer in the land, bucko, but the Guild's future is riding on this. The Guild wants the best gamer they can find on their side."

Ken looked up and found Lou gazing at him sternly.

"Kirk wants Richard Ross to play for the Guild. He was rated at the top when his accident occurred; as far as the Guild's concerned, the two of you are the best we've ever had."

Ken felt a prickling along his back. "I just spent several days with him. He didn't say a word."

"He doesn't know. Kirk knows he's going through an accelerated recovery program and didn't want to interrupt him. He'll find out whenever he gets home from the Resort."

"You, uh . . . you know I've only played against Richard once in a formal game."

Lou nodded grimly.

"Lou, did I ever tell you I've never shaken my old childhood feeling of intimidation by him? His knowledge of the field and history in general?"

"You didn't have to, Ken. I could see it."

Ken turned and began to pace around the office. This was what he had been waiting for, and running from, off and on for most of his life—a critical contest between the two of them. He knew he would have to play if the opportunity developed. Otherwise, he would wonder forever what might have happened.

"Lou, how soon can you get me a meeting with those people? The reform group."

Lou grinned suddenly and punched a fist into his other

palm. "That's it, bucko. Fix yourself a drink and sit down. I'll have somebody over here within the hour."

Ken sat on the couch and nervously swirled ice in a glass of water while Lou alternately shouted at and cajoled several people over the videphone. Lou clicked off and swung around his desk chair with that same broad grin. "They're on their way."

"Thanks, Lou. Look—what are they like? Are they hostile? Just because they have to deal with me doesn't mean they like it."

"I don't really know. But they are more than willing to deal—they've been coming to us. So if you find them unpleasant, stand up to 'em. They'll adjust."

"Well, I'll just wait here quietly. You go on with your work, and I'll unwind from the flight back up here."

"Fair enough."

Almost an hour later, Lou's receptionist announced the arrival of two visitors. Lou opened the door for them himself, while Ken set down his glass and stood cautiously by the couch.

Two people entered. The first was a slender woman in her mid-thirties, Ken guessed, very well dressed and carefully made up. She had wavy brown hair and the looks of many minor actresses. Her perfume reached him across the room almost immediately.

She was accompanied by a tall young man in his twenties who carried a briefcase and looked around earnestly through heavy, black-framed glasses, smiling readily. Ken guessed he was in sales.

"Ken," said Lou. "I'd like to introduce you to Jennifer Dubay and Jeff Retton, of Citizens Against the Guild Act. This is Master Ken Li."

"How are you." Jennifer Dubay extended her hand primly and shook with her fingertips for a moment before withdrawing it.

"I'm *really* glad to meet you!" Jeff took Ken's hand and pumped it heartily. "I've admired you for a long time."

"Well, thank you." Ken smiled in surprise. "I appreciate it."

"I even bought a tape of your game of Bosworth, with your masterplay in it."

"Master Li," said Jennifer firmly.

"Call me Ken."

"Ken, then. I assume Lou has told you what we want."

"He said you want me to play for your side if a game is granted over your lawsuit against the Guild."

"Exactly. We have your fee, and Lou has assured us that you are serious in your opposition to the Guild Act."

"Much to my disappointment, I might add," Lou growled. "Anybody want a drink?"

"No, thank you," said Jennifer. "Ken, are you interested?"

"Yes. In fact, I'd like to donate my services. If you will pay me, I will donate the fee back to your organization."

"Minus my percentage." Lou flashed a grin from where he stood at his bar.

"Oh. Well, that's very kind of you." Jennifer seemed to soften a little. "Um—tell you what. If you win, we won't need it, because CAGA's goal will be reached. If you lose, knock on wood, we'll appreciate it."

"All right." Ken offered his hand this time, and she shook with a little more spirit.

Jeff nudged Ken's elbow. "Another little incentive to win. But, of course, you're a master. I guess that's enough, huh?"

"Well, it's supposed to be. Look, I'm sorry the two of you came all the way down here for such a short time. Perhaps we should have clinched this over the phone."

"Oh, not at all," said Jennifer. "We wanted to meet you in person. I feel you're being honest with us, and frankly, our entire lawsuit hangs on your participation. The only other master who has actually been in touch with us is very new. She—oh!" Jennifer put her hand to her mouth. "Of course, Donna Wong. She was with you when you made your announcement."

"Yes, that's right."

"I'm sure she's good," Jennifer said quickly. "It's just that your stature and record will lend credence to our movement."

"Not to mention, he'll play better than she would." Lou chuckled and put his arm around Ken. "She is good but inexperienced, as you say. So—is everything set? If it is, I'll draw up the papers as soon as the court awards a game."

"Just one more thing," said Jeff, opening his briefcase. "Master Li, would you give me your autograph?"

CHAPTER
Twenty

Ken got home just before dinner time. Donna shrieked happily and dragged him into the living room, where the news was blaring from the screen set into the wall.

"Listen!" She said excitedly.

". . . has, as expected, decreed that a wargame be played under the sponsorship of the very Gaming Masters' Guild that is named in the suit." The announcer's voice came over a tape of Ken's press conference, with Lou, Ken, and Donna seated at the table before reporters. "Until recently, Citizens Against the Guild Act were unanimously against having a game played over this issue, according to spokesperson Jennifer Dubay. They felt that because they were against the Guild Act in principle, it would be hypocritical for them to force the Guild into a game under the provisions of the Guild Act. Their position only changed when Master Ken Li, the top-rated master in world, announced his support for their movement. He has reportedly agreed to play for their side, in this game that was made a top priority. . . ."

"He's not kidding that it was a top priority," said Ken. "I've never heard of court decisions coming down so fast. Guess it proves they can move right along if they have an emergency." He shook his head.

"Is it true, Ken? Did you?" She was giddy with excitement.

"Did I . . . ? Yeah. I told them I'd play their side just a little while ago at the Hall. They must have gone right to the media."

Donna reached up and hugged him hard. "I'm so glad. Really. This is just wonderful."

Ken laughed and pulled her arms down. "Easy, there. I could lose, you know. Then you'll all regret my joining in."

"Oh, stop it. That's crazy." She slid her arms around his waist.

"Well, guess who the Guild is asking to play for their side."

"Who?"

"The other top-rated gamer in the world."

"There isn't any. . . ." She looked up sharply. "Richard?"

Ken nodded. "He never lost his number-one rating. He got put out of action by the accident and off the ratings system."

"But he's still recuperating!"

"He's in an accelerated program, remember. And he looked very fit when I left him this morning. If I know him, he'll be ready . . . and no doubt anxious to get back into battle and prove himself."

"Now, look." She poked him playfully in the stomach with one finger. "Don't you start this old childhood terror thing again. You don't have any reason for it."

"I . . . I don't need a reason. It isn't rational, I know that. I just . . ." He shrugged.

"Ken, you've only played three games since you came to World Headquarters. In the first one, you were terrified of playing Richard—"

"And I lost!"

"And you came up with a masterplay. Then you said that before you played against me, you were all upset. That's silly."

"No, it isn't. We were playing for Richard's well-being, virtually his life, and yet I cared about how well you played, too."

"It was my first game as a master! How do you think I felt?"

"All I'm trying to say is that I *am* getting anxious again over playing Richard. And it's genuine, logical or not."

Donna walked away, shaking her head. "You ready for dinner?"

This time, Ken deliberately fought the uncertainty. He refused to dwell on his opponent's ability as he scheduled and played his practice games, and he did not speak again to Donna of his doubts. His heavy practice schedules always made him a little lonely, and did so now, but he told himself it was nothing unusual.

His practice games went well. He had harnessed his insecurity into a killer instinct that marshaled all his abilities; in a game of the Catalaunian Fields, he played Attila and utterly destroyed the allied force sent against him. His anxiety became a spur that also drove him, in another game of Culloden Moor, to destroy the army of Bonnie Prince Charlie from his role as the Duke of Cumberland. He could feel the momentum building for the first time since he had come to World Headquarters.

To Donna, he presented a carefully controlled facade. Her gibes had stung him, and he wanted to avoid any further discussion of the same kind. So he was breezy and casual, trying to exude a light confidence that would not go overboard into a transparent overcompensation for his nagging doubts. It seemed to work, as their companionship went smoothly. He was not feeling romantic, but he trusted that his heavy schedule would disguise his mood.

Ken and Richard, through their contractors, had agreed to a preparation time of moderate length. Richard's health was back, but he still needed to sharpen his reflexes, so he had refused the court's initial request to play on short notice. The gravity of the case called for a respectable contest, as well as a prompt one.

The media had a field day with the upcoming game, virtually a carnival. It was billed as the battle of champions, between two masters with legitimate claims to the number-one rating. Richard shunned reporters out of habit; Ken insisted to Lou that if he was going to have any chance in this game at all, he would have to be shielded from distractions.

Fortunately, Lou had little trouble drawing off the reporters, though he did arrange for uniformed guards and guard dogs to escort Ken in public a couple of times. Heavy snow and the bitter cold of winter helped discourage the media pursuit. The issue in the game was so large that the news media had enough work explaining the situation to the public. They ran documentaries on the history of the Guild, on Richard and Ken, and on the passage of the Guild Act. Whenever other masters were quoted, they unanimously supported Richard and the Guild against Ken.

Meanwhile, as the icy winds raged outside, the two masters went on practicing.

Finally the practice days wound down. As usual, Ken had left the day before the game free, and he awoke in the morning with a heaviness of mood that he had so far avoided. He should have made an exception, he suspected, and scheduled a game today, too, to keep his mind off . . . things.

Donna was already up and out of the house, to visit Sharon. Ken swung his feet out of bed and sat still for a moment. He wondered if he had been having bad dreams and was just not remembering them.

He got up groggily and went right to the shower. The stinging, steaming spray started to bring him around quickly. He let the hot water run over him, stimulating his circulation. By the time he had finished the shower and stepped out, he was wide awake but still burdened. He dressed quickly and went into the kitchen for something to eat.

He didn't feel like putting out much effort. A bowl of leftover Chinese noodles and pork would be an acceptable start. The flasher heated it and water for tea, and he sat down to eat, flicking on the news and swiveling the tiny kitchen screen toward him on its base in the table.

". . . tomorrow's game. Legal questions aside, who are the combatants, otherwise known as *master gamers*? Much has been said about them in recent weeks, but one fact has caught the imagination of the public more than any other. Masters Ross and Li were childhood friends long before they ever dreamed of fighting against each other in wargames, and—"

Ken shut it off and went on eating. Nothing had happened before they had dreamed of fighting each other in play; that sort of play had been the mainstay of their childhood friendship. It was just as well that the reporters had not succeeded in digging too deeply, though. They were both private people.

Fighting each other in wargames. Some of his many memories of childhood were no more than visual impressions of the way a scene had looked and who had been there. Fighting in play...

Richard had lived in a large old house on a sizable yard with towering trees and a hedge around the grounds. At various times, the expanse had held the city of Troy under siege, the field of Bannockburn, the plains outside Kadesh, the Great Wall, the hidden Inca fortresses of the Andes. Most of the sources they could read and understand at that age, however, told of England and English history.

Ken remembered one particular day when they had galloped about on imaginary horses as English knights, chasing imaginary villains and saving imaginary, but historically accurate, victims of injustice. He couldn't remember if they were in the reign of Henry IV, a time inspired by Howard Pyle's *Men of Iron,* or in the reign of Edward IV, a general of numerous victories. On this day, though, he knew they had not traveled on the Third Crusade, with Richard the Lion-hearted, another old standby.

Young Ken had been vaguely aware of Richard charging around nearby, but his attention had been focused on the invisible knight jousting with him. The two kids were carrying swords made of meter sticks and carefully decorated cardboard shields, despite the alarm this caused their parents and babysitters. Their experience with such toys was minor, but had taught them something of the rhythm of fighting with hand weapons and shields, and the effect of height and reach.

Richard came charging at him without warning, his sword stuck in his belt and an imaginary lance cradled in his right arm. Ken's ethereal foe vanished. He ran at his friend, holding his own sword in his left hand and swinging his old make-believe lance into position. In simultaneous, independent decisions, they both judged that the impact would unhorse themselves and went rolling to the ground from the nonexistent contact. Ken jumped to his feet and shifted his sword back to his right hand. Then he prepared for Richard to come—

The sound of the front door opening brought Ken out of his reverie. Quickly, he finished his modest breakfast and drank the last of the tea. Donna came in with a bright smile, carrying packages wrapped in white paper.

"Hi! I got some sandwich stuff for lunch." She started putting the packages away.

Ken nodded. Her good humor annoyed him.

"Is there anything you'd like to do today?"

He shrugged. "No."

She watched him for a moment. "What's wrong?"

He shook his head again. Then, anticipating another attack on his mood, he took the offensive. "What would you say if I backed out?"

She laughed. "It's a little late for that, isn't it?"

He kept a straight face. "What if I did?"

"Come on, Ken, you can't do that. You'd hate yourself. Besides, your professional reputation would be ruined." She was still smiling, going along with the joke.

"I feel terrible."

"I suppose you could get a postponement on health grounds," she said, now quietly.

"Suppose I said I was going to quit."

She watched him without speaking.

He felt cold, despite the warmth of the room, and relaxed—too relaxed—again, since he should not have been tired. . .

"An entire movement is counting on you to honor your contract."

"You could do it."

"What is this? What's wrong?" Her voice was sober now.

He shook his head.

"You're not a quitter. You never have been. Even after the last three games here at World Headquarters, where you got on edge before your games, you always came around. Why would you throw away the most glittering career in the Guild?"

"Second most glittering, maybe."

"No!" She said angrily. "I said I was tired of this routine, and I meant it. Every time a big game comes up, you work yourself into a frenzy for no good reason at all. I'm not going to debate facts with you any more. You *are* the hottest master in the guild, and you know it."

"I don't—"

"*Don't you*?"

He had never seen her this angry. "*If* I accept that," he said in a controlled quiver, "I'll get overconfident. Then it won't be true at all. Can't *you* see *that*?"

She started to retort, then stopped. When she spoke again, her tone betrayed a new realization. "You invent it. You deliberately invent it. The panic, the insecurity. You want to feel this way."

"Like a fool and an incompetent?"

"Like you have to prove yourself all over again."

"I do! We all do, every time out."

"Ken, I've heard you talk about killer instinct. That's what you want. You want to be so afraid of losing that you utterly destroy the other side."

"So they don't destroy me. What's wrong with that?" He jumped out of his chair and started pacing around the little kitchen, four steps one way, four steps back.

"It's a game, Ken. A game."

"With crucial decisions riding on it—like the future of the Guild Act. Isn't that why we're against the Act?"

"I'm not saying there's no pressure and no point to it. I'm

just saying that you're taking it all out of proportion personally."

He shot out an accusing finger. "You. You don't want a loser or a quitter, do you?"

"What are you talking about?"

"Don't tell me you didn't fall for a celebrity when we first met. That's what got your attention, isn't it?"

She looked at him, uncomprehending.

"First I thought I would just have to quit. When I saw that you were right about the Guild Act, I knew I couldn't go on supporting the Guild. That would make me a quitter, and you wouldn't respect that."

"You could do what I've been planning. Just play voluntary games and avoid the ones dictated by Guild Act provisions." Puzzlement showed in her face. "You already told Lou that was your policy now."

"That is still supporting the Guild and, indirectly, the Guild Act. Then, when this game came along, I figured I could play my best and get out of the trap by breaking the Guild Act. Only, I don't see how I can win. And I hate losing—always have. I don't think you want a loser around, either."

"*What?*"

He shrugged again.

"Ken, you're crazy," she said in quiet disbelief. "You're actually crazy. Do you mean to say that all this time you've been afraid of what *I* think?"

He started to shrug another time, then nodded slightly.

"Ken . . . I never said anything like that, did I?" She came around the table and stood next to him, resting a hand on his arm.

"Not exactly," he said huskily, in almost a whisper.

"Not at all, you mean. What made you think I care more about your career status than about you?"

Staring at the table in front of him, he shook his head very slightly, hardly a movement at all.

"It's not what I think. It's you and this whole competitive business. I'm not immune to it—remember how nervous I got before my qualifier? But the doubt is inside us, Ken, not outside. And I don't care if you ever play another game. I'll love you, win or lose or retire. And besides, how can you think I would put winning over principle? If you had quit the Guild rather than play when you no longer believed in it, that's . . . that's a very honorable decision."

"If I lose tomorrow," Ken whispered, "I may still have to do that." His eyes were stinging with tears.

Donna leaned down close and slid her arms around his neck. "You quit if you want to. And lose if you want to. I'll still be here. You can't get rid of me that easily."

CHAPTER Twenty-one

The next day Ken stood in the entry to the Marathon Gaming Arena with a feeling of lightness he had never experienced before. He felt like a monster—unbeatable, untouchable—and if that wasn't overconfidence, he was a Roman sandal.

He laughed to himself, uncaring.

He sauntered out across the floor, and a roar of cheers rose up from the packed stands and swirled around the great bowl above him. Spectators all across the stands were waving, shouting wildly, some even standing. He grinned and waved back heartily, in all directions. Donna was among them somewhere.

At the far end, Richard entered, and the din rose up again at his appearance. The moment seemed to freeze in time for Ken: the spring in the carpet, the deafening roar from the blur of excited fans, the knowledge that Donna and Lou were watching out there somewhere—and Richard taking his place against him in the distance.

Ken turned slowly, looking up at the high rows of seats surrounding him, smiling and waving at everyone.

"Sir?" An attendant shouted, smiling, in his ear.

Ken shook his head. "Everything's fine." Quickly, he mounted the steps and sat down in his gaming seat.

As soon as he sat down, years of professional habit took

over. He positioned the keyboard carefully, waving away the attendant who came to help. Then he fitted the sensory band over his eyes and ears.

The announcer was introducing the case, but Ken could barely hear him. At the mention of every name, every dispute, virtually every phrase, cheers and boos filled the arena again and drowned out even the massive loudspeakers. Ken had to watch the announcer, as well as listen, so he would know when the introductions were over.

Once again, media cameras were set up down on the floor. Ken saw one aimed at him and winked at it. Then the announcer was finished.

With one deep breath, he flexed his fingers and raised his hand for the attendant. His blood raced and a sweet pang of tension tightened in his chest. When Richard also raised his hand, the attendant opened the game.

The white playing field lit up with holographic color, mainly the lush green of an open plain. His keyboard screen read, "Bosworth Field. 1485. Henry Tudor, Earl of Richmond."

A flood of thoughts swept over Ken, led by the irony of the computer's random choice of battle. His dismay at playing Tudor, against whom he had developed his masterplay in this game, was followed by a quick return of professional judgment. His task was clear enough: he could not allow the conditions to arise for Richard to use his own masterplay against him.

Yet aren't you free of that old fear now? he asked himself. *Don't you have the freedom to lose now? Can't you accept losing now, if it seems ordained?*

The answer came back: *Not if you believe in your cause.*

The field activated. Ken began tapping the keys, taking control of his Lancastrian army.

Ken faced the royal army of Richard III, Plantagenet King of England. The Duke of Norfolk commanded the royal van where it was stretched across the forward slope of Ambion Hill; on the crest, the King led the main body of his army. Their combined 5,000 men were loyal and seasoned troops who were the critical danger to Tudor's rebel army of invasion.

Ken's Tudor van was commanded by the Earl of Oxford, who now led the rebels across Redmore Plain toward Ambion Hill. The rebel right would be anchored and protected by a marsh; the left would be unsupported. As Tudor, Ken had 3,000 French mercenaries—many of them riffraff from French gaols—and 2,000 Welsh supporters. He located his role, the Lancastrian heir Henry Tudor, on a small hill to the rear of his forces, accompanied by his guard and personal reserve of five hundred.

Tudor's real hope of victory lay in the conspiracy he had entered prior to the battle. The Earl of Northumberland commanded the royal reserve of 1,000 to the rear of King Richard's position on Ambion Hill, but he had promised Tudor he would not enter the battle. The computer would control his decision, but as the Earl had a long-standing grudge against the King and held Lancastrian sentiments anyway, he would probably stick to his agreement.

To the northwest, Sir William Stanley stood with his 2,000 mounted troops in a position to protect or attack Tudor's left flank. To the south, his brother, Lord Thomas Stanley, commanded another 2,000 horse, also nominally loyal to King Richard. Since they had secretly agreed to enter the battle on Tudor's side, Ken had a strong expectation of their support. However, the computer would also determine their actions. The Stanleys would join Tudor if his army was winning or in stalemate, but if the royal forces gained the upper hand, they would certainly take the royal side, and plead their loyalty to the King later.

Ken watched Oxford lead the van of his rebel army forward. The formation was still an inverted triangle, with the base forming the front line and the successive lines growing shorter and coming to a point, or apex of the triangle, in the rear. It had been effective historically and in games, so Ken let it stand.

He watched closely as Oxford's standard led the van into the range of Norfolk's chained serpentine guns, which began to fire. The rebel lines faltered, then continued. Oxford advanced, and the two sides released volleys of arrows from their deadly longbows. Openings appeared in the front lines of each side and were filled in again by the men behind.

As Ken expected, Norfolk waited to move until Oxford's front line began the clumsy ascent up the slope. Then the royal lines charged. Harsh voices screamed battle cries and steel crashed against steel in the arena speakers. Oxford's order was to press forward as hard as possible. Early success was required to bring the Stanleys in for Tudor, as they had agreed.

The writhing mass of holographic humanity fought in a thick and wavering line that first moved down the slope, against Oxford. Slowly the press of his numbers began to tell, and to drive forward again. Ken searched the field for an action from his opponent. So far, both gamers had simply allowed the programmed personalities in the game to fight as their historical predecessors had.

Oxford's van slowly battled Norfolk's center back, and back again. When Ken had played Richard III, he had responded with the King's own tactic, sending forward reinforcements in small blocks. Richard the gamer was not so conservative.

Three hundred loyal knights led by Viscount Francis Lovell, according to his pennon, charged down the hill. Two hundred billmen led by Richard Ratcliffe rushed after them. Norfolk's line parted and the stream of knights smashed into Oxford's van, driving it down.

Ken understood. Richard had chosen to gamble and to force the issue aggressively.

Oxford had no fresh men left. He had committed everyone early. Behind the van, Ken moved up the main body of his army in support. Richard had already committed a substantial and important portion of his army, and he sent forward another five hundred men as Ken studied the field. Richard was vying hard for the loyalty of the Stanleys, trying to break Oxford quickly.

Ken considered the implications of Richard's maneuvers.

The main rebel army under Tudor and the royal army under King Richard had both numbered about 5,000 originally, with a slight advantage in combat power to the royal side. Richard could fight Ken to a standstill, but the balance of victory would still belong to Northumberland and the Stanleys.

Ken was impressed with the gamble, though he hoped he could make it backfire. He had thought it too risky when he had played Richard III. Now, he wondered how the computer would treat the relationship between Northumberland and the Stanleys, since he had never seen this situation before. Though the traitors had entered a conspiracy with Tudor, none could be sure of the others, except that the Stanleys would act together.

Ken compared his numbers with those of his opponent. They were both committing their combatants as quickly as they could. It looked like it would be a short game, no matter who won.

The battle still raged in a deep, quivering line across the slope, not quite halfway up. Ken did not move Henry Tudor forward. Unlike the Yorkist King, Tudor had not been known for his prowess in battle, so the risk of losing him, and therefore the game, was much greater than the benefits of using him in combat.

Richard, meanwhile, was keeping Richard III safely out of the battle. He naturally would be hoping to avoid risking the battle on the final desperate charge to kill Tudor that Ken had used when he had played the royal side and established his masterplay.

Ken, as Henry Tudor, urged more of his men forward. Richard sent more of his units down the hill, and the carnage piled up. Quickly and constantly, men were falling on the field of battle.

Suddenly more royal reserves, led by King Richard himself, surged forward in a frightening charge down Ambion Hill. The great wave of knights smashed into the rebel lines and broke through almost completely. The banner of Oxford, a star with streams, fell. The rebels barely held their line, and the royal lines drove forward again.

Ken pounded the keyboard furiously, ordering his men forward. This phase of the battle could be critical; it was Richard's chance to take control and bring the Stanleys in on the royal side. Yet, in a horrible irony, Ken understood that if he withstood Richard's move now and at least kept the Stanleys waiting, he would simply set the conditions for Richard to use Ken's masterplay.

With his newfound emotional freedom, he admitted again: Richard was very good.

Ken had no time to ponder the conundrum. Every man of his army, except Henry Tudor's own reserve was committed now. He worked over the keyboard, sending and receiving messages as Tudor, eyeing the Stanleys anxiously. At any moment, the computer could judge that they would enter the fray on one side or the other and tip the balance.

Richard, too, knew the final moment was approaching. Behind his lines, the King was gathering his household troops. Ken's rebel lines had held; his opponent would have to use the masterplay.

In moments, Ken could see the two wings of his enemy riding out to the left of the battle. King Richard led the first wing, made up of his loyal household knights. The second wing would charge behind them at an interval, to break up the charge from the north of Sir William Stanley's men, if they should come in for Tudor at the same moment they had historically.

Here came the royal charge.

Ken activated the sensory band and found himself on the hill as Henry Tudor. King Richard's charge was still distant but coming on fast. Tudor's captains had spotted it and were shouting orders, wheeling about, trying to form their lines.

Though when Richard had played this side, he had taken Tudor in flight at this point, Ken did not dare do so now. If Tudor and his banner were seen fleeing by the men now fighting in the ranks, the battle would be lost on the spot.

Tudor's guards jammed in about him protectively, led by

Sir John Cheney, his personal bodyguard, who at 6′7″ was a true giant in medieval times. Ahead, the White Boar standard of King Richard led the charging knights.

The enemy smashed into the front row of Tudor's reserve. Horses screamed and reared; men fell; others shouted and laid on with their weapons. In the distance, Sir William Stanley had ordered his men to charge to the relief of Tudor, but Richard's second wing would blunt their attack, delay them, perhaps divert them completely.

Tudor could not flee; it was time for his own bold stroke. He was untried in battle, but Richard III had been untried at the battle of Barnet, where as Duke of Gloucester he had led the van in a great victory. Ken, knowing he was out of character for Tudor, charged the White Boar standard of King Richard.

The charge was ineffective. Clear battle lines no longer existed, and both sides now fought in isolated clumps. In the jumbled crowd Ken had to turn aside, blunting his charge, to avoid some of his own men.

Richard had seen his move, however, and now the King began fighting his way toward Tudor. Screaming men and stumbling warhorses crowded the way. Still the two advanced, forcing their way in the mass of steel-plated bodies and flailing weapons. Those in the center had no room to retreat.

Ken bent down low behind the shield on his left arm, holding a mace in the mailed glove of his other hand. He spurred his charger forward in the crowd at every opening. Just ahead on his right, Sir John Cheney towered over his liege as he swung his axe right and left, clearing a path. Behind them, the lightly armed standard-bearer carried the scarlet dragon of Cadwallader on a field of white and green, banner of the Welsh princes.

The banner of the White Boar dipped and rose ahead of them, maneuvering closer and closer. King Richard appeared in front of his standard-bearer on his charger White Surrey, holding his shield high and swinging his own great battle axe. A golden crown circled the outside of his helm.

Tudor raised his shield, tightened his grip on his mace, and spurred his horse. Just in front of him, John Cheney was toppled from his horse by the raging King. The riderless steed fled, and White Surrey plunged forward. The expressionless steel face of King Richard's helm rose up gleaming in the sunlight as he tossed away his shield. He raised the mighty war axe with both hands in a terrible arc, and he leaned toward his hated rival.

Young Ken ducked right, lifting the cardboard shield on his left arm to catch the blow. Richard's sword, a meter stick painted silver with a brown cardboard hilt, whacked against Ken's cardboard shield, which was painted yellow with a red paper falcon's head glued on it. Ken's arm stung from the blow, but he swung his own wooden sword in response.

Richard likewise caught it with his cardboard shield, where the red Cross of St. George shone on a silver field. The two of them stood by the side of Richard's house, wearing helmets of shirtboard sprayed silver, striking at each other in the summer afternoon with considerable spirit and vigor.

"Weakling," Richard taunted.

"Call for your horse," Ken yelled back. "'My kingdom for a horse,' that's you."

Ken and Richard were breathless and sweaty behind their cardboard visors. Most of the time, they traded sturdy, but predictable, blows in an easy rhythm, looking for an advantage. Ken tried a high stroke, over Richard's shield, but his friend was taller and caught the blow on his shield easily.

Richard responded with a similar high blow. Ken deflected it with the edge of his shield, but Richard's sword caught the top of Ken's helmet, knocking it crooked. Disoriented, Ken swung his sword blindly, lifting it in a backhand stroke that stabbed Richard's right armpit as he raised his sword again.

Richard yelled in pain, his voice muffled by the cardboard, and jumped back. Ken took the moment to straighten his helmet, and he raised his shield again just in time to catch Richard's next angry swing. They were not strong enough or vicious enough to hurt each other seriously.

Ken and Richard traded blows, right hand against left arm, like clockwork figures in the bright afternoon sun.

Tudor braced himself for the great two-handed blow from King Richard's axe. The axe swung down from left to right and smashed into Tudor's shield, splintering it. As the King raised it again on his other side for another strike, Tudor struck him in the chest with his mace.

This blow, struck with one arm and little weight behind it, was ineffectual against the thick steel plate of the King's armor. King Richard brought the axe down hard again, from Tudor's right his time. Tudor gripped his horse with his legs, clutched the reins, and leaned low to the left with his entire upper torso. The weight shift nearly pulled him free of the saddle, and the axe hit a glancing blow against his back plate, knocking him breathless.

Desperately, Tudor raised up in his stirrups, twisting back into the saddle again. In a wrenching upward backhand stroke he struck the spikes of his mace deep into the right armpit of King Richard, who had raised his arms yet again for another strike. The mace drove between the plates of steel armor, through the chain mail underneath. Blood spurted out. Tudor tore the mace free, shredding the King's right arm.

The King slumped sideways and then fell backward from his horse.

The holograms froze.

Ken pushed the sensory band up and looked at his screen. The screen read: "Victory Conditions: Lancaster."

He grinned, leaned back in his seat, and then laughed aloud. The sound was lost, though, in the roar of cheering that had arisen again on all sides, and echoed in the giant bowl of the arena. He looked across the field, where Richard was pulling off his sensory band and swinging his keyboard out of his way.

"Ken!" Donna was standing in an electric cart at the bottom of Ken's steps, smiling and waving. "Come on!"

Ken stood up, hesitating on the top step, and looked around one last time at the crowd. He had never enjoyed a game as much.

A moment later, he was sitting in the cart in Donna's arms as the attendant drove them out of the arena to the reception room.

Ken, unable to stop grinning, just looked into her own damp, smiling face. Neither of them spoke.

By the time they got to the reception room, it was already full of invited guests. Waving at everyone, they climbed out and Donna went to get punch while Ken settled into the lounger that had been reserved for him. Richard was already in his, sipping red punch from a tall glass.

"Crazy game, huh?" Richard offered his hand.

Surprised, Ken accepted it. "Yeah, it sure was. Fast and furious."

Richard gave him a wry grin. "Sorry you had to ruin your own masterplay . . . but if it doesn't work . . ."

"Then it wasn't a masterplay at all." Ken shook his head. "You know what's funny? Right now I don't even care."

"I'm not surprised. You sure won on a long shot. Who would have thought Henry Tudor could kill Richard III, King of England, Duke of Gloucester, and renowned master of arms?"

Ken laughed. "It wasn't them fighting; it was you and me. Say, you don't seem too unhappy with your loss."

Richard laughed suddenly and emptied his glass of punch in a sustained draft. "Well, you know, my performance was pretty solid, and after what I've been through with my health, I shouldn't complain. Even my rating should be pretty good."

"That's true."

"And, you know. . . ." He caught Ken's eye. "Something you said out at the Resort has been nagging at me, I guess. Along with the old saw about one crucial soldier on the field making the entire difference. Well, it came true today, but

I've been thinking about it, anyhow. When I think of my life hanging in the balance over this kind of situation . . ." He shook his head. "Maybe you have a point. The Guild Act shouldn't be forcing people to accept games."

"And it isn't, any more." Lou glowered at them both, looking down at them with his hands in his pockets. "So now what do I tell the rest of my clients? That one of my clients just knocked out a good portion of the games, making paupers of us all?" He was smiling by now. "Congratulations, Ken. I'm proud of you. Fine showing, Master Ross."

"I'm proud of him, too," said Donna, pushing her way through the crowd and kneeling by Ken. She handed him a cup of punch. "In fact, I—" She stopped short, looking past Richard.

Ken followed her glance, as did Richard and Lou. The people around them fell silent.

Kirk Emerald was standing by Richard's lounger, tall, slender, and dignified with his distinctive shock of white hair. He waited until the voices around him were all quiet.

"Master Li, congratulations on your victory. Congratulations to you, as well, Master Ross. You both played an excellent game, and one that will uphold the honor of the Guild in our next transition. Master Li, I just wanted to give you my assurance that the Guild holds no grudge over your personal stands in your recent games. Lou, if you get any sign of such a grudge from anywhere in the Guild, I want you to report it directly to me."

Lou nodded soberly.

Emerald smiled at all of them. "Sorry to interrupt. Excuse me." Then he was gone, into the crowd.

Donna hugged Ken. "Come on, champ. Let's celebrate."